William James Dawson

The Makers of Modern Prose

William James Dawson

The Makers of Modern Prose

ISBN/EAN: 9783337366346

Printed in Europe, USA, Canada, Australia, Japan

Cover: Foto ©Andreas Hilbeck / pixelio.de

More available books at **www.hansebooks.com**

The Makers of Modern Prose

A Popular Handbook to the Greater Prose Writers of the Century : *By W. J. Dawson*

LONDON : HODDER AND STOUGHTON 27 PATERNOSTER ROW 1899

Edinburgh: T. and A. CONSTABLE, Printers to Her Majesty

PREFACE

THIS volume constitutes the second of a series. About ten years ago I formed the ambitious project of writing what might prove a popular guide to modern English literature, and I published a volume dealing with the great poets. The project proved at the time too large for accomplishment, and for ten years this early book has remained unaccompanied by its proper comrades. At last I have been able to take up my plan again, and the present volume on the *Makers of Modern Prose* is the result.

The volume on the poets is now republished, and I hope to complete the trilogy by a similar volume on the *Makers of Modern Fiction*. Many friendly critics pointed out, on the appearance of the first volume, that its title, the *Makers of Modern English*, was misleading, since the book concerned itself with the poets alone, who certainly are not the only makers in modern literature. The justice of this criticism is incontestable. I have therefore amended my title, retaining the phrase, the *Makers of Modern*

English, as a generic title only, partly because it has already become familiar to my readers ; in the main, however, because it is now accurate as applying to the general scheme of these volumes.   That scheme, when completed, will include—

> Vol.   I. *The Makers of Modern Poetry.*
> Vol. II. *The Makers of Modern Prose.*
> Vol. III. *The Makers of Modern Fiction.*

W. J. DAWSON.

London, *June* 1899.

CONTENTS

CHAPTER I

JOHNSON'S ENGLAND

[Samuel Johnson, born at Lichfield, 1709. Published his *Dictionary*, 1775; *Lives of the Poets*, 1779-81. Died, Dec. 13, 1784.]

A FULL and accurate picture of the latter half of the eighteenth century would afford one of the most interesting studies to which the human mind could apply itself; but it cannot be said that any such picture already exists. We have many sketches of the period, lucid, brilliant, exhaustive, but all more or less partial, and affording merely so many hints and elements from which the true picture is to be combined. To the literary men of this period an imperishable interest attaches. We seem to see them as we see men who toil in soot and semi-darkness far down at the foundations of some huge building, lifting from the gloom at rare intervals a grimy head, and calling to us with a stentorian voice. We recognise in them the pioneers of popular literature, and feel for them the admiration which is due to that species of silent heroism which endures and labours without murmur in a cause which brings no personal reward, and whose triumph is deferred to an hour so distant that it is impossible that the original worker should behold it. There are those who reap and those who sow: for one, the golden weather and the joy of harvest; for the other, the bleak winds, the hard soil, and the labour done in hope, and only hope. It was the men of the eighteenth century who sowed the harvest which we reap to-day. It was Samuel Johnson and his contemporaries who abolished Grub Street, who raised literature in England into an honourable profession, who quarried through clay and rock to reach that gold of Golconda, of which they indeed secured little enough, but to which every man of letters can now help himself abundantly, and without restraint.

This England of the eighteenth century—Johnson's England, so to speak—was so entirely different from ours that it is difficult for us to arrive at a just understanding of its life. The French Revolution had not yet broken up the deadly stagnation which rested over Europe. It was an age of religion without faith, of politics without honour, and of life without morality. In forgotten pamphlets and remembered diaries, in the poetry of Cowper and the vindictive satire of Churchill, in the private correspondence of George Selwyn, the published diaries of Horace Walpole, the scanty records of the passionate invective of Burke, the sheets which hold the terrible eloquence of Junius, and even in the yellow pages of the old club-books, with their scrawling memoranda of bets and debts, we find a picture, only too vivid and startling, of the customs and manners of the time. We hear, as in some magic telephone, the confused hubbub of drawing-rooms, where dicers' oaths and dicers' gold rattle amid the whispers of the latest scandal or the next projected bribery; and we hear too, with even more terrible distinctness, the sea-like roar of the vast mobs which besiege the House of Commons, clamouring for Wilkes and the freedom of the press. We are face to face with corruption in politics, incompetence in council, and paganism in religion. It was Robert Walpole who said—not with noble scorn, but with sincere conviction—that every man had his price; nor is there any reason to believe that he ever found himself wrong in his estimate of those with whom he had to deal. It is Johnson who tells us that Walpole confessed that he always talked grossly at his table, because he found that was the only species of conversation in which everybody could indulge. There is no British statesman of to-day whose honour would permit him to use the secret intelligence of the Government for private purposes upon the Stock Exchange; but in the days of the Georges this was one of the most fruitful sources of income to a minister. There is not a page in the biographies of the period which does not bear witness to the venality and degradation of public life, and equally to the corruption of general morals. Out of their own mouths we convict statesmen who thought it no more dishonour to provide for themselves, and build up stately fortunes for their children, out of the public purse, than to ride after the hounds or eat a dinner. If we withdraw from the Parliamentary records of the age such noble names as Burke, Barré, Rockingham, Chatham, Wilberforce, and the faithful few who followed them, we have not only withdrawn the great lights from the firmament of debate, but all light from the firmament of public virtue. We walk amid a ghastly phantasmagoria of greed and envy; among men who have bribed their way to Parliament, and are

utterly unscrupulous as to how they vote or what
they do, so long as the literally golden goal of
official life is quickly reached. Almost the one object
of public life in those days was to make money, and
Cowper did not exaggerate when he wrote :

> The levée swarms, as if in golden pomp
> Were charactered on every statesman's door—
> ' Battered and bankrupt fortunes mended here.'

The public purse was only too public, for all hands
were as deep in it as circumstances would permit.
At the levée of a Grenville or a Grafton £200 bank-
bills were dealt round with lavish profusion, and the
position of a Government might be accurately determined by the amount it was willing to pay to be
supported.   It is calculated that every change of
Government added from nine to fifteen thousand
pounds per annum to the Pension List, and what
this means may be measured by a statement attributed to Burke, that ' five Prime Ministers maintained
themselves for an average of just fourteen months
apiece, from the day when they were kissed in to the
day when they were kicked out.'   That is, to put
it in round numbers, in less than six years from
forty-five to seventy-five thousand pounds per annum
were permanently added to the Pension List by
ministers who could not rise, and much less fall,
without pensioning all their dependants, from a
nephew or a secretary to a broker or a cook.   We
cannot wonder that Johnson, in his dictionary, defined
a pension as ' pay given to a State hireling for treason
to his country,' and a pensioner as ' a slave of the
State hired by a stipend to obey his master.'
Probably the one meritorious pension granted in the

latter half of the eighteenth century was the £300 per annum given to Johnson, and, as we all know, he was bitterly reproached for accepting it.

The social life of the period was little better than the public life. Drunkenness and betting were the most venial of its vices. Cabinet ministers were 'conspicuous for impudent vice, for daily dissipation, for pranks which would have been regarded as childish and unbecoming in a crack cavalry regiment in the worst days of military licence.' One Secretary of State was notorious as the greatest drunkard and most unlucky gambler of his age ; another official personage had established his reputation on one gift only—if gift it may be called—the power of out-drinking any man in the three kingdoms. A Prime Minister was permitted to appear at the opera with his mistress, and another Secretary of State was esteemed the very vilest public man of his century :

> Too infamous to have a friend,
> Too bad for bad men to commend,
> Or good to name.

The passion for gaming was at its height. Bets were offered upon everything : whether or not a ministry would last six months, a celebrated criminal would be hanged, a war with any given country would begin or end at any given time. Everything, from the state of the weather to the state of the world, was discussed to a running accompaniment of odds and guineas. The usual demoralisation ensued. In every drawing-room the ladies were the most eager players, and at the clubs the most reck-less were the younger men. The noblemen who thronged the clubs did not always trouble themselves to play fair, especially when the contest lay between a wealthy stripling and an impecunious profligate, and the losses sometimes were enormous. Life among the upper classes was of that species which is ironically described as short and merry. 'A squire,' says Mr. Trevelyan, 'past fifty-five, who still rode to hounds or walked after partridges, was the envy of the countryside for his health, unless he had long been its scorn for his sobriety.' Profligacy and drinking fill the earlier chapters of such lives: gout and premature decay the later. Even Horace Walpole ceases to be cynical, and catches something of the iron glow of Tacitus, as he paints the picture of cabinet ministers and statesmen 'reeling into the ferry-boat' at forty-five, worn out with drunkenness and gout. Walpole's caustic obituaries of celebrated libertines are not pleasant reading, but they are valuable for the lurid illumination which they pour on the character of the eighteenth century.

When the customs of the upper classes were what they were, it is not surprising that the life of the lower classes was inconceivably brutal and degraded. The most instructive commentary on lower-class customs is found in Hogarth's pictures and John Wesley's journals. In the Beer Street and Gin Lane of the great artist there is given the truest portraiture of drunkenness, in all its filth and madness, which the pencil ever drew, and we cannot doubt that the details of these terrible canvases were sketched from actual life. In the journals of the great evangelist there are chronicled the faithful reports of an eye-witness who saw many towns and many sides of life; who probably knew the village life of England as no other man has ever done; who had a thorough acquaintance with his country, from the Tweed to the Land's End ; and what impression do we gather from his pages ?   Everywhere we read of almost inconceivable ignorance and brutality among the poor : how the churches of those who should have aided him were closed against him ; how magistrates did all they could to silence him ; how violent mobs were always ready to rise at the first chance of mischief. The inhumanity of man to man encouraged moral callousness, and left little room for the blossoming of any refining sentiments or acts. Every week a host of young lads were hanged for theft, and the spectacle of a criminal riding through the streets to Tyburn, and getting as drunk as he conveniently could upon the way, was too common to attract attention. London was called the City of the Gallows, for from whatever point you entered it, by land or water, you passed between a lane of gibbets, where the corpses of felons hung, rotting and bleaching in the light.   Nor was crime suppressed by this stringency of the law.   Highwaymen rode into town at nightfall, coolly tying their horses to the palings of Hyde Park, and executed their plans of robbery in the very presence of the impotent protectors of the public peace. London was infested by gangs of youths, whose nightly pastime was to bludgeon inoffensive watchmen, and to gouge out the eyes of chance travellers. Dean Swift dared not go out after dark, and Johnson wrote :

> Prepare for death, if here at night you roam,
> And sign your will before you sup from home.

Ludgate Hill swarmed with mock parsons, and thousands of spurious marriages were celebrated every year. In the public prints of the time we read an advertisement like this: ' For sale, a negro boy, aged eleven years. Inquire at the Virginia Coffee-house, Threadneedle Street, behind the Royal Exchange.' So little was the public conscience alive to the wrong of slavery, that even George Whitefield thought it no shame to buy slaves as part of the property of his orphanage-house in America. The press-gang was a constant public terror. Smuggling was a respectable and lucrative employment ; brandy was four shillings a gallon, and port a shilling a bottle. In some parishes every fourth house was a tavern, and in the windows of many might be read the announcement, ' Drunk for a penny, and drunk with straw to lie upon for twopence.' The amusements of the people were characterised by a sort of rough jollity, and in Johnson's day football was still played in the Strand, and smock-races were run in Pall Mall. It is hard to believe that this England of Johnson is but a hundred years removed from us ; the chronological gulf of separation is slight enough, but the moral and social gulf immeasurable.

It is scarcely surprising that in such a period political liberty was not understood, and that the very foundations of right government were insecure. Freedom of speech was, in fact, hardly more possible under the Georges than the first Stuarts. Subservience to the court was as indispensable a condition of successful public life as the bribery of the constituencies. George III. never forgot a division or forgave an adverse vote. The most diligent and painstaking student of Parliamentary debates was the King himself, and the object of his studies was to discover and repress any opinion that conflicted

with his own. Brave men who had served under
the British flag with honour in every quarter of the
globe, were deliberately ignored and even deprived
of their commissions, because their political opinions
did not coincide with those of their royal master;
and the sovereign of a great empire could sink so
low as to request his Prime Minister to furnish him
with a list of those who had voted in the minority,
that he might turn his back upon them at to-morrow's
levée. 'If the spirit of service could be killed in an
English army,' said the indignant Chatham, 'such
strokes of wanton injustice would bid fair for it.'
When George III. said with bitter truth that 'politics
were a trade for a scoundrel and not for a gentleman,'
he forgot how much he himself had done to degrade
them, and how the worst scoundrels of politics were
those who stood nearest the royal person and ate
the royal bread. George III. was not above 'paving
the way for a new contest in a county by discharging
the outstanding debts of the last candidate, subsi-
dising the patron of a borough with a grant out of
the Privy Purse; and writing with the pen of an
English sovereign, to offer a subject some " gold pills "
for the purpose of hocussing the freeholders.' He
manipulated the constituencies with the unscrupulous
zeal and astuteness of a born electioneering agent.
With a king who openly dealt in every species of political jobbery, it is not surprising that there should be a
public demoralised to the last degree by bribery and
rapacity. It was really the rapacity of the placeman
which cost us our American colonies. Provinces
were repeatedly taxed to support sinecurists whom
they never saw, and in an evil hour the American
colonies were suggested as an admirable field for the

exploitation of the political jobber. The fiery pen of Junius protested 'that it was not Virginia that wanted a Governor, but a Court favourite that wanted a salary.' The debt of gratitude that the present generation owes to Junius it would be impossible to overstate. Often he may be envenomed, but he is seldom unveracious ; and it is to this man, who dwelt apart in honourable pride and scorn, condemning from his secret judgment-seat the evils of his time; who was more powerful than Cabinets and more feared than kings ; who lived his silent life with the iron mask ever on his face, and died and made no sign ; it is to this man that England owes much of her precious heritage of liberty which is hers to-day. Junius and John Wilkes were the political saviours of the eighteenth century ; Johnson and Wesley were its moral and religious saviours.

It is related that Johnson and Savage once walked the streets of London all night, because they were too poor to procure lodgings ; but, says Johnson, 'We were in high spirits and brimful of patriotism ; we inveighed against the Ministry, and resolved to stand by our country.' It is ludicrous enough—two ragged literary hacks, without a sixpence for their beds, resolving to stand by their country—and yet that was precisely what the country most needed, the loyal adherence of true and upright souls like Johnson's. For the problem Johnson had to face was that of a country fast going to pieces, and how to save her. The celebrated observation of Lord Chesterfield, that he saw in France every sign that preceded great revolutions, might have been applied with equal truth to England. For in England, as in France, Voltairism had infected the thinking classes, political blindness had fallen on the ruling classes, and the passion of revolution was already seething in the hearts of the lower classes. Add to this the spectacle of a Church whose spiritual power had waned almost to extinction because its priests had lost sincerity and merited contempt, a general scorn of literature, a general disbelief in virtue, and you have indeed all the conditions which precede and produce revolutions. Even men like David Hume and Horace Walpole believed in the imminence of some vast political convulsion, and Walpole had more than once seen London at the mercy of as turbulent and resolute a mob as ever tore up the paving-stones of Paris for barricades, and fought behind them with the wild ferocity of tigers. In such an age Johnson went to church, and Wesley went into the highways and hedges to care for those whom the Church neglected. If Walpole had visited Moorfields at four o'clock on a New Year's morning, he would have found thousands of people standing hushed before the appeals of Wesley; or had he gone to Bristol, he might have found still vaster crowds of grimy miners weeping under the impassioned oratory of Whitefield. The very enthusiasm and strength of character which would have made many a miner and mechanic a daring and dreaded captain of a mob, Wesley directed to the peaceful battlefields of righteousness, and thus changed the men who might have proclaimed a Commune into the most loyal subjects that the king possessed. Thus it happened that when the great Revolution came, fifty years of the great evangelical revival had done their work, and it was only the trailing edges of the storm-cloud that swept our shores. This is a conclusion now universally admitted by all competent historians, and it is

equally certain that what Wesley did in one domain
of national life, Johnson did, by very different means,
in another. Both were great conservative forces, and
incredible as it would have seemed to the men of
Johnson's day, yet it was from an obscure and excom-
municated clergyman, and from a ragged, neglected,
half-blind, and scrofulous scholar, who had known
what it was to work in literature for fifteenpence a
day, that the true salvation of England came.

CHAPTER II

IN this distracted England, what place was there for authorship? That was a hard question, but one which in due time Samuel Johnson was called upon to solve. It was in truth the very hardest age for authors that England had ever known. Shakespeare had had his Lord Southampton on whom to rely, and many a lesser man than he had had some patron, gracious or supercilious as the case might be, but who at least had stood between the poor author and want, and had thus made the profession of literature possible. But if the age of the patron had not altogether gone, it was fast going, and the age of the public had not come. The author was like some shivering minstrel who had been thrust out from the comfortable light and warmth of a tavern, where he had at least been per-mitted to sing unmolested, if unhonoured, and there was nothing before him but the bleak winds and the homeless waste. Where was he to go? Who wanted him ? He had no recognised place in the world : he was a dubious creature, for whom no chair was set at the board of life. His work was self-imposed, and questionable, understood by few and valued by yet fewer. Had he been a bricklayer or a hostler, the world would at least have credited him with a defi-nite vocation ; but authorship was a term of reproach, and the author was only a shade more reputable than the highwayman. Horace Walpole, although he dabbled in literature, hated authors : Burke's political career was actually hindered in its early stages by the fact that he had written a book.   It must ever be a matter for amazement that in such an age any man of spirit could have seriously thought of literature as a profession, and nothing but a miraculous endowment of that ethereal fire which men call hope could have sustained any man in such a purpose. Men turned authors only because every other livelihood had failed them : they were unwilling martyrs goaded on to an unheroic Calvary. He who turned his face toward the Calvary of literature by force of an inward and not an outward compulsion, could only do so because he was animated by some vision of a diviner joy that was set before him, some supremely noble purpose that at once inspired and gladdened him, and was its own exceeding great reward. Had a new Fox flourished in the eighteenth century, and set about writing a new Book of Martyrs, it is probable that he would have gone to Grub Street instead of Smithfield for his chronicles, and have found his heroes in literature, and not in religion.

The more thoroughly the eighteenth century is studied, the truer will these observations appear. The life of eighteenth-century authors is one prolonged Iliad of misfortune, misery, and shattered hope. Fielding died a broken man, in the very prime of life ; Smollett had to toil like a galley-slave for subsistence ; Richardson only succeeded in securing modest comfort for himself because he could print and sell books as well as write them. Burke said bitterly enough that figures of arithmetic were better

worth his while than figures of rhetoric; Goldsmith
was for years the literal slave of the booksellers;
Chatterton perished unhelped; Johnson had to solve
the problem of how to live in a London garret on
eighteenpence a day. The day was past when the
wit of Prior was rewarded with an embassy, and the
graceful humour of Addison was a passport to a
Secretaryship. Money might indeed be earned still,
and in profusion, by a certain species of political
authorship, but it was not money which any honourable man would care to touch. Walpole spent in ten
years fifty thousand pounds among the writers of
ephemeral articles and pamphlets, but not a single
penny on any man whose name is remembered in
literature to-day, except the pension he bestowed on
Young. A few of the names of these truculent
scribblers are still preserved in Pope's *Dunciad*:
notably Arnall, who received in four years nearly
eleven thousand pounds, and whose character may
be measured by Pope's stinging line,

> Spirit of Arnall! aid me whilst I lie.

Pope had indeed made a fortune by literature, but
Pope was the first poet of his day, and was one of
the shrewdest men of business who ever lived. But
even Pope had no pride in his authorship, and claimed
no dignity for the profession of man of letters. It
was the smart of personal vanity, writhing under the
reproach of authorship, which made him so meanly
anxious to dissociate himself from his poorer con-
federates in literature, and dictated the *Dunciad*.
Pope's great satire on Grub Street produces to-day
an effect the very opposite of that which he intended:
it reveals the malevolence of the poet, and holds up

Grub Street not to eternal scorn, but to commiseration and sympathy. A large-hearted man would have been softened by his very success into some compassion for the poor ragged drudges whose service of literature, such as it was, brought them no better reward than the garret and the sponging-house, or at least he would have refrained from insulting their misfortunes. But Pope was not a large-hearted man, and was too much under the traditions of literature by patronage to perceive that in Grub Street the foundations were being laid of a republic of letters, where the patron would be abolished and supplanted by the public.

This, then, was the state of things when Samuel Johnson, a lean, purblind, friendless scholar, made his appearance in London, humbly seeking from Mr. Edward Cave, of St. John's Gate, Clerkenwell, literary employment on the *Gentleman's Magazine*. There was little enough to recommend him, and he had little to hope for. He was literally what Boswell's father, years later, contemptuously said he was, ' A dominie who kept a school and called it an academy.' He was also a schoolmaster who had failed. Strange and rough in manner, odd almost to grotesqueness in appearance, liable to fits of self-absorption, quick in temper, keen and biting in speech, it is little wonder that his school had not prospered, and that after teaching Church history for many months to his pupils, one of these misguided students was under the impression that the monasteries were destroyed by Jesus Christ. Like Goldsmith, he was driven into literature by his necessities, and would gladly enough have escaped had he been able. One would like to know what were Johnson's first impressions of that strange, half-heroic, half-blackguardly, tatterdemalion world of letters into which he found himself introduced. The great light of the *Gentleman's Magazine* was a certain Moses Brown, and him he saw in an alehouse at Clerkenwell, wrapped in a horseman's coat, with 'a great bushy, uncombed wig,' much obscured in tobacco smoke; not an edifying vision, but one to be treated with due respect. Before long he was to find men of letters in far worse quarters than an alehouse: Derrick sleeping in a barrel, Savage finding his lodgings in the streets; Boyse in bed clothed with a blanket, through which holes had been cut that his arms might be thrust, in which pleasant position Mr. Boyse was accustomed to continue his literary labours with a somewhat imperfect success.

It was the custom of Boyse, as soon as he earned any money, to spend it on wine and truffles, after which he returned to his blanket and dry crusts, with a refreshing sense that life might after all be worth living. Drudgery naturally bred recklessness; and the darkness and sordid shifts of daily humiliation were occasionally illumined by flashes of wild gaiety such as this. And it was with the Boyses and Derricks that Johnson must needs begin his literary life. His companions were men who only occasionally knew the satisfaction of a full meal, and whose life alternated between gluttony and starvation. If Johnson had ever entertained any romantic notions of the glory of a literary life, a month of Grub Street was amply sufficient to undeceive him. But Johnson from the first had a perfectly clear vision of the life on which he was embarking. Romantic ideas of the pride of authorship did not trouble him;

he said with blunt common-sense that 'no man but a blockhead ever wrote except for money.' The problem was how to get money by means that did not involve a sacrifice of honour, how to maintain his independence against the seduction of the patron on one hand, and the bullying extortion of the book-seller on the other. That was the real task which Johnson set himself to accomplish: to make the world understand that the work of a man's brains was as worthy of remuneration as the work of his hands, and that among many professions literature is not the least honourable, nor the least productive of good to a nation.

Perhaps Johnson did not perceive the aim of his work as definitely as we do: it is not the soldier fighting in the thick of the battle smoke who knows best how the fight is going. It is pretty certain that Johnson had no objection to patronage in itself. Why, indeed, should he? That the man to whom fortune has accorded opulence should recognise that wealth has duties as well as privileges, and that among the very highest services which wealth can perform for a country is that of foster-ing and developing genius, is in itself an altogether right and noble thing. The connection between a Southampton and a Shakespeare is honourable to both, and most honourable to the patron. The doctrine that literary men should shift for them-selves, and that in the rough-and-tumble race of life they have as good a chance as anybody else, is very well for facile writers, gifted with commercial shrewd-ness; but in its application to the finer spirits of humanity, it comes perilously near Horace Walpole's cynical saying that poets are like singing-birds, who sing best if we starve them. Would it not have been a good thing for Goldsmith if a patron had secured him ease of mind, by freeing him from those sordid cares which wore his life out at six-and-forty? Have there not been delicate spirits in every age, whose genius has never reached its blossoming time, for want of some kindly shelter from the icy winds of penury? The false pride which prevents a man from accepting kindness, is little better than the callous heartlessness which prevents a man from bestowing it. It was the false pride of Chatterton that made him refuse a proffered meal when he was starving, and drove him into suicide; but a Johnson and a Carlyle knew how to receive graciously as well as give generously, and the former is more difficult than the latter. No, it was not the pride of stubborn independence altogether which made Johnson repudiate the patron. He dimly felt the drift of his times, and perceived that the day of the patron was over. Literature had outgrown the patron, and wanted a larger air, a freer environment. That same democratic force which at this very time was startling Chatham by the return of timber merchants to Parliament, and which was breathing its fiery summons through the lips of Wilkes, was also preparing a new era for literature. Henceforth books were not to be the solace of the rich, but the inheritance of the common people, and in the common people authors were to find a far more munificent public than in the select circles of the titled and the wealthy. The day was nearly over when Cowper dared not speak of Bunyan, lest so despised a name should earn a sneer. The reign of the common people was commencing, and the barriers which had hitherto divided authors from the public were about to be broken down. Johnson was the last great Englishman who endured the contempt which had been associated with authorship; and it was the advent of the democracy which freed authorship from reproach, and threw open to it the gates of a world-wide liberty.

The significance of Samuel Johnson in literature lies for us, then, in this one fact, that it was he who proclaimed the Republic of Letters, and in him a literary revolution centred. Two periods met in him: he was the last man of the one and the first of the other; the last great English author who wrote dedications to wealthy patrons, and the first to cast himself boldly on public appreciation for support. How Johnson, Tory as he was, at last was goaded into active rebellion, and proclaimed in stentorian tones, which still vibrate on the ears of men, this new Republic of Letters, we all know. When he wrote his celebrated letter to Lord Chesterfield, saying, 'Seven years have now passed since I waited in your outward rooms, or was repulsed from your door,' and went on to describe a patron as one who 'looks with unconcern on a man struggling in the water, and when he has reached the ground encumbers him with help,' Johnson rang the death-knell of patronage. It was a noble letter, worthy of the man and the occasion, breathing the spirit of proud independence, and touched also with a sort of rugged pathos, especially in those concluding epigrammatic sentences: 'The notice which you have been pleased to take of my labours, had it been early, had been kind; but it has been delayed till I am indifferent, and cannot enjoy it; till I am solitary, and cannot

impart it ; till I am known, and do not want it. I
hope it is no very cynical asperity not to confess obligations where no benefit has been received, or to
be unwilling that the public should consider me as
owing to a patron that which Providence has enabled
me to do for myself.' That letter marks an epoch in
English literature. It is the vigorous birthcry of a
new power: the Magna Charta, if you will, of authorship ; its Declaration of Independence, which, like
another similar document of modern times, seems to
state in no doubtful tones, not that American slaves,
but that English writers are then, henceforward, and
for ever free. It was in vain that Johnson signed
that letter, 'Your Lordship's most humble, most
obedient servant, Sam. Johnson': henceforth he
was no man's servant, and not obedient ; he had
elected to stand or fall by his own genius, and had
inaugurated a revolt not less important to the world,
perhaps, than John Wilkes' riots, or even French
Revolutions.

Perhaps, in a minor degree, that was not a less
significant service to literature which Johnson performed when he knocked down Thomas Osborne,
the bookseller, with one of his own folios, for daring
to bully him for negligence in some miserable hack-
work he had undertaken for him. That a poor
author should knock down a bookseller was certainly
as startling to shabby, dim-eyed, drudging Grub
Street, as that he should insult an earl. It was much
like a schoolboy who had been sent up to be
thrashed, turning round upon the master and thrash-
ing him instead ; and was received with the same
species of jubilation. The folio with which this prodigious act was performed is still in existence, and

should certainly be preserved as literally one of the most famous instruments by which liberty has been achieved. For when the worst has been said about patrons, there is still worse that might be written about publishers. If it were a hard thing to eat the bread of charity at a patron's table, it was incontestably a harder to earn one's bread amid the rapacious tradesmen of Paternoster Row. There were publishers who were honourable, and even generous, as Johnson testified ; but there were others of the Griffith species, who bought men like Goldsmith at so much a week, and grew rich and even kept two carriages, as is reported of Griffith, by the lucrative process of sweating poor authors. Not less ignorant than rapacious, such men knew just enough of books to perceive that they might be produced for little and sold at a good profit, and their function was to pick the brains of authors and then kick their skulls down Paternoster Row. Their contempt for literature went far to make literature itself contemptible, and the famished Grub Street drudge might well look back to the days of patronage as to a shining Paradise, and feel that the most scornful charity of the patron was better than the dull avarice of the hack bookseller. This insolence of the man to whom literature was known only as a commercial commodity, Johnson had also to fight, which he literally did when he knocked down Osborne. His task was a hard one : it was to convince a reluctant world that the man who wrote books deserved well of mankind, that he would no longer be content to work for nothing, that he was about to emerge from his sordid Inferno and Valley of Humiliation, and become a power to be reckoned with, and that henceforth he would vigorously refuse to bare his back to the

Whips and scorns of time,
The oppressor's wrong, the proud man's contumely,
The insolence of office, and the spurns
Which patient merit of the unworthy takes.

Alone, unaided, asking neither charity nor pity, Johnson set himself to his appointed task, and opposed to the shocks of time and fate a stubborn, unvanquishable patience, altogether noble, memorable, and heroic. If to-day the man of letters is honoured and even opulent, if it be his great vocation to mould the minds of myriads through the press, and to preach in a secular temple as wide as the horizons, it was old Samuel Johnson who won for him this liberty, and by his poverty and sorrow made many rich.

CHAPTER III

BOSWELL'S JOHNSON

THE story of Johnson's life has been told by many writers, writing from various points of view, and with various degrees of insight and sympathy, but it has never failed to be interesting. Macaulay has given us his Meissonnier-like picture of the man and his times, a brilliant portraiture from the outside wrought up with consummate patience of detail and vividness of colouring. Carlyle has given us his sketch of the moral significance of the man and his times, by virtue of his intense insight and sympathy going far deeper than Macaulay, and touching-in his portrait with more lifelike realism and effect. Other and minor hands have again and again assumed the task, and few have altogether failed, because the man himself is so full of interest that it is hardly possible for any one to be quite dull in writing of him. Boswell's *Life of Johnson* has held its place for a century as a classic biography, and is not likely to be displaced. It is one of the few books which a man would choose for lifelong companionship, a book which fascinates the scholar and student not less than the common people who run and read. It has the superb merit of being graphic and alive in its every detail. Boswell has no need to describe his hero: we see him for ourselves. There is no reticence about James Boswell; he tells us all he knows. His worship for his burly hero is touching in its thoroughness and simplicity. He is quite willing to acknowledge that his one function in life was to gather up the scattered conversational gems of Dr. Johnson, and he reckons it a task worth living for. Vain as he is, he has no vanity in the presence of his idol. He is his most devoted humble servant. He enjoys being insulted by Johnson more than he would relish being flattered by any other man. All other men he reckons to be poor creatures beside the surly old philosopher of Bolt Court, and he is at no pains to conceal his estimate of them. The result of this hero-worship on the part of Boswell is a book which has interested the English-speaking people of the earth for a century, and seems likely to interest them for many a century to come. Mr. George H. Lewes has said that Boswell's Johnson was a sort of test-book with him; according to a man's judgment of the book was the judgment he formed of him. And he has also said with equal felicity and truth, that 'the charm and value of such a work must be in the delightfully dramatic conversations, crowded with wit, humour, and wisdom; and in the moral significance of the picture thus presented of a noble soul struggling with difficulties, moral and physical, a strong and affluent nature in which many infirmities were blended.'

Johnson was a great author in more senses than one, but when we name Johnson we think of the man rather than of his writings. Not that his writings are not worth careful perusal. There are lines in his poetry which have become classical, and there are pages in his essays which are unmatched in their own ponderous and elaborate eloquence. His Dictionary is a monument of indefatigable industry and critical acumen. His *Lives of the Poets*, narrow and unsympathetic as they are in certain essential points, are nevertheless nobly conceived and nobly written. Cast off as they were with rapidity and ease by a man who no longer had a reputation to make or penury to fear, they are less stilted than his earlier writings, and are in every way more vivid, more graceful, and more perfect in structure and workmanship. But when we have said all that can be said about Johnson's voluminous writings, we are still face to face with the strange phenomenon of a man whose reputation as a writer is forgotten, still living in the imperishable regard and interest of posterity. For this singular state of things Boswell is answerable. But for Boswell, Johnson would now be a mere shadow and a memory. But Boswell, when he took it upon him to dog and eavesdrop the steps of Johnson, to report his conversations and treasure up his witticisms, redeemed Johnson from the decay which has fallen on his contemporaries and postponed for him indefinitely the encroachments of oblivion.

When we ask what it is that has made Boswell's book a great classic, we are bound to concede to Boswell himself the credit of having inaugurated a new style of biography, conceived with true originality, and carried out with conspicuous success. Toady, sycophant, braggart, eavesdropper—all these and more Boswell may have been, but he had one great gift, the faculty of recognising greatness, and of suppressing himself in the presence of greatness. His introduction to Johnson was not auspicious, and a prouder man would have keenly resented Johnson's mode of reception. 'It is true,' said Boswell, with great humility, 'I am a Scotchman, but I can't help it.' 'That is what a great many of your countrymen cannot help,' retorted Johnson. More than once Johnson tired of his sycophancy, and on one occasion said to him, 'You have only two subjects, myself and yourself, and I am sick of both of them.' On another occasion, when they were discussing how to get rid of an awkward friend, Johnson said, 'We'll send you to him. If your presence doesn't drive a man out of his house, nothing will.' Johnson alternately lectured, bullied, and quizzed him, all of which Boswell endured with exemplary meekness, for had he not the memory of that beatific hour when Johnson said, 'I have taken a fancy to you'; and was not that sufficient to encourage and fortify him under the worst caprices of his hero? It was the very insignificance of Boswell that gave him his unique fitness for the post of Johnson's biographer. Johnson stood on no ceremony with him : he never restrained himself, he concealed nothing, he followed his variable whims as he pleased, without any uneasy sense of being observed, and in fact disported himself with an unreflecting abandonment which displayed the whole man. Johnson had no company manners for anybody, but it is pretty certain that he talked in the presence of Boswell with a freedom which he felt in no other presence. The result of this strange comradeship was that Boswell saw Johnson with a completeness which was granted to no other man, and his biography is a vivid portraiture of Johnson in all his moods. We see him in his domestic as well as his public life, in his prejudice and narrowness as well as his nobility and sympathetic breadth of nature, in his chivalry and rudeness, his pugnacity and kindliness, his strong-mindedness and superstition, his irascibility and patience, the humorous cynicism of his public talk, and the concealed and shamefaced charities of his private life. To this uninterrupted and minute study of Johnson, Boswell devoted the best years of his life, and behind that seemingly foolish face of his there was concealed an extraordinary vigilance of observation which was capable of producing with photographic exactitude all that passed across the area of its vision. The singular merit of Boswell's book is that we always see the hero and never think of the author. We are annoyed by no tedious dissertations on Johnson's character and merits; Johnson is his own expositor, and lives and moves before us with extraordinary reality and vividness. It is these qualities which make Boswell's book the greatest of biographies, and which justify us in describing this idle, vainglorious, Scotch gossip as the father of all modern biography.

There is even something in the very simplicity of Boswell himself which is fascinating. He reveals himself with the same unconscious art with which he paints Johnson. He makes it abundantly evident what a terrible bore he often proved himself, and half of Johnson's smartest sayings were provoked by the irritating interrogatories of Boswell. When Boswell grew sentimental and talked of retiring to a desert, Johnson instantly suggested Scotland to him as a suitable locality. When he ruefully informed Johnson that the wine he drank overnight had made his head ache, Johnson sarcastically replied it was not the wine which made his head ache, but the sense he had put into it. 'Will sense make the head ache?' said Boswell. 'Yes, sir, if you're not used to it,' retorted Johnson. Those continual gibes against the Scotch, which afforded Johnson's friends so much amusement, were more often than not devised for Boswell's benefit. When a Scotchman apologised for Scotland by saying God made it, Johnson replied that 'comparisons were odious: God made hell.' The first night he was in Edinburgh, Boswell and he walked arm-in-arm up the High Street. 'Well now, doctor, we are at last in Scotland,' said Boswell. 'Yes, sir,' was the answer, 'I smell it in the dark.' When Boswell pressed him to admit that there was at least plenty of meat and drink in Scotland, he replied, 'Why, yes sir, meat and drink enough to give the inhabitants sufficient strength to run away from home.' It was one of his habitual jokes that the finest prospect a Scotchman ever saw was the road that led him to England, and when some one once said that England was lost, he retorted that it was 'not so much to be lamented that England was lost as that the Scotch had found it.' He was reconciled to Wilkes by a story which that astute demagogue told him of a privateer which had completely plundered seven Scotch islands, and sailed away with the booty of—three-and-sixpence. It must have cost Boswell something of a patriotic pang to narrate these stories, but he never hesitated to narrate any sort of gibe, either against his country or himself, if it only illustrated the wit and humour of Johnson. The wonderful thing is that with all his admiration of Johnson, he never tried to soften in the narration those asperities of speech from which he must often have suffered. He reveals Johnson's defects with the same simplicity with which he reveals his own. When Hannah More entreated him to delete from his biography the stories which showed Johnson's temper at the roughest, he replied, ' I will not make my tiger a cat to please anybody.' This real love of truth which distinguished Boswell was his most memorable quality, and it wrought in him an unconscious artistic insight, out of which there was produced a book which is still unrivalled, unapproached, and perhaps unapproachable.

The charm of Dr. Johnson lies in his uncurbed and fearless individuality. When he emerged into fame, those peculiarities of demeanour and temper which had always made him grotesque were too deep-seated and long-indulged for modification, nor did he seek to modify them. In his long and solitary struggle he had suffered much, and suffering had given edge to his temper and asperity to his speech. In those hard and bitter years, when he had been as famished as Derrick and as badly housed as Boyse, when he had lain in sponging-houses, and had huddled behind a screen in an eating-house that his rags might not be observed, he had learned many lessons, and chief among them this—an independence of soul which utterly refused to be imposed upon by the cant and conventionalities of life. He had learned to see men in their native worth, or worthlessness, and crouched and fawned to no man. He had found greatness of soul in the outcast, and littleness of soul in the great; heroism hiding under rags, and meanness concealed under coronets. Such experiences had developed his natural power of insight, his bluntness of speech, his fearlessness of the conventions of society. When

he told men to clear their minds of cant, he recom-
mended a process by which he himself had profited.
He aimed at pleasing nobody by his civilities, and
conciliating nobody by his friendship. If he thought
a man was a fool, he told him so with uncompromising candour. When some one defended drinking
because it drove away care, and made men forget
what was disagreeable, Johnson retorted to the
question whether he would not allow a man to drink
for these reasons, ' Yes, sir, if he sat next *you*.' When
an antiquated beau asked him what he would give
to be as sprightly as he was, ' Why, sir,' was the reply,
' I think I would almost be content to be as foolish.'
When a lady congratulated him on the absence of
nasty words from his dictionary, his acute but
uncomplimentary retort was, ' Oh, then you 've been
looking for them, have you ? ' The noblest element
in the strange conglomerate of Johnson's nature was
this untamable honesty. He had passed at a single
step from Grub Street to the society of the wealthy
and the scholarly, but he retained amid the incense
of daily flattery the same resolute independence
which had supported him in the long outlawry of
his beggary. He had brought with him from Grub
Street also many habits which were quite as startling
as the freedom of his speech. It is not difficult to
understand how Mrs. Boswell resented his over-
bearing manner, his uncertain hours, his strange
voracity, his method of snuffing candles ·with his
fingers, and dropping the wax upon the floor. But
he was no less strange an apparition in the well-
ordered house of Mrs. Boswell than he was in society
itself. There he was, a rough, untamable man,
irascible, dogmatic, contentious, saying things no

one else would dare to say even if he could, doing things that were permitted to no other, and men might take or leave him as they pleased. But there was also in him a great kindly-beating heart, a rugged nobleness of nature, a lambency of pure genius, playing with fitful splendour over all his thought; and for these things men might well forgive, as the most discerning did, defects of manner and deficiencies of temper and behaviour.

Another reason which has contributed to the lasting popularity of Johnson is that he was a typical Englishman. He was what would be called to-day a Philistine. He had no more respect for literary than social conventions, and outraged both with the same energetic delight. He was full of prejudice, thoroughly insular in his habit of thought, and narrow in the area of his vision. He applied the test of blunt common-sense to everything— except, perhaps, the Cock Lane ghost. And yet such is the humour with which he clothes all his opinions, that the very insularity of Johnson becomes a new charm, and his prejudices delight us. He gloried in the fact that he had accomplished single-handed a work over which French lexicographers had exhausted years and numbers; but then, 'What can you expect,' said he, 'from fellows that eat frogs?' He said that the first Whig was the Devil, and when he wrote Parliamentary reports he always took care that 'the Whig dogs should get the worst of it.' He at once absolved from uncharitableness a man who was throwing snails into his neighbour's garden, when he found his neighbour was a Whig. He brought the same prejudices into play in his literary criticisms. When he was asked if he thought any other man could have written Macpherson's *Ossian*, he replied, ' Yes, sir, many men, many women, and many children.' Gray was dull in company, dull in his closet, dull everywhere: when he wrote his poems he was simply dull in a new way, and that made people think him great. When some one claimed for David Hume that he was at least luminous, Johnson replied that undoubtedly he had light—just enough to light him to Hell. He saw no beauty in Percy's *Ancient English Ballads*, and ridiculed the simplicity of their metre in the well-known parody:

> As with my hat upon my head
> I walk'd along the Strand,
> I there did meet another man
> With his hat in his hand.

For some obscure reason he hated Milton's *Lycidas*, and when Miss Seward told him she had read it with a delight that grew by what it fed on, and asked what was to become of her, he replied, ' Die, then, in a surfeit of bad taste.' In relation to art and music he displayed the same obstinate dislike to conventional opinions. When a young lady tried to secure his admiration for the music she had just played by saying it was difficult, ' Difficult,' he exclaimed, ' would to Heaven it had been impossible!' So one might go on recounting stories which afford ample illustration of the Philistinism of Johnson. In all these stories, however, two things are obvious: the workings of a strong but prejudiced mind, so careless to conceal its defects that its very candour is humorous; and a power of shrewd, piercing commonsense, which is equally successful in ascertaining the qualities and defects of men and things, and in the exposition of both is entirely unrestrained by any considerations of average and conventional opinion.

The humour of Dr. Johnson, springing as it does from intellectual force and being based on sterling common-sense, is precisely that species of humour which the Englishman never fails to relish. It is often rude and rough, but it always goes to the point, and puts to rout the adversary. The oddity of the whole performance is that when Johnson has delivered his most knock-down sort of retort, he is never conscious that he has been rude at all. He was not a sensitive man, although he was a man of deep feeling, and he had no compassion to spare for the pangs of wounded vanity. He even prided himself on being a particularly gallant and polite man. If he was not exactly that, we may at least say that there was no malice in his wit. He usually fought for the mere sake of victory, and it is easy to see that he loved these controversial battles for their own sake. Nothing delights him so much as to find a foeman worthy of his steel, or we might more appropriately say, of his bludgeon. His controversial battles were all conducted upon the pattern of his famous tussle with Thomas Osborne. When he had knocked Osborne down he exclaimed, ‘Lie there, thou son of dulness, ignorance, and obscurity’; and he further observed to the truculent bookseller that he need be in no hurry to rise, for when he did so he proposed kicking him downstairs. He always aimed at disabling his adversary, and when his blood was up never stopped to consider whether his words would hurt. Johnson’s wit is no sharp rapier thrust, no splendid fencing; it has no delicacy, no ironical banter, no concealed satire, nothing of that elusive half-meaning which makes Swift's wit so searching and formidable. He uses the most terse and stinging phrases, and is a master in the art of covering his adversary with ridicule. And yet, however hard he hits, his epigrams are so bathed in paradoxical humour, that it is impossible to be seriously offended with him. Even when he is in his most contradictory and prejudiced mood, it is rarely that we cannot recognise some redeeming quality of good sense in his criticisms. Many of his sayings have the sententious wisdom of proverbs, as, for instance, when he said in reference to theological disputes that the man who would not go to heaven in a green coat would not get there any quicker in a grey one; and when he compared a preaching woman to a dancing dog—the wonder was not that the performance was well done, but that it was done at all. He could even accept the laugh when it went against himself with a surly grace. But it must be owned that this was a rare occurrence. He was the very Napoleon of conversation, moving with lightning-like rapidity upon his adversaries, and defeating them in detail. He overwhelmed them with the sheer brilliance and velocity of his attack; with all his massiveness, was far too alert ever to be caught napping; and visited with the most summary castigation any one who was foolish enough to suppose him capable of such stupidity.

But, after all, no mere description, however vivid and incisive, can paint Samuel Johnson. For the perfect portraiture of Johnson we must go to Boswell's ponderous book, and there, reading slowly and many times, till the impression has had time to saturate itself into the memory, we shall at last find the figure of the old doctor emerging from the shadows of the past, with all the freshness and vitality of an immortal creation. Gradually, as we look through Boswell's pages as through a magic crystal, the mists are withdrawn, and all that strange, crowded, fascinating life of the eighteenth century transacts itself again before our eyes. We see the old club-room where Burke and Reynolds, Beauclerk and Goldsmith are familiar faces: we hear Goldsmith's modest speech, Burke's sonorous eloquence, Johnson's stentorian verdicts, while Reynolds listens with attentive trumpet, and Beauclerk smiles with satiric mirth, and Boswell rubs his hands and chuckles at the smart thrust and parry of his hero. We follow Johnson as he sallies forth into Fleet Street; we laugh at the superstitious care with which he touches the posts in passing; and there is moisture in our eyes as we see him stoop to put a coin into the hands of sleeping children, whose outcast lives know no softer pillow than the stones of London. We see him do a stranger and nobler thing still: from those filthy kennels he lifts a diseased and outcast woman, and carries her away upon his back to that old house in Bolt Court, which is already an asylum for all species of distress, that he may there nurse her back to life and virtue. What strange depths of tenderness and compassion there are in the heart of this old stoical philosopher! Who else would ever have stood bare-headed in the rain, amid the jeers of a market-place, because forty years before he had there inflicted an unkindness upon a father long since dead? How many other famous men of letters have we had who would have watched beside a servant's sick-bed as he watched beside the bed of Catherine Chambers, have called her his dear friend, and have written, 'I then kissed her. She told me that to part was the greatest pain she had ever felt, and that she hoped we should meet again in a better place. I expressed, with swelled eyes and great emotion of tenderness, the same hopes. We kissed and parted; I humbly hope to meet again and to part no more.' It is for things like these that we love, and can never cease to love, Samuel Johnson. Well might Goldsmith say of him that there was nothing of the bear about him but the skin. Hidden under that uncouth exterior, that seamed face and shabby dress, there was not merely a great genius, but a great nature, a profoundly religious, upright, heroic soul. 'The world passes away, and we are passing with it; but there is doubtless another world which will endure for ever. In the meantime let us be kind to one another,' he writes in one of his last letters. His final thoughts were how to arrange an annuity for his servant Frank, and having found that fifty pounds per annum was considered a handsome legacy from a nobleman to a favourite servant, he resolved to leave Frank seventy. To the last his social nature manifested itself. He filled his sick-room with friends, and when Burke feared the number might be oppressive to him, he replied, 'I must be in a wretched state indeed when your company would not be a delight to me.' Burke replied with the tremulousness of unshed tears in his voice, 'Dear sir, you have always been too good to me.' He did not disguise his honest love of life, his honest dread of death; but he who had known how to endure the one with fortitude learned how to meet the other without dismay. To him, as he lay dying, men and women came for benediction, and his last words were to say to such a visitor, a young girl in the freshness of her maidenhood, 'God bless you, my dear.' Such was Samuel Johnson, a great man, and what is more than that, a good man ; one of those rare spirits, who not only do much to illumine the minds of men, but who do more still to kindle and sustain their best impulses, and whose memories thus become a glory and an inspiration.

CHAPTER IV

OLIVER GOLDSMITH

[Born at Pallas, Ireland, Nov. 10, 1728.   Published the *Citizen of the World*, 1760; the *Traveller*, 1764; the *Vicar of Wakefield*, 1766. Died, March 25, 1774.]

IF the interest excited by Dr. Johnson has been great and lasting, not less permanent is the interest which attaches itself to Goldsmith.   But it differs altogether in quality.   Johnson is in all things the strong man, a Hercules wrestling with his seven labours, rude and rough, but rarely less than heroic in a stolid and indomitable fashion, and above all a humourist, whose humour was a weapon, with which he fought his way to fortune.   He tells us that he was once touched by the description which a ragged female beggar gave of herself—'an old struggler'; and he was touched because the phrase applied itself with curious felicity to his own arduous life.   We are fascinated with the spectacle of Johnson storming his way onward to esteem, as we should be with the spectacle of a forlorn hope pushing its way upward against flaming battlements: he touches the soldier instinct in us. But Goldsmith was not a strong man, nor a wise man, nor a successful man.   His qualities were precisely those which do not help a man to overcome the world, but through which the world is able to inflict severe suffering and much secret torture. His two dominant characteristics were simplicity and sensitiveness, and the hard discipline of life never taught him how to barter the one for worldly shrewdness, or the other for worldly callousness. It was his simplicity which Walpole jeered at when he called him 'an inspired idiot'; it was his sensitiveness which laid him open to many of those conversational disabilities which Boswell recounts with such malicious glee. No experience of the venomous jealousies of the world ever cured Goldsmith of his native habit of wearing his heart upon his sleeve; no experience of the ingratitude of the world ever soured the native kindliness of his nature. In sweetness of heart, in tenderness of feeling, in all that constitutes charm of character, Goldsmith, with all his faults, was and still remains the most lovable man whom English literature has produced.

The whirligig of Time brings strange revenges, and it is one of the revenges of Time that the very qualities which were the secret of Goldsmith's earthly troubles are now the sources of his fame and fascination. A soft, unfading radiance clothes him, and our hearts go out with unfailing affection towards one to whom we owe so much. For, in a wider sense than we can readily conceive, the simplicity and sensitiveness of Goldsmith were the forces which shaped all the really memorable work which he has done in literature. Who but a tender-hearted man could have written the *Deserted Village*, who but a man of guileless simplicity could have wandered through those many sharp experiences which find such delightful reflection in the *Traveller, She Stoops to Conquer*, and the *Citizen of the World*? More than any other writer of his time, more even than professed novelists like Smollett and Richardson, Gold-

smith drew upon the wealth of his own experiences
in all that he wrote of abiding interest. None but
a simpleton would have mistaken a squire's house
for an inn, but out of that ludicrous misadventure
his best comedy was born. None but a man of
ineradicable guilelessness of nature would have
entertained the idea of fluting his way through
Europe, but the fruit of those strange wanderings
was one of the loveliest and most perfect poems in
English literature. A man less sophisticated and
world-hardened than Goldsmith could never have
conceived such a story as the *Vicar of Wakefield*,
a story on which, to quote a phrase of Bunyan's, 'the
very dew of heaven is still fresh.' It may be that
in the ordinary sense Goldsmith was not a wise man,
but there is a frequent wisdom in simplicity which is
denied to profundity, and in the truest sense simplicity may be the last art of profundity. Certain
it is that for the production of the most delicate
bloom of literature the childlike mind is needed, and
Goldsmith was an eternal child. Amid all the rude
and violent influences of his time, he still retained
something of the child's divine innocence and grace,
the child's sensitiveness and impressionability, and
for us he possesses also all the child's lovableness.
If he occasionally manifested also the foibles and the
petulance of the child, these are faults which can
be readily forgiven him. Without the foibles, the
harmless egotism and amusing vanity, the love of
fine dress and incapacity of understanding the duty
of paying for it, the careless generosity, the total lack
of prudence, the unforeseeing pleasure in the hour, the
gay neglect of the lessons of the past and the stern
monitions of the future, he would not be Goldsmith,

he would not be the man whose simplicity is more attractive, and whose folly is more endearing, than the heroism and wisdom of far greater men.

The life of Oliver Goldsmith may be described as a prolonged misadventure, a comedy with tragic shadows always lurking in the background, a tragedy lit up to the very last with sunny flashes of comic mirth. What a series of immortal pictures glow before us, in living vividness and colour, as we read his history! From the first our sympathies go out to the little, ugly, pock-marked child, under whose clumsy demeanour so rare a spirit is concealed. We laugh at his innocent college excesses, his elation in the possession of a guinea, his prodigal wanderings, and return on his 'fiddle-backed Rosinante,' his excuse that after so much trouble to reach home his mother might at least have been glad to see him, his futile efforts to study law and medicine, his still more futile attempt to become a cleric, his reckless generosity, his insouciant philosophy, his light-hearted way of following delusive hopes and attempting foolish enterprises. There was never so lovable a ne'er-do-weel, so innocent a prodigal. But it often happens that our laughter comes perilously near to tears, and the picture of Goldsmith standing in the shadows of the Dublin streets listening eagerly to some street hawker singing his songs, is as immortal in its pathos as the picture of Goldsmith spending his last guinea in buying tulips for his uncle Contarine is immortal in its humour. Throughout the life of Goldsmith the pathos and the humour go together, and the ludicrous and tragic chase each other in his history, as cloud and sunshine in an April firmament. To him, however, that was often enough tragic which is ludicrous to us. In the world's great school he was one of those awkward scholars whose fate it is always to be imposed upon by shrewder, and bullied by stronger, natures. Like all sensitive people he had a great capacity for love, a thirst for recognition which the undiscerning mistook for vanity, a desire for sympathy which the callous interpreted as egotism. Even Johnson misunderstood and was unfair to him, and often caused him poignant if unintentional pain. No one else tried to understand him, and no one took him seriously. To the members of the Literary Club he was what he had been at Trinity College, Dublin, at Dr. Milner's Academy at Peckham, at Mr. Griffiths' dingy shop—a person of no particular account, whose amiableness invited imposition, and whose awkwardness was a theme for ridicule. Those who knew him best had recognised his genius so little, that when he published the *Traveller*, it was difficult to persuade them that he had written it himself. He was throughout life the butt of inferior wits, and in the arts which secure earthly success was completely distanced by inferior men, because he had no power of impressing himself as others. He had the finest wit, but it was not at command ; he had genius and eloquence, but an invincible awkwardness and timidity prevented the display of either when their display would have won him respect. In conversation he was like a man who has a purse of gold, but who cannot produce the single silver coin which is wanted at the moment. The same illustration may be applied to his entire life. With a heart rich in affection, a nature incomparably wealthy in noble qualities, he possessed nothing of that exterior fascination by which friendship is invited and retained. Misunderstood, repulsed in his affections, the hunger of his heart was satisfied with no human food; and therefore to his loss, but to our infinite gain, he transferred his love to the creatures of his fancy, and let the restrained kindliness and yearning of his nature overflow in pages which are the delight of the world to-day, not less for their literary beauty than for their moral tenderness and sweetness.

If Goldsmith's life had been less chequered, if he had possessed personal charm as well as genius, his writings would have been very different, and possibly we should miss much that is our delight to-day. He was so intensely individual that the reflection of his own life is seen in everything he wrote. Even in his meanest hack-work we come ever and again on passages saturated with personal feeling, passages which, like some still pool in a barren moorland, hold in their depths the clouded blue of his own troubled life. It is not only in his private letters that he talks of starving in the streets of London, where Otway and Butler starved before him, and says that no one cares a farthing for him. Buried in the reviews which he wrote for Griffiths in the earliest period of his drudgery, we find sentences like these, which at once arrest the ear with the ring of personal experience: 'The regions of taste,' says he, 'can be travelled only by a few, and even those find indifferent accommodation by the way. Let such as have not yet a passport from Nature be content with happiness, and leave the poet the unrivalled possession of his misery, his garret, and his fame.' Here again, in his *Inquiry into the State of Learning*, is a passage which is too clearly wrung from his own bitter knowledge of life, and is but too faithful and prophetic a transcript of his own career. He says that the author is 'a *child* of the public in all respects; for while so well able to direct others, how incapable is he frequently found of directing himself! His simplicity exposes him to all the insidious approaches of cunning ; his sensibility to the slightest invasions of contempt. Broken rest, tasteless meals, and causeless anxiety shorten his life, or render it unfit for active employment ; prolonged vigils and intense application still further contract his span, and make his time glide insensibly away. Let us not then aggravate those natural inconveniences by neglect : we have had sufficient instances of this kind already. It is enough that the age has already produced instances of men pressing foremost in the lists of fame, and worthy of better times, schooled by continual adversity into a hatred of their kind, flying from thought to drunkenness, yielding to the united pressure of labour, penury, and sorrow, sinking unheeded, without one friend to drop a tear on their unattended obsequies, and indebted to charity for a grave.' He cannot even write his *Natural History* without this touch of heartfelt humanity :—' The lower race of animals, when satisfied for the instant moment, are perfectly happy ; but it is otherwise with man. His mind anticipates distress, and feels the pang of want before it arrests him. Some cruel disorder, but no way like hunger, seizes the unhappy sufferer, so that almost all those men who have thus long lived by chance, and whose every day may be considered as a happy escape from famine, are known at last to die, in reality, of a disorder caused by hunger, but which in the common language is often called a broken heart. Some of these I have known myself, when very little able to relieve them ; and I have been told by a very active and worthy magistrate, that the number of such as die in London of want is much greater than one would imagine — I think he talked of two thousand a year.' In passages like these we have not only gleams of poetry and pathos, but we have Goldsmith's own life. All the reward he obtained for his poetry was his misery, his garret, and his fame. Tasteless meals and mean distresses in Green Arbour Court, threats of arrest from Griffiths, midnight vigils and ill-paid drudgery, a life whose every day was a happy escape from famine, were the actual elements of Goldsmith's lot, and wore his strength out in the very prime of his years. That strange disorder called a broken heart, of which two thousand persons died annually in London, including some he had known and could but little relieve, was his destined end also ; for were not his last words the confession that his mind was not easy? and was it not that united pressure of labour, penury, and sorrow which weighed him down into the grave? How much does it say for the true nobility of Goldsmith's nature, that hard as his life was, one of its unhappy results at least he never knew : he never flew from thought to drunkenness, or was schooled by adversity into a hatred of his kind.

There is another respect also in which the nobleness of Goldsmith's nature was displayed. He had a higher vision of the functions of a man of letters than even Johnson had, and, with far less natural strength of character than Johnson, was equally sturdy in the maintenance of his own honour and independence. We are accustomed to praise Marvell for refusing a king's bribe, and Milton for turning his back upon a king's messenger, but in Goldsmith's life there occurred an equally striking but less-known scene. We have seen that while men of genius starved, political pamphleteers of the meanest abilities rolled in luxury, and there came a time when the Government made a bid for the pen of Goldsmith. The infamous Sandwich had a certain Parson Scott as chaplain, and Scott was sent to Goldsmith to induce him to write in favour of the administration. 'I found him,' says Scott, 'in a miserable set of chambers in the Temple. I told him my authority: I told him that I was empowered to pay most liberally for his exertions, and would you believe it, he was so absurd as to say, " I can earn as much as will supply my wants without writing for any party; the assistance you offer is therefore unnecessary to me." And so,' said the reverend plenipotentiary, with unstinted contempt, 'I left him in his garret.' What Goldsmith's exact earnings were at this time, it would be interesting to know: what sum it was that he found sufficient for his wants; but we know that this offer came at the close of twelve years' desperate struggle for bread, during which his first work had brought him little profit, and the *Vicar of Wakefield* had been sold for £60 to pay his landlady. He was now forty, and had but a few more years to live. Eight years before he had made despairing attempts to free himself from the unsought yoke of literature, and had thus described himself: 'Years of disappointment, anguish, and study have worn me down. Imagine to yourself a pale melancholy visage, with two big wrinkles between the eyebrows, with an eye disgustingly severe, and a big wig; and you have a perfect picture of my present appearance.' It was this man, who had toiled like a galley-slave, and with scarcely more honour, who had produced some of the finest things in English literature for the wages of a porter, who had been bandied from pillar to post by booksellers and editors, hustled, bullied, threatened, a miserable drudge whose only familiars were ignominy and hunger—it was this man who was now tempted with the vision of opulence, and he refused it. It may seem little enough to some ears to-day to say that Goldsmith refused to sell his pen to a party, but let us measure the temptation rightly that we may rightly measure the heroism of the refusal. There were few writers of that time who would not have welcomed the Reverend Chaplain Scott on such an errand. In many a garret not more miserable than Goldsmith's, his advent would have seemed like the birth of light itself after long darkness. Had he gone to Chatterton's garret in Brooke Street, Holborn, he would have been welcomed, for Chatterton, boy as he was, had measured the world with cynical correctness enough to say that any man was a fool who could not write on both sides of a question. Neither Marvell nor Milton was tried by so terrible a test as this, for neither touched the depth of miserable poverty in which Goldsmith dwelt. Yet forlorn as he was, Goldsmith was proof against the bribe. Much as he had lost in the long struggle, he had not lost self-respect ; broken as he was in hope, he was not broken in noble pride : with prompt magnanimity he said 'No' to Parson Scott, and that covetous intriguer and pluralist left him to his misery, his garret, and his fame.

Horace Walpole once said, with characteristic coxcombry, to a correspondent, 'You know how I shun authors, and would never have been one myself if it obliged me to keep such bad company. They are always in earnest, and think their profession serious, and dwell upon trifles, and reverence learning. I laugh at all these things and divert myself.' When Goldsmith shut the door upon Parson Scott, he performed the last definite act which bound him to authorship. He had begun life with far different hopes, he had become author only by compulsion, but at last he had come to see that authorship was the one vocation for which he was supremely fitted, and he regarded it with seriousness and earnestness. The special fitness of Goldsmith for authorship lay in two things, and the first of these was style. He touched nothing that he did not adorn: if he had written upon a broomstick he would have written beautifully, said Johnson, and it was no more than the truth. Where did this careless idler, this unscholarly scholar, this poverty-stricken waif, pick up the secret of his style? We do not know and cannot tell, for in truth literary style is born and not made. Clumsy as Goldsmith was in conversation and unskilled in repartee, no sooner did his hand hold a pen than he was at once master of a most delicate humour, a rare felicity of thought, a diction of exquisite purity and grace. Open where we will in Goldsmith, we come on passages as clear as running water, and as full of refreshing music. He never tries to be eloquent: all is simple, natural, unaffected, and yet all is expressed with such concision and polish of phrase that we feel in every line the skill of the true artis   When he said that if Johnson had written of little fishes he would have made them talk like whales, he exactly hit the fault of Johnson's prose—its wearisome pompousness, its artificial and grandiose pretension. But Goldsmith could make little fishes talk like little fishes; in other words, he was master of a perfectly supple and lucid style, and always wrote not only with engaging simplicity, but with a true artistic perception of the adaptation of the means to the end. A perfect finish characterises even his most hasty and lightly-considered work. His *Animated Nature* was little better than hack-work, but it contains passages like this: 'It is the landscape, the grove, the golden break of day, the contest upon the hawthorn, the fluttering from branch to branch, the soaring in the air, and the answering of its young, that gives the bird's song its true relish. These united improve each other, and raise the mind to a state of the highest yet most harmless exultation. Nothing can in this situation of mind be more pleasing than to see the lark warbling on the wing, raising its note as it soars, until it seems lost in the immense heights above us; the note continuing, the bird itself unseen; to see it then descending with a swell as it comes from the clouds, yet sinking by degrees as it approaches its nest, the spot where all its affections are centred, the spot that has prompted all this joy.' Here is the hand of the true artist, who writes well because he feels exquisitely, and whose phrases have the spontaneous eloquence which springs from true feeling, alike charming to the intellect and the heart. In freshness, elegance, grace of style, Goldsmith is unrivalled, and he who desires to write noble English cannot go to a better school than that of the *Citizen of the World* and the *Vicar of Wakefield.*

But it needs more than a fine mastery of language to make a great writer ; and the second source of Goldsmith's literary greatness is his temper. He breathes the spirit of a noble benevolence, an unaffected piety, a heart-moving compassion. His own rough experiences of life, so far from teaching him aversion to his kind, had bred in him a boundless sympathy. 'Were I to be angry with men for being fools,' he writes, 'I could here have found ample room for declamation ; but alas! I have been a fool myself, and why should I be angry with them for being something so natural to every child of humanity?' This sentence is admirably characteristic of Goldsmith. With the child's fascinating artlessness he is the historian of his own folly, he laughs at his own blunders, he reveals his own most secret affections. He finds something of gold in the poorest dross of human nature, and refuses to speak meanly of the lowest, or harshly of the worst. He himself has been a fool : why indeed should he laugh at the folly of others? He himself has also found out, by living contact and experience, that human worth and kindness are to be found everywhere, and most perhaps in the least-expected quarters. No one ever understood the poor better, or has treated them with so touching a reverence. For Goldsmith's feeling for the poor was not mere sentimental pity ; it was a profound respect. He was the son of a country clergyman 'passing rich on forty pounds a year' : he had seen the austere nobleness of poverty, as well as its mean shifts ; and in those early wanderings of his, he had often broken

bread with some such peasant saints as he describes :

> At night returning, every labour sped,
> He sits him down the monarch of a shed ;
> Smiles by his cheerful fire, and round surveys
> His children's looks that brighten in the blaze.

It was of his brother's humble life he wrote :

> Blest be those feasts with simple plenty crown'd,
> Where all the ruddy family around
> Laugh at the jests or pranks that never fail,
> Or sigh with pity at some mournful tale,
> Or press the bashful stranger to his food,
> And learn the luxury of doing good.

The luxury of doing good was the only luxury
Goldsmith ever knew. Perhaps it compensated him
for the lack of many other things which most men
esteem luxuries. He believed in goodness and
practised it, and it was out of that temper of unrestrained love for humanity that all that is noblest
in his work sprang. Its most direct fruit is the
Vicar of Wakefield. Who that has ever read those
immortal pages, who that has laughed at the harmless simplicities and vanities of the little group, has
not also felt the presence of something beside humour
and pathos in the book, a sunny humanity, a divine
atmosphere of compassion, the pulsations of a pure
and boundless sympathy? Is there in the whole
realm of English literature anything more profoundly
touching than that scene in which the old Vicar
suddenly stops himself in the curses which he has
uttered on his daughter's betrayer, and says, ' I did
not curse him, child, did I ? ' ' Indeed, sir, you did ;
you curst him twice.' ' Then may Heaven forgive

me and him, if I did.'   It is a great power to touch at will the sources of tears and laughter, but it is a yet greater to breathe into the very spirit of a man something of the charity of God, and that is what Goldsmith has done in the *Vicar of Wakefield.* The fresh wind of Eden blows across its pages ; it is the picture of a lost Paradise, and the lesson of how it may be regained.   Goethe has recorded how great a blessing the book was to him.   He read it in his youth ; he has recorded his obligations in his autobiography; and 'standing at the age of eighty-one on the very brink of the grave, he told a friend that in the decisive moment of mental development, the *Vicar of Wakefield* had formed his education, and that he had recently, with unabated delight, read the charming book again from beginning to end, not a little affected by the lively recollection of how much he had been indebted to the author seventy years before. When we think of this noble spirit of piety which breathes through all Goldsmith's writings, and of its effect in softening the emotions and purifying the thought, we may say of Goldsmith, as he has said of the great poets whom he loved, " To such would I give my heart, since to them I am indebted for its humanity." '

Much of Goldsmith's writings must perish, but his best writing is secure.   The impression which he made upon the men of his own time was deeper even than they knew, and it was only the hour of bereavement that revealed to them all that they had lost. When the unexpected news of his death came, Burke burst into tears, and Reynolds threw away his brush ; but more affecting still, as a token of what his life had meant to many, was the crowd of unhappy creatures who thronged the staircase, and wept bitterly, because the only friend they had ever known lay dead above. Perhaps he would have valued the tears of these poor retainers at a higher rate than the praises of posterity; and yet, too, there was a fame which Goldsmith sought, and to which he knew himself entitled. There is nothing more pathetic in his history than that keen tormenting consciousness which possessed him of capacity squandered in uncongenial toil, of genius equal to the highest tasks but bound to the meanest by the need of bread. He did his hack-work, but he loathed it; he did it as hack-work was never done before, but he chafed under its degradation, and still more under this sense of conscious waste of power; and if he had stopped there, we should not be writing of him to-day. But deep in the heart of poor Goldsmith there was that fiery thirst for fame which is the portion of all great spirits, and without which it would be impossible for genius to endure the hardships and reproaches of its lot. The foolish call this thirst vanity, and the undiscerning name it egoism, but it is in truth neither one nor other: it is simply the effort of a great mind to attain its greatest, to be worthy of itself, to secure the recognition which it feels that it may justly claim, to live again in the life of distant ages as an influence and a power, secure in an eternal esteem, immortal in the power of doing good. ‘There is,’ says a modern writer, ‘a kind of life after death which is enviable; such as Apuleius had all over the cities of the East; the fame which bent down before it alike the Pagan and the Christian world, which united in it all the glories and all the forces of the pontiff, the poet, the orator, the teacher, the seer.' Apuleius lived in the flesh eighteen hundred years ago, but he lives to-day in the spirit, in the mind of every scholar. Can we think of the sweetness of Psyche without remembering her poet ? Can we even hear an ass bray in the streets without a vague fancy that the heart of Lucius is beating under his shaggy skin ? That is fame, because it is indissoluble attachment with the minds of men, and a power over their emotions, which is secure amid all changes of time and taste. It is this vision of a place in the

> Choir invisible
> Of those immortal dead who live again
> In minds made better by their presence,

that has been the divine, sustaining hope of all those great spirits whose thoughts yet move us, and whose memories are dear and vital to us. It has been also their reward. When Goldsmith toiled in secret on the *Traveller*, he had a definite aim before him ; it was to 'catch the heart and strike for honest fame.' He could not better have described his claim to immortality. He has caught the hearts of men in the charmed web of his exquisite and tender simplicity, and has found honest fame in the love of multitudes made not merely wiser but better by his presence. The first instalment of that fame was paid in the praise of Goethe, and each succeeding generation has followed where he led, and has been eager to pay its tribute of affection and acclaim at the shrine of Oliver Goldsmith.

CHAPTER V

EDMUND BURKE

[Born in Dublin, Jan. 12, 1729. Published *A Vindication of Natural Society*, and *Philosophical Inquiry into our Ideas on the Sublime and Beautiful*, 1756; *Reflections on the French Revolution*, 1790. Died, July 9, 1797.]

THE last of those great men who formed the Johnsonian circle is Edmund Burke, and he is the greatest of all. In mere bulk of genius he easily overtops all his contemporaries, and is second only to Johnson himself. The testimony to the greatness of Burke is singularly impressive and complete. Johnson said that if a man had to shelter from a shower under a shed, and had Burke as his companion for ten minutes, he would go away saying, 'This is an extraordinary man.' Goldsmith spoke of Burke's inimitable fashion of winding his way into a subject like a serpent. Fox said of him on a memorable occasion, 'If all the political information I have learned from books, all which I have gained from science, and all which my knowledge of the world and its affairs has taught me, were put in one scale, and the improvement which I have derived from my right honourable friend's instruction and conversation in the other, I should be at a loss to decide to which to give the preference. I have learned more from my right honourable friend than from all the men with whom I have ever conversed.' Mackintosh said that

Gibbon might have been taken out of a corner of Burke's mind without ever being missed. To the splendour of his oratory no witness is needed. It is true that he often spoke amid the hootings of tipsy squires, and he spoke too often for his own fame in the House. But, like another great Parliamentary orator of our own time, it was unanimously felt that while it might be safe to treat him with unseemly contempt on small occasions, when a great occasion came he was the only man really competent to deal with it. Burke's mind was one of those full and powerful minds which are perpetually restless to express themselves, and seize every occasion and an infinite variety of subjects on which to lavish their stored-up wisdom. It was this that Johnson felt when he said once, during an illness, ' that if he were to see Burke then, it would kill him,' because Burke called forth the full powers of his mind. Burke's was, in truth, one of the great fountain-minds of the eighteenth century, and from him there streamed forth intellectual influences which produced profound effects upon his times that are still felt.

That Burke's success in life was not equal to his deserts is a common observation, and there are many circumstances to account for the fact. He entered public life with the taint of the adventurer attaching to him, and that is precisely the one thing which stiff and formal politicians find most difficult to forgive. To this day no one has unravelled the mystery of his purchase of the Gregories; all that we know is that he seems to have passed at a single stride from indigence to comparative opulence, that one week he is glad to earn an extra hundred pounds by writing for Dodsley, and the next he is a landed proprietor with a position which could not be sustained on less than two thousand a year. Throughout his life he was profuse in his expenditure, and both Rockingham and Reynolds helped him with princely generosity, and ordered that their heirs were to destroy all bills which they had received from Burke. But perhaps this taint of impecuniosity would not have hindered Burke's career seriously, if he had not also displayed many glaring defects of temper and judgment, which rendered him a difficult political colleague and an awkward friend. In his philosophical judgments he was profound, brilliant, far-reaching; but in his personal judgments of men and things, he was apt to be hasty and violent. He hated to be thwarted: he did not know how to be conciliatory, and thus he often became politically impracticable. In much of this there was the natural irritability of genius in conflict with slow and stupid natures, but much also must be attributed to a temper inherently defective. We can understand his breach with Fox, but it is lamentable to find him refusing to ride in the coach of a man who spoke a good word of Fox. We can understand his chivalrous interpretation of political friendship, but it shocks us to find him using all his eloquence to defend two defaulting clerks in his own department, who were indubitably guilty. Burke was as lavish of his friendship as of his money, and one reason why his party never rewarded him with cabinet rank was, as Elliot puts it, that 'Burke has now got such a train after him as would sink any one but himself,' and goes on to name four discredited Irishmen, of whom he says mankind is quite 'nauseated.' This cardinal lack of discretion not merely spoiled Burke's political chances, but it did something to spoil his literary style also. His violence of feeling often leads him to the use of grossly exaggerated phrases, and occasionally of phrases whose vulgarity is but a poor substitute for force. Fox said, and with truth, that he had ransacked the controversial writings of Milton and Salmasius, that he might give fresh currency to the violent language of Salmasius against Milton, and the still worse language of Milton against Salmasius. When Goldsmith spoke of Burke giving up to party what was meant for mankind, this was what he meant. Burke allowed his whole nature to be so thoroughly mastered by partisanship, that his noblest qualities had only incidental opportunities of display, and his errors of taste were remembered with malicious exactitude, when the greatness of his genius was forgotten.

These are faults which go far to explain the comparative failure of Burke's political career, because in political life dexterity and adroitness are qualities which go much further than genius. But when all possible allowance has been made, it must be confessed that Burke had about him that grand style which, whether in life or literature, always distinguishes the really great man. There was a magnificence about the man which awed men into admiration, even in spite of themselves. He moved upon the stage with a certain largeness of action which no other had, and when he chose he completely dominated it. In the small scuffles of Parliamentary life he was awkward and useless, simply because he was one of those rare men who demand a great stage for the display of their powers, and are never seen to advantage on any other. Burke required great questions to call forth his greatness, and it is a pity that he ever deigned to speak on any others.

Let a question be such as rose out of the realm of party advantage into the ampler air of imperial solemnity and moral consequence ; let it be something which touched the life of nations, the sources of virtue, the inalienable rights of justice; let it above all be a question which touched the deepest springs of sentiment, and purified the passions by terror and pity — and then the full stream of Burke's genius was unloosed, and he became an intellectual giant, lifting the most tremendous burdens of thought with easy mastery, probing their profoundest depths with superhuman power and insight.   In such moments Burke was 'clad in sudden brightness like a man inspired.'   The central force of his genius was a brilliant imagination, and it was not until his imagination kindled that his whole mind woke into activity.   But when once his imagination caught the flame, his whole mind seemed to flow like molten ore.   He touched the supreme heights of thought, of passion, of feeling, without an effort.   He was swept away upon the current of his own strong passion, and was its slave rather than its master.

Across his sea of mind
The thought came streaming like a blazing ship
Upon a mighty wind.

Men looked on with awe, as upon some supernatural display.   They asked whether this could indeed be the man whom they had jeered at with tipsy wit the night before last, and who had been able to find no jest in reply.   It was Burke indeed, but it was Burke transfigured.   It was Burke with the grosser and lesser elements of his nature purged away in the flame of humanitarian passion, and with only the essential genius left. When we read the greater passages of Burke's speeches and writings, we are still full of wonder at their brilliance and grandeur ; and by that we may judge how enormous their effect must have been when the questions of which they treat were living questions, and the words we read at the distance of a century were spoken with a voice of thunder into the ears of living men.

It is this grand style, this quality of magnificence, which has raised Burke's Parliamentary speeches into permanent literature. He first roused the English mind to the appreciation of the vastness of that Indian Empire which England had won for herself, and to the truth that conquest brings responsibility as well as glory. He brought into the politics of his time a just and humane tendency, which has increased and strengthened ever since. He hated all forms of oppression and despotism with a perfect hatred, and was never roused to such noble eloquence as when he was pleading the cause of the oppressed. The derision with which the House often treated him was, in truth, the measure of his moral greatness. Dull natures resented—as dull natures only can— the fierce goadings of a man who was full of the enthusiasm of humanity. Why did Burke perpetually preach to them the wrongs of India? What was India? It was the prize of British conquest, and should be treated as a prize. What possessed Burke to talk about the rights of Hindus? Men who refused civil rights to the American colonists were not likely to admit that Hindus had any rights to be outraged, or any code of honour to be abused. All the barbaric insularity of British ignorance and prejudice rose up against Burke when he pleaded the claims of India, and his opponents found it easier to hoot him down than to answer him. In fact, he could not be answered. He was right, and men knew that he was right.

The magnificent detachment, the singular and almost sublime isolation of the man, was not less impressive than his eloquence. The eloquence itself was like nothing that the House of Commons had listened to before or since. It possessed a peculiar richness of quality, beside which the sparkling speech of Sheridan seemed jejune, and the eloquence of Fox unfinished. It abounded in a species of sublime imagery such as no other English orator has ever commanded. It was, in fact, the unrestrained outpouring of a great intellect, perhaps the fullest and ripest intellect of his time.

We cannot wonder at the sort of impotent fury which possessed the minds of his adversaries, whose only notion of governing India was to suck her lifeblood out by infamous rapacities and spoliations, when they listened to such a passage as this. He pictures the sort of men who were sent out to govern India thus: 'Animated by all the avarice of age, and all the impetuosity of youth, they roll in, one after another, wave after wave, and there is nothing before the eyes of the natives but an endless, hopeless prospect of new flights of birds of prey and passage, with appetites continually renewing for a food which is continually wasting.' Then they return home, glutted with wealth, 'and their prey is lodged in England; and the cries of India are given to seas and winds, to be blown about, in every breaking up of the monsoon, over a remote and unhearing ocean.' In India, he bitterly exclaims, all the vices operate by which sudden fortunes are acquired, while in England are often displayed by the same person the virtues which dispense hereditary wealth, so that 'here the manufacturer and the husbandman will bless the just and punctual hand that in India has torn the cloth from the loom, or wrested the scanty portion of rice and salt from the peasant of Bengal, or wrung from him the very opium in which he forgets his oppression and his oppressors.' Such masterpieces as these have long since been recognised as among the noblest passages of English literature. They are kept alive not merely by their rhetorical brilliance, but by the intense flame of moral power which animates them. They are models of declamation, and more than this, they are models of magnificent style, of the power and stateliness to which the English language can attain when it is wielded by the hand of a great master.

The common peril of what may be called the grand style is grandiloquence, and this peril Burke has not always escaped. The purple patches are not always introduced with good taste, or with a correct eye to the general harmony of effect. Like most artists who produce broad and powerful effects, his workmanship is sometimes coarse, and his colours are sometimes crude and hot. Burke's temperament was that of the poet, and that was why everything was seen through the golden haze of imagination. His first book, the memorable essay on the *Sublime and Beautiful,* is the manifesto of a poetic genius. It is the index to Burke's mind, and sufficiently declares on what food he had nourished his thoughts. The finest passages of ancient poetry, especially of Hebrew poetry, are there cited and explained ; and when Burke cannot

find an adequate translation, he makes one for himself, as in the admirable transcript of the lines of
Virgil which describe Vulcan's cave in Etna : ' *Three
rays of twisted showers, three of watery clouds, three of
fire, and three of the winged south wind : thus mixed
they in the work terrific lightnings, and sound, and fear,
and anger, with pursuing flames.*'

But it would be a mistake to suppose that Burke
always uses one style, and that a style of superb
rhetorical adornment.   He uses whatever style best
suits his immediate purpose.   He can be terse, unadorned, homely, colloquial, as well as gorgeous,
ingenious, and philosophical.   He can concentrate
his passion into single vivid phrases, as when he
speaks of the ' living ulcer of a corroding memory.'
He is never monotonous, because he is always various.   He can write in the clearest and most un-
coloured of prose, as in his *Thoughts on the Present
Discontents* ; or in glowing diatribe, as in his *Reflections on the French Revolution* ; or with an overwhelming passion of scorn and anger, as in the famous
Letter to a Noble Lord, which Mr. Morley has called
the most brilliant repartee in the language.   So
diverse is his power that one of his critics has said,
and scarcely with exaggeration : ' Burke's writing is
almost unrivalled for its combination and dexterous
interchange of excellencies.   It is by turns statistics,
metaphysics, painting, poetry, eloquence, wit, and
wisdom, it is so cool and so warm, so mechanical and
so impulsive, so measured and so impetuous, so clear
and so profound, so simple and so rich.   Its sentences
are now the shortest and now the longest ; now bare
as Butler, and now figured as Jeremy Taylor ; now
conversational, and now ornate, intense and elaborate

in the highest degree. He closes many of his paragraphs in a rushing thunder and fiery flood of eloquence, and opens the next as calmly as if he had
ceased to be the same being.' The only exception
that we need take to this description is the use of the
words 'wit' and 'mechanical,' as applied to Burke.
Dr. Johnson said with truth that Burke's wit was
blunt, that in fact it was a quality which he did not
possess. As for being 'mechanical,' this is the very
thing that Burke could never be. On the contrary,
he did more than any other writer of the eighteenth
century to break the bonds of mechanism which
Johnson and his school had laid upon literary expression. The very critic who has thus called him
mechanical has in another place said, with a clearer
perception of the truth, that 'all good and vigorous
English styles since Burke's—that of Godwin, that
of Foster, that of Hall, that of Coleridge, that of De
Quincey, are much indebted to the power with which
Burke stirred the stagnant waters of our literature,
and by which, while professing himself an enemy of
revolutions, he himself established one of the greatest,
most beneficial, and most lasting—that of a new,
more impassioned, and less conventional mode of
addressing the intellects and hearts of men.' But the
greatest quality of his writings must still be recognised in that species of spiritual aloofness which held
him, as it were, poised high above his immediate
subject, with his eye fixed on the broader issues and
relations of things, in something of philosophic, but
still more of prophetic intensity of vision. Greatness
of style arises after all not from accidental grace or
glow of expression : it springs from something deeper
—the great mind and the noble temper.

The greatest of Burke's writings, and the one which produced the most profound effect upon his times and his own fortunes, was his *Reflections on the French Revolution.* Nothing that he wrote has been more widely read, and in it the best and worst qualities of his genius are displayed with singular abandonment. Its literary qualities are great and undeniable. Few passages in English literature are better known than that marvellous description of Marie Antoinette as he saw her in her happy days, and of that burst of mournful anger against the foes who had humiliated her. 'But the age of chivalry is gone. That of sophisters, economists, and calculators has succeeded, and the glory of Europe is extinguished. Never, never more shall we behold that generous loyalty to rank and sex, that proud submission, that dignified obedience, that subordination of the heart, which kept alive, even in servitude itself, the spirit of an exalted freedom. The unbought grace of life, the cheap defence of nations, the nurse of manly sentiment and heroic enterprise is gone! It is gone, that sensibility of principle, that chastity of honour, which felt a stain like a wound, which inspired courage while it mitigated ferocity, which ennobled whatever it touched, and under which vice itself lost half its evil by losing all its grossness.' The spectacle of Burke suddenly transformed into the panegyrist of the French Court might well prove an astounding one both to his friends and foes. But in reality the change was not a change of principle. In all that touched the higher sentiments of life, Burke had always been intensely conservative. He still professed to love a ' manly, moral, regulated liberty,' and in this he only said afresh what he had said ten years before—'The liberty, the only liberty I mean, is a liberty connected with order.' Burke was simply the first great Englishman to perceive the violence which was being bred in French politics, and to walk in that pathway of unpopular renunciation which was afterwards to be trodden by Wordsworth and Coleridge.

But the really remarkable thing about Burke's pamphlet was that it displayed a political foresight which was little short of prophetic. It was published in 1790, when the foremost minds of Europe entertained nothing but the most brilliant hopes of the Revolution. The dreadful spectre of the Terror had given no sign of its advancing footsteps. The very word Republic had not yet been breathed, and the king still believed constitutional government possible. Robespierre was an obscure name. Marat had somewhere about this time been convicted of theft at the Oxford Assizes. Danton was unknown. The little Corsican who was to change the map of Europe was a youth still learning the rudiments of military science. At the hour when Burke wrote, not one single voice had been lifted up in warning of any such catastrophes as these. The very wisest and most cautious of men had 'golden hopes for France and all mankind.' Burke's book was a storm-bell rung when the sky was clear, when a new day of the brightest and most reasonable hope seemed breaking over Europe. We may admit now that Burke wrote from imperfect information, and with an entirely imperfect realisation of the real causes which worked out the Revolution. We may lament that he who had so nobly championed the native rights of Hindus should find nothing to say on behalf of the French serf, to whose famine-stricken appeal the reply of the French aristocracy was that he should eat grass. But however imperfectly Burke realised the true causes of the Revolution, he accurately perceived its course when he prophesied that its end would be a new despotism, fiercer, mightier, and more intolerant than Europe had ever known or dreamed of. There is no instance of political prescience in English history so remarkable as this. Three years later, in the January of 1793, the news of the execution of Louis XVI. reached London, and it then seemed as if a great unheeded prophecy had come true. The whole nation put on mourning, and Burke found himself at once the most famous and most powerful man in the country. It was then that the full fruit of his pamphlet began to be seen. It is scarcely too much to say that it was Burke who directed the course of foreign politics for the next twenty years, that that long series of wars which culminated at Waterloo began in that wave of intense feeling which swept over the country when men read Burke's pamphlet, and found three years later that its terrible verification had commenced.

For himself, however, the vindication of his opinions was a heavy price to pay for that wide disruption of friendships which ensued. He had become popular with the men who had hated him all their lives, and he had lost the love of men who had honoured him with the friendship of years. He was vindicated, but he was solitary ; he was undismayed, and was sustained doubtless by his unconquerable love of truth ; but when a man reaches the borders of age, the loss of friendship cannot but leave its sorrowful mark upon him. He was not indeed the sort of man who could tolerate a friendship which ignored what he felt to be convictions of solemn and almost religious gravity. He would hold out his hand to no man who approved of that which he had denounced with all the power of an intensely earnest nature. He made his creed the sword of division, which cut through every bond of ancient love, of lifelong fellowship, of mutual service. To argue whether he was right or wrong in this is futile : it was for him a simple necessity of his nature. It was the price he was prepared to pay in what he deemed the service of truth, and he paid it with unflinching fortitude. But to those who had so long loved and trusted him, all this seemed not so much fortitude as obstinacy, not so much a change of view as the recantation of every principle on which his life had been built up. They looked upon him with sorrowful eyes, and perhaps felt that they might well quote of him the great lines which he had expounded with so much force in his earliest book :

> He, above the rest
> In shape and gesture proudly eminent,
> Stood like a tower : his form had not yet lost
> All its original brightness, nor appear'd
> Less than archangel ruin'd, and th' excess
> Of glory obscured : as when the sun, new ris'n,
> Looks through the horizontal misty air,
> Shorn of his beams ; or from behind the moon
> In dim eclipse disastrous twilight sheds
> On half the nations ; and with fear of change
> Perplexes monarchs.

To the last, disappointment pursued Burke. When at length his lifelong labours for his country were about to be rewarded by a peerage, his only son died after a short illness, and the arrangements for the peerage broke down. Few passages in literature are more touching than that in which he laments his son, saying : ' The storm has gone over me, and I lie like one of those old oaks which the late hurricane has scattered about me. I am stripped of all my honours ; I am torn up by the roots, and lie prostrate on the earth. I am alone. I have none to meet my enemies in the gate. I live in an inverted order. Those who ought to have succeeded me have gone before me. They who should have been to me as posterity are in the place of ancestors.' The image which Burke used is at once a grand and true one ; and this element of magnificence, which had always distinguished him, characterised him to the end. He is as impressive in his solitary old age as in the height of his power, and presents to the mind's eye to the last a singularly picturesque and striking figure. He stands out among the men of his time with a grandeur of outline such as distinguished Sir Walter Raleigh among the writers of Elizabeth, and the same vivid personality reveals itself in all his writings. He was one of those men of whom posterity finds it difficult to form a judgment high enough to be accurate, simply because the man was far greater than his works, and his works are but fragments of a mind which might have achieved far higher results, had his life been free from the cares and vexations of party warfare. We have, however, to take him with the defects of his qualities ; and if he has not the calm incisive force of Bacon, nor the strength of Milton, he comes near to the one in his profound grasp of principles, and the other in superb force of expression, and is entitled to be ranked with those who have used the English language with the noblest flexibility and music, and for the service of the greatest moral purposes.

CHAPTER VI

EDWARD GIBBON

[Born at Putney, April 27, 1737. First vol. of *Decline and Fall* published, 1776, the last 1788. Died, 1794.]

WHEN we pass from Burke to Gibbon, the sensation which we experience is like a change from the tropic to the temperate zone. The life and individuality of Burke are full of vivid colour, and impress us with a sense of power and splendour. It is easy to say that they are sometimes clothed in a certain meretricious glitter, as it is easy to find fault with tropic scenery for a gorgeousness that oppresses us, and a fulness of light which is monotonous. But when we enter the region of grey seas and clouded skies, we at least remember with regret the glory of the realm which we have left, and we find it difficult to accustom ourselves to the flat outline and drab colour of an environment so different. Burke's life moves through a region of swift and magic transitions, and is fascinating from first to last: Gibbon's travels on a plane of rigid commonplace. Johnson and his friends impress us differently, but each figure is instinct with life, and allures us with a tragic or pathetic interest. Gibbon is a great author, but we do not feel him to be a great man. It is in vain that we read his letters or study his journals, to catch some gleams of that alluring individuality

71

which has often made the lives of far less famous
men a subject of perpetual interest. We have no
report of his conversations, nor is there upon record
a single saying of his which is remembered for its
wit, its insight, its brilliance, or its epigrammatic
force. He appears in the pages of Boswell, but it
is only as a lay-figure on that crowded stage. Virtu-
ally he lives only in the immortality of his one great
book, *The Decline and Fall of the Roman Empire.*
When we have mentioned the book, we have summed
up the life of the man.

On the other hand, it may be said that such a
statement is in itself impressive. There is not
another example in English literature of a man
who dedicated himself with such entire devotion
to a single task, and who so completely subordinated
himself to one profound literary ambition. When
we look at Gibbon's life from this point of view, we
cannot help feeling that it is after all illumined by
a faint and yet real glow of poetry. For the devotion
of the scholar is not less noble than the ardour of
the poet, and his steady fulfilment of a dominant
purpose is scarcely less impressive than the more
rapid and public triumphs of the statesman. We
see in Gibbon a noble example of what one great
and solitary purpose, clearly conceived and reso-
lutely followed, can make of a life that otherwise
might have been wasted in epicurean sloth, or
futile and confused ambitions. In the sickly and
dilletante youth of Gibbon there was nothing that
promised greatness. At Oxford he learned nothing,
and of that period of his career said with bitter
truth : ' To the University of Oxford I acknowledge
no obligation, and she will as readily renounce me

for a son as I am willing to disclaim her for a mother.
I spent fourteen months at Magdalen College: they
proved the most idle and unprofitable of my whole
life.'   But Gibbon had that which Oxford could
neither give nor take away—the inborn ardour of
scholarship.   He says that he took with him to
Oxford a stock of erudition which might have
puzzled a doctor, and a degree of ignorance of which
a schoolboy might have been ashamed.   For this
state of things the desultory character of his previous
education is to be blamed.   A great or finished
scholar he never was, in the sense in which we
reckon Porson or Bentley great and finished, or
indeed in the degree to which many other men of
his generation attained.   But he brought with him to
the toils of scholarship a literary instinct and a power
of using knowledge which men like Porson lacked ;
and thus his comparatively unfinished scholarship
was of far greater service to the world than the un-
circulated wealth of their more recondite learning.

It may, indeed, be well doubted whether a university training does not do more to impede the growth
of literary genius than to develop it.   It is a striking
fact that a brilliant university career has rarely been
the portion of those who have become the greatest
forces in our literature.   Among poets, Shakespeare
knows little Latin, and less Greek ; Byron's residence
at university is more notorious for its dissipation
than its scholarship; and Shelley is expelled from
Oxford while yet a mere boy.   Among novelists,
Scott finds his education in the free life of the
Border, and Dickens in the streets of London, while
the foundations of the wide scholarship of George
Eliot are laid in the quiet life of a Warwickshire

farmhouse.   Among our modern historians, Grote, who perhaps was the most scholarly, was not trained in a university.   The list might be indefinitely extended.   In Gibbon's own day the lives of Burke and Goldsmith furnished striking examples of the growth of literary genius to which the ancient seats of public learning had contributed nothing.   The truth appears to be, that while a university may do much in the way of scholarly training and discipline, it is apt to repress originality, and to turn out scholars who are moulded after a common pattern Had Gibbon pursued a distinguished university career, it is probable that he might have become a fellow of a college, or even a bishop, but he would never have been the historian of Rome.   He has himself almost lamented, in one of those curiously frank confessions which occasionally enliven his memoirs, that he did not choose 'the fat slumbers of the Church' as the goal of his ambition.   The lamentation is to us almost as ridiculous as the chagrin of Robert Blake when he failed in becoming a Fellow of Merton.   We can perhaps as little conceive Gibbon swaying the crozier of the bishop, as the great admiral of the Commonwealth restraining his energies within the decorous limits of an Oxford Fellowship, but we can now perceive that such disappointments were part of that eternal law of fitness which works in human affairs.   Perhaps the two circumstances that did most to fit Gibbon for the labours of his life were, first, that his university career was brief, and second, that his removal from Oxford resulted in a residence of five years at Lausanne.

It was in Lausanne that Gibbon discovered the bent of his own genius, and began to train his powers after a method of his own. He read voraciously in the ancient classics, and did not trouble himself about the minuter details of scholarship. His tutor wisely left him to himself, and his reading thus became not a drudgery, but a delight. In Greek he made but slight progress, and from 'the barren task of searching words in a lexicon withdrew to the free and familiar conversation of Virgil and Tacitus.' He easily adapted himself, not merely to the methods of Continental life, but to the ways of Continental thought. When we consider that these five years covered the most formative period of youth, we can appreciate the effect they would have in giving freshness of outlook and originality of reflection to a mind like Gibbon's. They freed him from any trace of insularity, and moulded his thought to a European breadth. French became the language in which he habitually thought, and of that contempt for foreigners which was so common even among educated Englishmen in Gibbon's day he was wholly emancipated. The result of these combined influences was that when he approached the great work of his life, he brought to it a mind trained to singular breadth of vision, and his writings have always been among those which have been best known and best appreciated by Continental peoples.

A great deal has been written about Gibbon's coldness of nature, but one can be by no means sure that there is any real ground for the charge. A careful recapitulation of some of the cardinal points in his life would lead us to a different conclusion. At sixteen he has enough religious enthusiasm to embrace the doctrines of Rome, and to take up precisely the intellectual position into which Newman was driven ninety years later. In all his family relationships his conduct was perfect. It is not an easy position for a son and heir to return after some years of foreign education to find a stepmother in possession, and his own prospects embarrassed and seriously threatened. But the amiability of Gibbon smoothed all difficulties; his affection for his stepmother was deep and constant, and to the last he was always willing to make sacrifices that her jointure might be made secure. He was able to inspire so much love in his friend Deyverdun, that after years of separation Deyverdun could say that he had not passed a single day without thinking of him, and could imagine nothing more conducive to the happiness of both than that they should spend their old age together. Years later, when he was greatly enfeebled in health, the news of Lady Sheffield's death was sufficient to make him break up his home at Lausanne, and travel home post-haste that he might console Lord Sheffield in his sorrow. In this journey he was accompanied by the son of a deceased friend, who was proud to act as his courier, and Gibbon remarks, ' His attachment to me is the sole motive which prompts him to undertake this troublesome journey.' These are scarcely the incidents which we should expect to find in the life of a cold-hearted man. And over against such facts as these what is there to set, except his account of the reasons which prompted him to renounce his boyish love for Susanne Curchod, afterwards Madame Necker: ' After a painful struggle I yielded to my fate; I sighed as a lover, I obeyed as a son.' It is not an unusual thing for youths of twenty, who are entirely dependent on their parents, to be driven to a similar conclusion, though they are rarely able to describe it with such artistic terseness. Yet it is upon this circumstance, and the unfounded gossip of Rousseau which sprang from it, that the charge of cold-heartedness against Gibbon is based. It is difficult to know what the accusers of Gibbon want. So far as one can judge, they are aggrieved because he did not defy his father and elope with the lovely daughter of the Genevese pastor. The comments of Rousseau are both spiteful and ridiculous. He is glad that Gibbon left her alone, and he detests him for doing so. If he had taken her to England she would have been miserable, and because he did not take her to England he is a heartless trifler. That is the head and front of his offending. If the charge means that Gibbon was not reckless and romantic, that he did not spoil his life to gratify a boyish attachment, and an attachment which later years proved to have been anything but deep on either side, then we may freely admit it, and all that it implies. Gibbon's was a singularly equable and amiable nature, and those solid qualities of affection which characterised his conduct in the most difficult circumstances of his life—circumstances, moreover, in which romantic people are often apt to display considerable cupidity and selfishness—may very well be set off against that lack of unconsidered passion which Rousseau and his followers so much deplored in Gibbon.

A much stronger case can be made out against Gibbon on the score of his lack of political insight and enthusiasm. He has told us that he entered Parliament without patriotism and without pride.

On the great public questions which agitated his
generation, he had no opinion and uttered no voice.
He never once opened his lips in the House, and his
services were limited to strict party docility. He
gave his vote as occasion required, without troubling
himself with any inconvenient scruples of conscience.
He never grasped the political facts of his time, and
was therefore absolutely destitute of any real vision
of their meaning. He did not perceive the real
issues of the American War. Even a trifler like
Horace Walpole had a clear view of the case, and
spoke of it not merely with statesmanlike prescience
and sagacity, but with urgent patriotic passion.
Gibbon looked upon it with aggravating nonchalance.
He appears to have had no interest in a struggle
which was dismembering the empire and creating a
new nation, and he could never make up his mind
on the great issues which were involved. He was
for a little time a member of the Board of Trade,
with a salary of £1000 per annum. He says that
he never received so much, but whatever he received
it was more than he earned, for the duties were
purely nominal. This was one of the abuses which
Burke attacked with his most brilliant vehemence
in his great speech on Economical Reform. 'This
board,' said Burke, 'is a sort of temperate bed of
influence, a sort of gently ripening hothouse, where
eight members of Parliament receive salaries of a
thousand a year for a certain given time, in order to
mature at a proper time a claim for two thousand,
granted for doing less.' No one was more ready to
concur in the truth of this description than Gibbon
himself. He was cynically frank about the motives
which led him into political life, and the price he

put upon himself. The only excuse for his conduct is to be found in the fact that he lived in an age of political corruption, and that is but a shambling apology for an historian of Rome who lived in the age of Burke. But the truth of the case is that Gibbon never ought to have entered Parliament at all. His was the temperament of the scholar who lives in the past, and is without vital interest in the present. His friend Deyverdun knew him better when he wrote: 'I advise you not only not to solicit a place, but to refuse one if it were offered you. Would a thousand a year make up to you for the loss of five days a week?' It is impossible to grudge Gibbon the two or three thousand pounds which he received from the Government, when we recollect the sort of men who grew wealthy through the life-long plunder of the public purse, but his best friends must always regret that he ever accepted it. The Parliamentary life of Gibbon was a mistake from first to last, and it is impossible to think of it in any other way.

When Gibbon turned his eyes from the affairs of English politics to the great drama of the *Decline and Fall of Ancient Rome*, he became a different man. Unable to discern the drift of English politics, or to understand the latent forces which were rapidly preparing the French Revolution, he pierced at once to the secret causes which broke up the greatest empire of antiquity, and he surveyed that tremendous scene with an intellectual insight which genius alone could confer. Hitherto he had engaged in no pursuit which had really liberated the highest qualities of his mind or truly interested him. He had been indifferent to love, indifferent to the military duties which absorbed his early manhood, and he was indifferent to the public life of England. But the idea of the mighty empire of ancient Rome, the glory of its power, the disintegration of its strength, the long record of battles and sieges which dragged it to its fall, the internal movements which undermined its despotism and shook its pride, the five centuries of that sure and splendid decay, and the final pathetic contrast between the Rome of the Cæsars and Rome as it is to-day—a spoliated glory, a ruined splendour, yet still magnificent and imposing in its very desolation—this was the spectacle which suddenly broke the lethargy of Gibbon's mind, and emancipated it with a glorious liberty. It is not infrequent to find a really great mind sunk in apathy for want of a compelling thought, a dominant idea, a commensurate ambition. Then something rouses such a mind, and at the touch of a magic wand its slumber is broken. Some hint drops like a seed into its prepared soil, and the mind becomes so renewed and vitalised that henceforth it scarcely seems the same. This was precisely the history of Gibbon's intellect. The moment when his imaginative sympathy was touched with the thought of the past glory and present degradation of Rome, was the moment that freed all the latent powers of his genius, as ice is thawed by the sudden burst of summer warmth. And in that moment, also, his years of wide and irregular study bore fruit. A point of combination had been found for his immense knowledge. He had builded better than he knew, and on that foundation of undisciplined scholarship which he had laid by his own unaided industry, there was to rise the edifice of an imperishable fame.

There are two noble passages in Gibbon's writings which are known to all readers. The first is the narration of the inception of his work. ' It was at Rome,' says he, ' on the 15th October 1764, as I sat musing amid the ruins of the Capitol, while the barefooted friars were singing vespers in the Temple of Jupiter, that the idea of writing the decline and fall of the city first started in my mind.' The other tells the story of its conclusion. It was ' on the day, or rather the night, of the 27th of June 1787, between the hours of eleven and twelve, I wrote the last lines of the last page in a summer-house in my garden. After laying down my pen, I took several turns in a berceau, or covered walk of acacias, which commands a prospect of the country, the lake, and the mountains. The air was temperate, the sky was serene, the silver orb of the moon was reflected from the waters, and all Nature was silent. I will not dissemble the first emotions of joy on the recovery of my freedom, and perhaps the establishment of my fame. But my pride was soon humbled, and a sober melancholy was spread over my mind, by the idea that I had taken an everlasting leave of an old and agreeable companion, and that whatsoever might be the future ate of my history, the life of the historian must be short and precarious.' The real story of Gibbon's life—all that the world desires to know— lies between these years. He has himself told us that at first he surveyed his project at ' an awful distance.' He began with the idea of writing the history of the decline of a city, and did not realise how vast was the field which he was destined to occupy. If he had foreseen in that moment of sympathetic musing, under the shadow of the Temple of Jupiter, the immense toil of his undertaking, perhaps he would have renounced it ; and if he had not wandered among the ruins of the Capitol, and the melody of the vespers had not touched some finer chord in his nature on that eventful evening, perhaps his great book would never have been written. But we may call a truce to such conjectures. It is by such seeming accidents that great minds are prepared for great achievements, and in that October evening Gibbon found his life-work, literally the task which was henceforth to absorb every working moment of his life.

The abiding significance of Gibbon's great book lies in the fact that it is the first great history of modern times. It was not until the middle of the eighteenth century that historic studies assumed a large importance. The materials of history existed in abundance, but the art of combining into one homogeneous whole the scattered memoirs, chronicles, and documents, in which the past had received a sort of piecemeal entombment, was yet in its infancy. Great historic collections, like those of Rymer and Leibnitz, existed ; but the art of writing history had scarcely passed beyond the stage of rudimentary chronicle. Voltaire commenced the new historic epoch in his *Age of Louis XIV.*, published in 1751, and David Hume with his *History of England*, the first volume of which was published in 1754. But it can hardly be questioned that these histories were in themselves but tentative experiments in a new method. Hume made little pretence to research, and Robertson, who followed in his footsteps, made less. Both wrote excellently, and Hume's *History* is still a masterpiece of style. What still remained to be

done was to approach the study of history in the
spirit of scholarly inquiry, to treat it with a true
comprehension of principles, and in a broad and
impartial temper. For this task Gibbon was admirably fitted. In an unconscious fashion his whole
life had been his preparation for it. He did not
aim, like Hume, at writing merely a lucid record,
notable for its literary qualities rather than its
research ; nor did he simply take a theme, and write
upon it for the sake of its picturesque possibilities, as
did Robertson. He brought to his task a mind that
had been steeped from boyhood in literature of the
past. He had spared no pains to qualify himself for
his work. He had sedulously profited by every
means of preparation that the scholarship of his time
afforded. In this he was the forerunner of Grote
and Macaulay, and stands in the field of history as
the first modern. Later historians have improved
upon his methods and corrected his judgments, but
his method has nevertheless been generally adopted ;
and no higher testimony to his work can be found
than the verdict of Mr. Freeman, that 'whatever else
is read, Gibbon must be read too.'

Gibbon's idea of history was a great series of imposing scenes, a vast panorama, full of movement, life,
and brilliance, but buttressed at all points by solid and
competent scholarship. There is a gorgeousness and
pomp about Gibbon's history which has never been
surpassed. The sentences move with stately measure,
as it were, to the sound of some vast and reverberat-
ing music. He never drops into commonplace or
becomes colloquial. It would perhaps be better if
he did. There is something in the acute criticism
of Porson, 'that he draws out the thread of his

verbosity finer than the staple of his argument, and occasionally reminds us of that great man Mr. Prig, the auctioneer, whose manner was so inimitably fine that he had as much to say upon a ribbon as a Raphael.' The style naturally becomes oppressive from its very stateliness, and the mind wearies of its sustained pomp and splendour. His epigrams are wrought with laborious skill, and his sentences move from climax to climax, in a long and majestic procession, which suggests the phalanx of a Roman army. It is pre-eminently an artificial style as distinguished from a simple style. But when this is said, the worst is said that can be said. Pompous as it is, the style is appropriate. The whole story is so magnificent, it commands such an extraordinary retrospect of human greatness, that an historian may well be pardoned if he lavishes upon it all the adornments of a splendid rhetoric. And it must be added also, in all justice, that an admirable lucidity characterises it from first to last. If it is never colloquial, it is never slovenly ; if it is sometimes grandiloquent, it is always clear ; and if it is not supple, it is always powerful and impressive.

The great blot on Gibbon's *History* is the entirely misleading and offensive account which he gives of the early Christians in the two famous chapters which conclude his first volume. From his early enthusiasm for the Church of Rome he soon relapsed into a sort of complacent and good-humoured Voltairism, and this temper characterised his entire life. He has none of the gibing bitterness of Voltaire, none of his airy wit: he is simply full of good-natured contempt for religion. The religious side of his nature, like Darwin's, seemed to have suffered from permanent atrophy. His whole mind had been occupied with other subjects, and he was really incapable of understanding the sublime enthusiasms out of which Christianity was born. Thus, when he is forced to deal with the rise of Christianity, he is consistently unjust because he is ignorant, and his ignorance is of that species which no scholarship could overcome. He does not understand the heart of man, and is a stranger to its spiritual aspirations. He attributes the growth of Christianity to the zeal of the Christians ; but he does not tell us how that zeal was kindled. He says that the doctrine of a future life made Christianity a fruitful force, but he does not tell us how it was that the doctrine, which had never been more than the vague hope of ancient poets, suddenly became the intense conviction of vast masses of people, who were ready to stake their whole lives upon it. He attributes the noble virtues of the primitive Christians to their care for their reputation, as if the fear of Mrs. Grundy could ever have been sufficient to turn the current of notoriously dissolute lives, in a notoriously dissolute time, and inspire the austerest chastity and purity in the hearts of millions. He says that the union and discipline of the Christian republic were the sources of its growth ; but he forgets to tell us what was the basis of the union, and out of what compelling forces the organism of the Christian Church arose. The spirit of the mystic, the saint, and the martyr is incomprehensible to him. He had no spiritual sensitiveness, no pious aspiration, and he cannot understand them in others. Admirably fitted as he was in all other respects for his great task, he was absolutely unfitted, by the very nature of his own mind, for this most important section of it. These two chapters mark the limitations of Gibbon's mind, and are an impressive revelation of the essential earthliness of his nature. They have long since ceased to be of any controversial value, and are remembered to-day not for any damage they did to the Christian faith, but for the reproach they cast on Gibbon's historic fairness.

Complacent, epicurean, studious, Gibbon was essentially a man of the pre-Revolution time. A drama not less marvellous than the fall of Rome was preparing round him ; but he ignored it, and failed to comprehend it, for the same reason that he failed to understand the origin of Christianity—a radical ignorance of the human heart. Within two years of the completion of his *History*, on the very night his friend Deyverdun died, the Bastille fell, and the great Revolution began ; but he seems to have seen nothing extraordinary in this first act in the tragedy which was to remake the map of Europe. He lived his life after his own fashion, and saw nothing of the world that was travailing in the birth-throes of a new era. His books, his pen, his lettered ease were all in all to him. It is a perfect picture of the pre-Revolution littérateur that is given us in this vivid little etching of Colman : ' On the day I first sat down with Johnson in his rusty-brown suit and his black worsted stockings, Gibbon was placed opposite to me, in a suit of flowered velvet, with a bag and sword. The great historian was light and playful— still he tapped his snuff-box, still he smirked and smiled, and rounded his periods with the same air of good-breeding. His mouth, mellifluous as Plato's, was a round hole, nearly in the centre of his visage.'

It is the picture of a cheerful epicurean, quite at home in the world, and contented on the comfortable assurance that it is the best of all possible worlds. He was no seer, with a vision of the deeper forces which move the springs of human history ; no leader of men, to whom men could look as a tower of strength in difficult times. And therefore it is that we remember him as a writer, not as a man ; but, nevertheless, as the writer of a book which cannot be displaced. Professor Freeman's verdict is his highest praise : 'Whatever else is read, Gibbon must be read too.'

CHAPTER VII

LORD MACAULAY

[Born Oct. 25, 1800. Entered Trinity College, Cambridge, Oct. 1818. Obtained his Fellowship, 1824. *Milton*, his first essay, appears in *Edinburgh Review*, August 1825. Member for Calne, 1830. Made his first great speech on Reform, 1831. Accepts post of legal adviser to the Supreme Council of India, and sails for Madras, Feb. 15, 1834. Returns to England, 1838. Gives up writing for the *Edinburgh Review*, 1844. First volume of his *History of England* published Nov. 29, 1848. Raised to the peerage, August 1857. Died Dec. 28, 1859; buried in Westminster Abbey, Jan. 9, 1860.]

THERE are two pictures which irresistibly suggest themselves with the mention of Macaulay's name. The first is of the Clapham Sect, among whom his childhood was spent. The sect consisted of a group of men, most of whom were deeply pledged to evangelical principles of religion, all of whom shared the fervour of great philanthropic enterprises. Sir James Stephen has sketched the group with vividness and fidelity, and has given the hint of how noble a history might be written of its character and work.

It was in the house of Henry Thornton, the member for Southwark, that the group oftenest met, and were to be seen at their best. There was found William Wilberforce, the master of a silver-tongued eloquence unrivalled in his day; Granville

Sharp, equally remarkable for the resolution with which he dedicated himself to public purposes, and the grave and chivalrous tenderness of his private character; Gisborne, known by his love of Nature; Lord Teignmouth, the Governor-General of India; Charles Simeon, the head and representative of Evangelical Churchmanship; occasionally Mackintosh, beloved for his benignity, as well as admired for a genius which never found adequate expression in his writings; and Brougham, whose versatile ability secured an admiration which his character did not support. But in all this memorable group, the most remarkable man was old Zachary Macaulay himself. Silent, austere, heavy-browed, there was a simple grandeur about him which marked him the chief of all that brilliant circle, and excited a faith approaching to superstition, and a love rising to enthusiasm. No man was ever troubled less than he with a thirst for the fickle honours of publicity No man ever cared less for the applause or fashion of the world. He was one of those rare men who are content to toil and be forgotten if the cause to which they have devoted their lives succeeds. No stain of self-seeking was ever discovered or suspected in his public life. He did right with a noble fearlessness, and the dignity and heroic temper of his character arose from its simplicity, its concentration and its rectitude.

The second picture is of that group of Edinburgh Reviewers among whom Thomas Babington Macaulay was to occupy so brilliant a position. It is not easy for us nowadays to understand what gave the *Edinburgh Review* its great reputation and authority. It professed, of course, to be the organ of Whig opinions, but there is abundant evidence that it had no very violent passion for Liberalism. Scott, who was as sound a Tory as one could well imagine, contributed to its pages for years, and ' so late as the end of 1807 invited Southey, then developing into fiercer Toryism, as became a "renegade" or a "convert," to enlist under Jeffrey.' Nor is the secret of its early success to be found in the brilliance of its literary achievement. Most of the articles were hastily written by men who had other fish to fry, and bear the marks of shallowness and carelessness. Jeffrey himself, great as was his pretence to critical ability, was in reality as bad a critic as one could well find. He echoed rather than guided popular opinion ; he did not create conditions of popular appreciation, but obeyed them. He gravely discusses the immortality of Mrs. Hemans' poetry, and says (in 1829): ' The rich melodies of Keats and Shelley, and the fantastical emphasis of Wordsworth, and the plebeian pathos of Crabbe, are melting fast from the field of vision.' The only poets of his day for whom he predicts fulness of fame are Rogers and Campbell—the very poets who in fact have melted fastest ' from the field of vision.' Still more flagrant is his error in selecting the finest of all Wordsworth's poems, the *Ode on the Intimations of Immortality*, as hopelessly absurd ; and in declaring Goethe's *Wilhelm Meister*, which Carlyle had just translated, to be ' so much trash.' The real reason of the success of the *Edinburgh Review* was that it was fresh, independent, and afforded an open door for new writers who manifested anything like talent. When the *Review* was started, no one conceived of magazine articles as other than ephemeral, and consequently such work as deserved to be called litera-ture—work that was solid and noble in quality, first-rate in style and research—was only to be looked for in books. It was Macaulay who did most to set the new fashion. He and Sydney Smith were the first to use the magazine as a stepping-stone to Parnassus. Yet even he apologises for the republi-cation of his essays, and explains that the action of American publishers has made it necessary.[1]

Yet, when all deductions are made, it cannot be denied that the Edinburgh Reviewers make almost as fascinating a group as the Clapham Sect. Jeffrey had a certain pertness of intellect, an amusing vivacity, and a real kindliness of nature, which make him both interesting and lovable. The sunny fresh-ness of Sydney Smith's genial humanity, together with his quaintness, his unforced humour, and his rollicking laugh, are sure passports to the favour of posterity. Brougham is interesting in another way. He was probably the most terrible contributor that a Review ever had. He could not be said to lose his temper—he had none to lose; a more irascible and conceited mortal never lived. There was no limit to his powers of vituperation and objurgation. It was impossible to satiate his appetite for praise, and he was not particular as to the quality. Yet Brougham was a force, and is a unique figure both in politics and letters. The least notable of the group was Horner, of whom Sydney Smith said he had the Ten Commandments written on his face, and looked so virtuous that he might commit any crime with impunity.

----

[1] This whole subject is admirably treated by Mr. Leslie Stephen in the third series of his 'Hours in a Library.'

The most brilliant was Macaulay. With the
appearance of his article on Milton in August 1825,
the *Edinburgh Review* entered on a fresh lease
of life. Jeffrey asked in astonishment where Macaulay had picked up such a style. It was the lot of
the young essayist to wake up and find himself
famous. His articles so impressed Lord Lansdowne
that five years later he offered him a seat in Parliament for the borough of Calne. Previous to this, in
1828, Lord Lyndhurst had made him a Commis-
sioner in Bankruptcy. At thirty years of age he
had already achieved a splendid reputation, and was
on the high road to fortune.

English literature certainly records no more successful life than Macaulay's; the current of fame ran
from the first with a steady and increasing volume,
and knew no obstacles. He did not experience
what it was to wait for the tardy recognition of an
undiscerning public. One reason for this was that
he wrote in a form which was admirably calculated
to appeal to the average intelligence. He was
neither too high nor too deep; without writing as a
party hack, he yet managed to be judiciously
partisan, and to echo popular opinion; without
being original, he had struck out a new path for
himself, and was the inventor of a new method.
His was not one of the great 'seminal minds' of
literature: his popularity was sufficient token of
that. He travelled along a broad and well-trodden
road, but with distinction and splendour. The very
trials of his life became new factors in the furthering
of his success. It is curious for us to learn, in these
days of high-priced magazine articles, that Macaulay
never earned more than £200 per annum from the

Edinburgh Review. But the narrowness of his means drove him to India, and his residence in India broadened his views, and gave him leisure for study, and a grasp of practical statesmanship. Two of his most famous essays, those on Clive and Warren Hastings, could scarcely have been written without his Indian experience, and when he returned from his brief exile it was as a man of fortune. Nothing, indeed, ever seems to have gone wrong with Macaulay. He had a sound head, a sound digestion, and a comfortable assurance of himself. He stepped into the arena amid a peal of praise, and the plaudits never ceased while he occupied it. Laborious as his preparation for writing often was, he was insensible of the labour, and he wrote in pure joyousness of heart, and out of a redundant fulness of knowledge. It would be difficult to find any parallel to the even, unbroken, and consistent success which characterised his career.

It is unnecessary to dwell upon the well-known incidents of Macaulay's life. Sir George Trevelyan's fascinating biography is within reach of all. Such a triumph as Macaulay's could not be repeated in our own day, because many of the conditions have passed away. It is not in the power of statesmen in our time to reward famous essayists by the presentation of pocket-boroughs; nor is literature generally considered a happy apprenticeship to political power. But fortunate in this, as in everything else, Macaulay appeared just in time to profit by the best qualities of a social system which was passing away, and to inherit the opportunities of a better condition of things which was beginning to exist. He early obtained admission to that brilliant circle which gathered round Lady Holland. It says much for the sturdy manhood of Macaulay that Lady Holland never attempted to practise on him those imperious airs and petulant caprices, which so often made her drawing-room a place of torture to the more sensitive guest. It says much also for his social charm that Lady Holland wept, protested, and refused to be comforted, on his departure to India, and altogether behaved as if her assemblies would be intolerable without him. But Macaulay had the knack of captivating all sorts of people— even Samuel Rogers. He had homeliness and good humour as well as genius. No man of great parts was ever afflicted less with a sense of his own importance. Carlyle once observed his face in repose, and said: 'I noticed the homely Norse features that you find everywhere in the Western Isles, and I thought to myself, "Well, any one can see that you are an honest, good sort of fellow, made out of oatmeal."' In the same spirit Goldwin Smith speaks of the homeliness of Macaulay's appearance, and says that, but for the eyes, his was the sort of face you might expect above a cobbler's apron. He inherited something of old Zachary Macaulay's simplicity of nature, and had no pretence about him and disliked it in others. He was thoroughly honest in his loves and hatreds. He had a refreshing way of taking his own course, and of being entirely oblivious of current opinion. He was never guilty of hypocrisy in matters of taste. Thus, whatever we may miss of finer quality in Macaulay, we are always conscious of the sincerity of his character; and to whatsoever heights of fame we follow him, his nature remains unperverted and impresses us by its solid simplicity and strength.

As an author, Macaulay attempted three rôles, and in each he won phenomenal success. He was at once poet, essayist, and historian. His *Essays* are practically one with his *History* in spirit, method, and style. They are what the rapid sketch is to the complete picture, or, it would be fairer to say, what the small canvas is to the larger one. His method as historian and essayist is very simple: it is to tell a story of facts in such a way that it shall be more interesting than a novel. He says, 'There is merit, no doubt, in Hume, Robertson, Voltaire, and Gibbon. Yet it is not the thing. I have a conception of history more just, I am confident, than theirs.' The main difference in his conception was that he aimed at more minuteness, vividness, and artistic setting; thus he was more pictorial and dramatic, and for this reason more effective. 'For this,' says Dr. J. Hutchison Stirling, 'he amassed, even while at college, and year after year industriously afterwards, all those great stores of reading and information which bore directly or indirectly on this great subject. For this he tried himself in relevant periodical papers, and feared no waste; for he said to himself, cheerily and proudly: 'One day, in the long evening of my life, I will throw over these, connecting them into oneness, the bulk of an entire history; and this history over these essays shall be as the great dome of a cathedral that closes unitingly over its many rich and splendid chapels.' Perhaps, in this conception of how history should be written, the weakest point is the immense accumulation of detail. The five volumes which he wrote cover only fifteen years; and had he carried out his original idea of bringing the history down to the reign of George IV., and upon the same scale, at least fifty volumes would have been needed. It may therefore be justly doubted whether, in the conception of how history should be written, Macaulay is really superior to Hume and Gibbon.

There is no doubt, however, that in the picturesque grouping of material, Macaulay has no superior, as we shall have occasion to remark further on. This, indeed, is the most striking quality of his poems, as of his prose writings. In the highest sense of the word, Macaulay was not a poet, and did not claim to be one. He had no ear for the more delicate music of words, for the nobler effects of rhythm. This is sufficiently evident in his prose, where the sentences do not grow out of each other in natural order, but are accumulated one above another, and often fall on the ear with a sort of disagreeable, metallic harshness. But the power of pictorial effect which made him so consummate a story-teller, served him equally well in the *Lays of Ancient Rome*. Nothing fascinated him so much as civic state, the greatness of heroic deeds and names, and here he is in his element. His power of painting a picture could not be better displayed. But he does something more than this : he succeeds in kindling a real enthusiasm in his reader. His lines are terse, clear, ringing ; his narration is perfect. The force of these splendid ballads is greatly increased by their simplicity of structure, and the fact that they are almost unadorned. It is not surprising that they achieved a phenomenal success, eighteen thousand copies being sold in ten years. The very lack of the higher qualities of poetry would help their sale, as really as the very distinct and remarkable qualities which they possessed. While we admit, then, that Macaulay was not a poet, yet it was his happy fortune to invent a species of poetical writing that was as captivating as his prose style, and is still unequalled of its kind. Essentially, the qualities which underlie the *Poems* and the *History* are the same: lucidity of statement, vividness of perception, and unique power of picturesque effect.

It is now the fashion to attack, not merely the style of Macaulay's *History*, but its accuracy; but with this latter attack we have but little sympathy. It is naturally a very easy task to find instances of erroneous statement and imperfect judgment in a history executed on so vast a scale, yet with such minuteness of detail. He would be more than mortal who could tell the long story of warring factions and intricate statesmanship, the rise and dissolution of parties, the disintegration and rebirth of empire, the intrigues of courts and cabinets, the secrets of embassy and diplomacy, the individual force and impression exerted on their times by actor after actor in one of the most crowded, various, and exciting periods of history, and commit no error of fact, pass no unjust judgment, and be led into no misinterpretation of act or motive. Undoubtedly there are errors, and serious errors, in Macaulay's famous *History*. But, on the other hand, the merits are conspicuous and unique. He marshals his facts with a masterly precision and orderliness. Never was history designed on so vast a scale before, yet with such attention to minute details. It has been happily likened by Mr. Cotter Morrison to a Gothic cathedral, where every separate stone, and even those least likely to be observed, has been carved with exquisite fidelity to art. Every paragraph is crammed with information, and information drawn from the most obscure and unlikely sources. It is perfectly amazing to reflect on the immense amount of historical information which the diligence of Macaulay has accumulated, and the grasp and tenacity of the memory in which it was stored. Darwin, in his autobiography, describes his own mind as a sort of machine for grinding out general laws from the mass of facts and observations which it had accumulated; and it may be said in the same way that Macaulay's mind was a sort of machine for the accumulation and digestion of immense masses of historical information. But Macaulay is a consummate rhetorician, which Darwin was not. All this enormous mass of knowledge is shaped and used with the finest literary skill, and with excellent literary judgment. He never wearies his reader, and never retards the progress of his story by his erudition. Every fact is fitted to its place, and has its exact bearing on the elucidation of his theme. It has been said that no poet but Milton could have moved under the weight of learning with which his poetry is loaded, and it may be said with equal truth that no historian but Macaulay could have borne with ease the gigantic burden of knowledge with which his *History* familiarises us. He never betrays the slightest sign of weariness or exhaustion. The very structure of his sentences is full of life and briskness. They give the impression of an eager and alert intellect, impatient to get on rapidly with its task. If there is any quality in Macaulay's style which produces a sense of weariness, it is that it is almost too brilliant : the antitheses come in too rapid and dazzling a succession, the rhetorical artifice is too little concealed, and we feel that a little homeliness, an occasional lapse into simplicity, would be a welcome relief.

Yet how vivid and clear the style is! Jeffrey might well wonder where he had picked up such a style. It glitters like burnished steel. It travels from climax to climax without a pause to draw breath and rest. There are no intervals of shadow, it is true; and that is why the mind tires with it, as the eye is oppressed by the continuous glare of too strong a light. But it is a sustained and splendid pageant, which makes all other modes of writing history seem flat, stale, and unprofitable. Its pages are a long succession of Rubens-like pictures; and if they lack the grandeur of Rubens, and are, like his pictures, often coarse in colour, they are always bold and vivid, and often splendid and superb. It is not the sort of history to touch the heart. The pictures of Rubens are not the pictures which touch the heart. They amaze us with their wealth of colour, their magnificent scale, and their mastery of execution. So Macaulay amazes and delights, he excites and interests, he holds us spellbound with the witchery of his art; but he seldom touches the emotions, and sensation succeeds sensation so rapidly that we have scarcely time to feel deeply. We are hurried on as men are hurried on in the shocks and charges of a great battle, and the excitement is too great for reflection. Few novelists have ever displayed half the art of sensationalism, in its really legitimate sense, which Macaulay manifests. He is a master of plot, and he makes the commonplace facts of history more fascinating than romance. And occasionally, too, he is profoundly moved, and his words quiver with genuine enthusiasm and pathos. His description of the acquittal of the Seven Bishops, and of the siege and relief of Londonderry, are among the finest instances of this rare display of emotion in Macaulay. They are not merely fine examples of pictorial power, but they palpitate with genuine moral earnestness and enthusiasm. They mark the highest points of the *History*, and are the best possible proofs of Macaulay's historical genius.

The limitations of Macaulay's genius are many, and are distinct to the most casual observer. Qualities and defects alike appear with a singular definiteness of outline. Perhaps his worst defect was a habit of imputing motives to those with whom he disagreed. This is, perhaps, as it has been well described, 'a vice of rectitude;' but it is not a pleasant vice. It leads him to see all things in black and white, to catalogue the characters of men and women in cast-iron categories, and to miss those finer and more delicate shades of distinction which can only be discovered by a sympathetic insight. His world is full of sheep and goats, and he is fond of antici- pating the last assize in his methods of summary separation. For the alpacas, those curious creatures, which, as a brilliant writer in the *Nineteenth Century* once remarked, are half sheep and half goat, and belong wholly to neither class, he has no sympathy. He is intent on driving them into one or other of his pens: he insists that whatever art of simulation may be theirs, they are either good or bad, and must be judged accordingly. Perhaps the strict Calvinistic basis of his early training had something to do with this. The theology of his youth was clear, hard, and logical, and it left its impress for ever on his mind. But in the later years, when he became a literary artist, it limited his view, and gave him a touch of pharisaism, a dogmatic assertiveness of superior virtue in his judgments of men, which was at the least uncharitable, and was often positively offensive. We miss in him that genial humanity which charms us by its catholic kindliness. He repels us by this vice of rectitude. This, for example, is his view of Sir Walter Scott: 'In politics, a bitter and unscrupulous partisan ; profuse and ostentatious in expense ; agitated by the hopes and fears of a gambler; perpetually sacrificing the perfection of his compositions, and the durability of his fame, to his eagerness for money ; writing with slovenly haste of Dryden, in order to satisfy wants which were not, like those of Dryden, caused by circumstances beyond his control, but which were produced by his extravagant waste or rapacious speculation : this is the way in which he appears to me. I am sorry for it, for I sincerely admire the greater part of his works ; but I cannot think him a high-minded man, or a man of very strict principle.' There is, of course, some truth in these strictures ; but Macaulay's way of putting the truth is so exaggerated that the general effect becomes untruthful. This is not the real Scott, the genial Sir Walter, whom we know and love. And even if the half of this description were justified, who can read it without a sense of its shocking lack of urbanity, its rudeness, and its coarseness of expression?

Such a passage as this is the clue to Macaulay's character, or at least to a certain side of it. What annoys him in Scott is what he is pleased to term his 'extravagant waste,' his 'ostentatious expense,' his 'rapacious speculation,' his agitation by 'the hopes and fears of the gambler.' He could scarcely have used stronger terms if he had been dealing with a bankrupt tipster or a convicted welsher. The explanation lies in the fact that Macaulay's own temperament was wholly dissimilar. He had a horror of extravagance ; and, to do him justice, was prodigal only in his benefactions. He loved quiet and simple life. He had been trained in a hard school, and knew the value of money. He had never been tempted by risky financial speculations. It was said of him in later life that no man in the city of London possessed a sounder business judgment. His integrity had never suffered the shadow of a stain ; he was upright, and proud of his uprightness. All this is to be accounted to him for righteousness ; but out of it was bred that dogmatic virtue which made him hard upon all who did not quite come up to his own standard. What was openhandedness in Scott appears to him extravagant waste, what was generous thoughtlessness is thriftless folly, what was the realisation of boyish dreams—the building of Abbotsford, and the founding of a territorial name—is merely ostentatious expense. He fails to recognise that vein of romance which coloured Scott's life, simply because he himself was the least romantic of men. He calls by hard names what were at the worst amiable weaknesses. And his judgment of Scott is paralleled by many other judgments which disfigure his *Essays* and his *History*. He sees all things from a comparatively narrow standpoint. He is so confident of his own justness and omniscience that he admits no mitigation of penalty, no palliation of error. And the consequence is that he often exceeds his brief, and falls into exaggerations, which not merely annoy us by their unconsidered violence of temper, but seriously weaken our faith in his historical judgment.

It must not, however, be supposed that Macaulay was ever intentionally unfair. On the contrary, he strove to be studiously just. But even Sir George Trevelyan has to admit that 'vehemence, over-confidence, the inability to recognise that there are two sides to a question, or two people in a dialogue,' were defects inseparable in him from the gifts with which he was endowed.

> To him
> There was no pain like silence—no constraint
> So dull as unanimity. He breathed
> An atmosphere of argument, nor shrank
> From making, where he could not find, excuse
> For controversial fight.

When Crabb Robinson describes him as possessing 'not the delicate features of a man of genius and sensibility, but the strong lines and well-knit limbs of a man sturdy in mind and body,' he does much to reveal the character as well as to recall the presence of Macaulay. The faculty by which he understood men was a certain luminous shrewdness, and it took the place of genial sympathies. And it must be confessed that he used this faculty with excellent effect. His letters and diaries are full of notes and memoranda on great personages, clear and rapid etchings, which convey at a stroke his impressions, or the reported impressions of others. He notes the table-talk of Rogers with evident delight, and putting aside the acrimony of Rogers, the two men closely resembled each other in this gift of luminous shrewdness. Rogers told him that Byron was 'an unpleasant, affected, splenetic person,' of whom thousands of people ranted who had never seen him, but that no one who knew him well ever mentioned him with a single expression of fondness ; and Macaulay remarks that the worst thing he knows about Byron is the very unfavourable impression which he made on men who were not inclined to judge him harshly. It is with a touch of something like cynicism he notes later on that his article on Byron is very popular, and is one among the thousand proofs of the bad taste of the public. But Macaulay was anything but a cynic ; he was far too good-humoured to be really spiteful or bitter. He was, as Crabb Robinson says, a man of sturdy mind, robust in thought, clear-headed, dictatorial in temper, honest and just according to his lights, but a little hard, a little lacking in delicacy of literary perception, and altogether too positive and controversial in his opinions to conceal his dislikes, or veil them in urbanity.

'There never was a writer,' says Mr. Gladstone, 'less capable of intentional unfairness,' and the biography of Macaulay affords plentiful proof of the pains which he took to be accurate. He complains bitterly of the unfairness of Gibbon, and indorses this peculiarly stinging paragraph of Porson's. 'Gibbon,' says Porson, 'pleads eloquently for the rights of mankind ; nor does his humanity ever slumber, unless when women are ravished, or the Christians persecuted. He often makes, when he cannot really find, an occasion to insult our religion, which he hates so cordially that he might seem to revenge some personal insult. Such is his eagerness in the cause, that he stoops to the most despicable pun, or to the most awkward perversion of language, for the purpose of turning the Scriptures into ribaldry, or of calling Jesus an impostor.' But Macaulay is quite as prejudiced and unfair in another way. It is not that he has written his *History* in a spirit of vehement partisanship, as is constantly alleged. It cannot be said of him that he wrote the *History of England* to prove that God was always on the side of the Whigs, as it was said, with some justice, that Alison wrote his history to prove that God was always favourable to the Tories. On the contrary, when we consider the strength of his own political convictions, it must be owned that he has shown remarkable self-restraint and equity of statement in his treatment of parties. He blames Whigs and Tories alike, and visits them with an equal severity of castigation. His most enthusiastic praise is often awarded to high-minded Tories, as, for example, Bishop Ken and Jeremy Collier. If he has spoken harshly of the Stuarts, he has not spoken untruthfully, and the great majority of competent historians share his views. But it is in relation to individuals that his unfairness is apparent. His personal likes and dislikes govern him ; his prejudice makes him come to the worst conclusions about persons he dislikes, upon the most insufficient evidence. He can find no invective strong enough to express his loathing for the knavery of Marlborough, the foolish vanity of Boswell, or the polished hypocrisy of Penn. Having arrived at the conclusion that Marlborough was a knave, Boswell a fool, and Penn a liar, he is incapable of recognising any counterbalancing qualities of good, and every

time he speaks of these men his anger and derision
become more violent.   Thus, his description of
Brougham's vindictive partiality is often the description of his own conduct: ' All the characters are
either too black or too fair.   The passions of the
writer do not suffer him even to maintain the decent
appearance of impartiality.'

CHAPTER VIII

LORD MACAULAY (*continued*)

So strangely is human nature constituted, that it is necessary to correct any false impression which Crabb Robinson's words may create, by stating that in some respects Macaulay was among the most sensitive of men. If we are conscious of a certain glittering hardness of mind in his controversial diatribes and literary verdicts, we must also recollect that his letters and diaries give us perpetual evidence of the goodness and tenderness of his heart. His whole life was a sacrifice in the interests of his family, and a sacrifice which gains much in magnanimity by its unconscious and uncomplaining dignity of endurance. When his friend Ellis loses his wife, he sits for hours listening to his confidences, and not attempting to console him, because he feels that the only consolation he can offer is the sociable silence of the sympathiser. When he stands in Santa Croce, he notices in the cloister a monument to a little baby, and remembers his three-months-old niece, and says, 'It brought tears into my eyes. I thought of the little thing who lies in the cemetery at Calcutta.' He is easily affected in the same way by great historic memories, or by pathetic novels. When he stands for the first time in St. Peter's, he says, 'I could have cried for pleasure.' He is much moved beside the tomb of Michael Angelo, and at the grave of Dante says : ' I was very near shedding tears as I looked at this magnificent monument, and thought of the sufferings of the great poet, and of his incomparable genius, and of all the pleasure I have derived from him, and of his death in exile, and of the late justice of posterity.' On his journey through the Pontine marshes in this same Italian tour, he reads Bulwer's *Alice*, and is affected by it in a way he has not been affected for years. ' Indeed,' he continues, ' I generally avoid all novels which are said to have much pathos.   The suffering they produce is to me a very real suffering, and of that I have quite enough without them.' His passion for *Clarissa Harlowe* is well known. How many times he read that prodigious novel, and how often he wept over the sorrows of its heroine, no one knows. Every one will remember how he justified his melting mood by the story of the way in which the book was read by his friends at an Indian station in the hills : ' The Governor's wife seized it, the Secretary waited for it, the Chief-Justice could not read it without tears ; and, finally, an old Scotch doctor, a Jacobin and a free-thinker, cried over the last volume till he was too ill to appear at dinner.'

Perhaps one explanation of some of these defects which we have enumerated, is that Macaulay injured his literary faculty by his political activity.   No man can serve two masters, and it was not till late in life that he chose what he knew to be the better part.   The practical grasp and decisiveness of his judgment were admirable qualifications for a great party leader.   It is very easy to imagine Macaulay, had he started with different social advantages, becoming an ideal Premier. As a parliamentary orator he ranks with the highest: the cry that Macaulay was 'up' was always sufficient to secure a crowded House. His admirable lucidity, his power of picturesque narration, his definiteness of view, his practical grasp of the main issues of a debate, his hard-hitting, his vivacity, his eloquence, were precisely the forces which the House of Commons most appreciates, and which do most to lift a debater into power. But these very qualifications for political life were disqualifications for literary pursuits. The oratorical style and temper are fatal to the perfection of literary style. In oratory it is necessary to paint with a broad brush and strong colours, because immediate effect is the aim. The more delicate gradations of colour are not noticed, and are not needed; but in literature the very opposite is true. It is delicacy of perception, sympathetic insight, gradation of colour, that makes style. No one knew this better than Macaulay; he felt that the political and literary lives could only be united to the detriment of both. But he was unable to shake himself free from the influences of the House of Commons. The sharp divisions of opinion which politics had taught him were carried with him into literature. He was destitute of philosophic calm; the whole force of his training made him take a side, and the exaggerations of colour which had served him excellently in parliamentary oratory were still retained in historical disquisition. Had Macaulay never entered Parliament, had he been content with a life of literary production from the first, there can be no doubt that his work would have been far more finished, and his temper far calmer, and therefore better able to deal with those great problems of personal character in which history abounds.

It is really the parliamentary debater, rather than the littérateur, who speaks in such an essay as that on Robert Montgomery. Montgomery was a bad poet, and an absurd poet, and his popularity was a public absurdity which deserved denunciation. Yet, after all, Macaulay's castigation was out of all proportion to the offence; but it was the case of a good opportunity of attack, and Macaulay seized it, as he would have seized a similar occasion in the House. One suspects that in this and in many other instances, he was carried away by his own immeasurable copiousness of vocabulary. Adjectives crowd upon him as he writes, and he uses not the most suitable but the most sonorous. He soon lashes himself into a fine simulation of anger, and is the victim of his own deception. He lives upon antithesis—he sees human life itself, and human character too, as a vast antithesis. He has a sort of schoolboy delight in the use of a telling phrase, and he has a schoolboy's carelessness of verbal exactitude. He is not content to inform us that some one was a bad man: he tells us that the turpitude of his conduct was only equalled by the malignancy of his temper, and that the meanness of his character was paralleled by the corruption of his thought—or some other equally sounding phrase. To use the right word—the one right word in all the English language —which illumines with a flash of light the whole subject, is an art whose rudiments he has never learned. He excels in sonorousness of language— not in precision; and in this respect his style resembles Johnson's. But he cuts Johnson's paragraphs up into sparkling sentences, and uses full stops where Johnson used colons. He retains the balance, the antithesis, the pomp, but he adds a new vivacity and glitter. When he says that Johnson's style is 'sustained only with constant effort,' and that his 'big words are wasted on little things,' he is unconsciously describing his own defects. His own worst literary vice is his lack of proportion, and his entire inattention to those laws of light and shade which regulate the highest literary art.

Macaulay's essay on Johnson is in itself an almost perfect example both of the greatness and the limitations of his power; it displays his unrivalled faculty for the collection of details, and equally his all but total lack of real insight. He sees Johnson, as he sees all the personages he describes, entirely from the outside. He categories all his peculiarities, his slovenly disorder, his boorishness, his voracity, his oddities of speech and gesture, his superstitions, his humorous petulances, his grotesque absurdities, and thinks that he has painted the man. 'Macaulay is never more at home than in such scandal,' it has been well said; 'the eating, drinking, and clothing of men, their mistresses, their warts, their bandy-legs, or their red noses—Macaulay has, in such curiosities, absolutely the *furore* of a collector.' But he never once recognises the grandeur of that spirit which is concealed beneath this uncouth exterior. We must go to Carlyle for that vision. *He* has the prophetic insight which interprets the whole nature of a man in a single significant phrase. His power is the power of understanding the soul of a man. Carlyle paints a portrait which lives, Macaulay constructs an elaborate mosaic. Any historic personage, even the humblest, who has once been bathed in the searching light of Carlyle's imagination, is henceforth known to us, and is instinct with vitality. But the most we learn from Macaulay is how such a person dressed his hair, ate his dinner, or treated his wife. Carlyle gives us the essential man ; Macaulay enumerates the mere accidents of the man's life. It is infinitely vivacious, entertaining, and fascinating ; but it is, after all, an inferior form of art which addresses itself to inferior intelligences. The fact which stands out most clearly about Johnson in Macaulay's essay, and which is most distinctly remembered after many years, is that he tore his food like a famished tiger, and ate it with the sweat running down his forehead. And that is not the cardinal fact of Johnson's personality. It is not the thing which is best worth recollecting, or even worth remembering at all. But it is things like these, obscure and trivial traits in a man's person or habits, which Macaulay exalts to first-rate importance, and which are offered us in place of a real analysis of his character, a true insight into his soul.

Not that Macaulay is without imagination, however ; it is simply the quality of the imagination that is at fault. He has 'epic clearness,' if he has not dramatic intensity. He has photographic vividness, if not creative genius. There is ample evidence that he did not even understand some of the noblest productions of the human imagination. He derides Spenser, and calls the poetry of Wordsworth interminable twaddle. He is incapable of soaring into the higher heavens of vision. He had no hours of stillness and brooding fancy, out of whose depths there was at length evolved the true image of a man or a period. He loved the concrete, and his mission was to illuminate and vivify it. That species of imagination which fuses a vast mass of facts and details into one glowing whole, was his in perfection. We have already seen that he aimed at making history as fascinating as a novel, and that he has done. To do so he treated it as a vast portrait-gallery, and did not trouble himself with the deeper currents of thought which characterised a period. For the subtler forms of criticism he felt himself unfitted, and owned his defect with that perfect candour which is so engaging a feature in his character. He says, ' Such books as Lessing's *Laocoon*, such passages as the criticism on *Hamlet* in *Wilhelm Meister*, fill me with wonder and despair.' There is no limit to the labour he will undergo to unearth those picturesque details which are the stage properties through which his most striking effects are produced. But when he has collected his details he is content. He does not sift and resift evidence, till he knows exactly how a case stood : that is Carlyle's method. He does not aim at expressing himself with the originality of dramatic insight. He simply arranges his picture with a consummate sense of effect. He has not called spirits from the vasty deep, but he has constructed an imposing panorama, in which the great actors of the past move with an excellent simulation of life. The appeal from first to last is to the eye, and nothing can be more brilliant, vivid, and effective in its way. The only thing is, it is not the highest way ; it is panoramic, but not dramatic art.

Macaulay has been compared with Burke, but there is no likeness between the two men, save that which is purely superficial. Both were orators, writers, parliamentarians, but there the likeness ends. Burke was an original force, with something of the freshness of Nature in him : the real basis of Macaulay's mind was commonplace. Burke was a profound thinker, and Macaulay was in no sense whatever a thinker. Burke was an incompleter, but a far greater man : a man of the Titanic order, whereas Macaulay has nothing of the Titan in him. It is precisely when we compare Macaulay with a man like Burke that we become most conscious of his real inferiority, of his comparative littleness. We see then that what Macaulay lacked was that powerful individuality which is inseparable from the highest genius. He was not one of those who are set for the rising or fall of nations, the potent source of new thoughts and ideals, new impulses and forces for times and peoples. He exercised nothing of the fascination of real greatness over his contemporaries. They never speak of him as we speak of Carlyle, or as Reynolds spoke of Johnson. They all acknowledged his brilliant powers, but he inspired neither animosity nor devotion, division nor discipleship. His conversation was typical of the man. Sydney Smith complained that it had 'no flashes of silence,' and Carlyle said contemptuously, 'Flow on, thou shining river!' It was a vast stream of erudition, good sense, good humour, occasionally of sententious wit, but it displayed none of those larger human qualities which invest the table-talk of Johnson and Carlyle with a perennial charm. Somehow we are always conscious of an air of precocity in all Macaulay's displays. His power of memory is greatly in excess of his power of reflection, and this is one of the common vices of precocity. But be this as it may, it is as a superb literary artist that Macaulay must stand or fall. What he did he did excellently, but again we repeat it was not the highest kind of work. Nor was he one of the highest kind of men, and that is why we feel it to be an impertinence to include his name in the category of Burke, and Johnson, and Carlyle. His English prototype is Hume or Gibbon; his Latin, Sallust.

Perhaps the most pleasant feature of Macaulay's character was his intense enthusiasm for literature. It was a real and beautiful enthusiasm, and it gave a certain dignity to his thoughts, and is the source of all that is best in his writing. It is not the enthusiasm of a large intellectual life, however; real as it is, yet it moves in a comparatively restricted area. He seems to have had no interest in science, in modern poetry, or in the social and religious problems of his day. To the subtler influences of thought he was simply insensible. He was impatient of philosophy, and indifferent to religion. But he loved books with an almost indiscriminating passion. He read again and again those ancient classics which most interested him, and the list of books he read in a single year of his Indian life is simply astounding. He was fond of walking, but he always walked with a book in his hand. In a walk of sixteen miles he once re-read six books of Homer. When he crosses the Irish Channel, he amuses himself by sitting on deck all night and repeating the *Paradise Lost* from memory, noting with pride that he can still recite six books, and those the best. He was a genuine hero-worshipper. In his Italian tour his chief pleasure is not found in the beauty of the country, but in its historic associations. It thrills him with an exquisite delight to tread in the steps of Cicero or Hannibal, and his immense erudition invests every place he sees with vivid interest. No one but a hero-worshipper could have written the essay upon Milton. The note struck in that famous essay is the note struck in all his writings, or all that is noblest in them. It was always with a sigh of relief that he turned aside from public duties to the companionship of books, and he said that he could covet no higher joy than to be shut up in the seclusion of a great library, and never pass a moment without a book in his hand. And this confession declares the man. To acquire information was the real passion of his life. He was not interested in the study of human nature, and had no love or aptitude for meditation. A man with genial interest in his fellows, and in life as a whole, would not have walked the streets of London with a book in his hand ; and a man with any faculty of meditative thought would scarcely have employed a long starlit night on the Irish Sea in a recitation of Milton.

Great powers and great qualities Macaulay had, but one great deficiency is always felt : he has no sense of the Infinite. He has no sense whatever of the mystery of life, of its eternal environments, of what Shelley felt when he conceived that

> Life, like a dome of many-coloured glass,
> Stains the white radiance of Eternity,

or of what Shakespeare felt when he wrote the great soliloquy of Hamlet. His 'foible is omniscience,' that complete knowledge of the surface of life which supposes that it has looked into 'the very heart of the machine' when it has enumerated the outward characteristics of human life, but has no corresponding intuition of its inner movements. We look in vain in Macaulay for any of those sudden flashes of light which reveal the deep heart of the writer, and instantaneously send the thoughts of the reader soaring into the firmament of the Infinite. He never asks Whence am I?—Whither am I going? He never makes us feel the solemnity of the thought that all these generations which he pictures have trodden the dusty road of death, and lie silent under the drums and tramplings of succeeding ages. He does not feel, with Wordsworth, the grandeur of the suggestion that the soul

> That rises with us, our life's star,
> Hath had elsewhere its setting,
> And cometh from afar,

or with Shakespeare the pathos of the thought that 'we are such stuff as dreams are made of,' and our 'little life is rounded with a sleep.' He does not close his *History* as Raleigh closed his, with any magnificent apostrophe to 'eloquent, just, and mighty death.' The 'still, sad music of humanity' is a music he has never heard. There is no eternal dome of heaven arched over his history, there are no watchful Presences that look on us from other worlds; all is gross, palpable, commonplace, mundane. Life passes before us like a glittering pageant, and we are conscious only of its buzz and tinsel. He is content that it should be so; he aims at no higher effect. It is in the *mise en scène* of the theatre he excels; he has no eye for the starry spaces and deep profound of Nature which allure and impress us outside the theatre door. If he can make us clap our hands before his scenic show, it is enough; we must look to others for guidance in the eternal mystery of things, for interpretation of the heavenly silences.

We do not ask for spirituality in an historian, and we can do without philosophic depth ; but the lack of this sense of the Infinite unmistakably dwarfs the subject, and makes the noblest effects impossible.   It is like the lack of atmosphere in a painting—everything is too rigid in outline, too near and distinct, and the charm of distance is wanting.   The grandeur of Carlyle's *French Revolution* arises from this very quality, his intense sensitiveness to the nearness of the Infinite.   Everything is seen against a background of infinity.   We are reminded again and again of those solemn abysses of eternity on the brink of which men sport.   We see the drama of human life played out in an awful environment of immensities and eternities, and are the more fascinated with its

> Shifting fancies and celestial lights,
> With all its grand orchestral silences,
> To keep the pauses of the rhythmic sounds.

And there is no great writer in modern literature who has not had this sense of the Infinite.   It gives solemnity to the fancies of De Quincey, as well as to the history of Carlyle ; it bathes the pages of Ruskin, and Tennyson, and Browning, not less than those of Newman, with a celestial splendour.   But no gleam of that light which never was on sea or land illumines the writings of Macaulay.   In the ordinary sense of the world he was not a worldly man.   He was not avaricious, self-seeking, or immodestly proud.   He was simple in his tastes, and moderate in his ambitions.   But if he was not a worldly man in this orthodox sense of the word, he was distinctly a mundane man.   He never felt what Burke felt when he said, ' What shadows we are, and what shadows we pursue !'   He never looked over the barriers of the world into that eternal sea which flows round all, and he never heard its undertone of melancholy music. What the deepest hearts have felt, he never felt ; what the clearest eyes have seen, he never saw ; and the problems with which great thinkers have wrestled all their lives in an agony that yearned without pause for the breaking of the day, never so much as troubled him with a suggestion of their presence. Macaulay had never met the wrestling angel and prevailed. He was an unconscious but complete materialist in all his thoughts and ideas ; he was like Gibbon, ‘ of the earth earthly.’

A very mundane man, no doubt ; an eager-minded, strenuous man, with an honest delight in life, and a pleasure in its rough tussles for pre-eminence ; but for all this, a man who, in his private conduct, was capable of being quietly heroic in a way which more unworldly spirits have often found it difficult to emulate. Perhaps we can afford to barter some of the higher qualities of literary sympathy for the fortitude and unselfishness which can endure banishment for five years, at a time when political prospects are brightest, for the sake of putting himself and his family on a basis of independence. There have been many literary artists who were exquisitely discerning and sympathetic in their taste, but who were utterly cynical and selfish in their private relationships ; and when we choose between nobility of conduct and finish of intellect, we know which ranks the higher. ‘ At Christmas,’ he writes from India, ‘ I shall send home a thousand or twelve hundred pounds for my father and you all. I cannot tell you what a comfort it is to me to know that I shall be able to do this. It reconciles me to all the pains—acute enough sometimes, God knows!—of banishment. In a few years, if I live—probably in less than five years from the time at which you are reading this letter—we shall be again together in a comfortable, though modest home; certain of a good fire, a good joint of meat, and a good glass of wine; without owing obligations to anybody, and perfectly indifferent, at least as far as our pecuniary interest is concerned, to the changes of the political world. Rely on it, my dear girls, that there is no chance of my going back with my heart cooled toward you. I came hither principally to save my family, and I am not likely while here to forget them.' The letter is of the earth earthly, no doubt, but there is surely a touch of noble feeling in it also. It was not Macaulay's way to wear his heart upon his sleeve; he was inclined rather to simulate a bluntness of feeling which was not real, and to conceal his deepest emotions under the mask of worldly shrewdness. But that those emotions were there, and that a real sensitiveness of heart was allied to his native shrewdness of mind, no one can doubt. The jovial anticipation of 'the good joint and the good glass of wine' does not enable us to forget the sore heart of the exile, nor are we likely to overlook his silent self-sacrifice.

It is scarcely necessary to add more. Macaulay was so thoroughly honest, genuine, and sweet-natured that it is with regret one has to say so much of his defects. He was 'a lump of good-nature.' It has been well said that we must beware of either praising or blaming him, for the praise becomes blame and the blame praise before we know it. Thus if we say that he had no strong passions, we must immediately recollect the depth and tenderness of his affections, and his noble loyalty to such duties as sprang from the affections. The very defects which close to him the doors of the highest renown are the qualities which ensured him his immense and undiminished popularity. He wrote not for people who think, but for the mass of people who prefer what is interesting to what is profound. He did his work with an honest delight in it, and spared no labour to make it as perfect as his conception of it permitted. He certainly invented a new style and a new method of writing history, and the charm of both is that they are infallibly interesting. Perhaps the compliment which he most appreciated was that conveyed in an address from some working-men, who thanked him for being the first to write a history which the common people could understand. To have done this is to have done much, but to have written a history which is equally the delight of the learned and the cultured is a unique achievement. And he deserved his success; no man ever worked with more singleness of aim and devotedness of purpose. The faults of his work are the defects of the man himself, they are inseparable from his endowments, and are not the blemishes which come by intention, or can be removed by determination. If he was not a great man, he was a man of great genius; and a long period of time must elapse, and public taste and human nature become much changed, before his work can pass into desuetude, or his name be forgotten.

CHAPTER IX

WALTER SAVAGE LANDOR

[Born at Warwick, January 30, 1775. Educated at Rugby and Oxford. Published his poem, *Gebir*, 1798. Went to Spain as volunteer in the Spanish cause against Napoleon, 1808. Married Miss Thuillier, 1811. Wrote his poem, *Count Julian*, in same year. Published first instalment of *Imaginary Conversations*, 1831. Examination of Shakespeare, 1854. *Pentameron*, 1837. Collection of Latin Poems, 1847. Died in Florence, September 17, 1864.]

'I CLAIM no place in the world of letters; I am alone, and will be alone as long as I live, and after,' wrote Landor in one of his late confessions. Equally characteristic is his proud saying, 'I shall dine late; but the dining-room will be well lighted, the guests few and select.' In each instance the prophecy is likely to be fulfilled. Landor still speaks to the few, but they are the best judges of literature : he still stands alone, but it is because there is no one capable of disputing his peculiar pre-eminence with him.

In mere weight and mass of genius Landor stood high among his contemporaries, and in the final form which he adopted for his expression, he has neither prototype nor imitator. Carlyle rightly described him as an 'unsubduable old Roman'; Swinburne, with more delicate felicity of epithet, distinguishes the Greek grace of manner which he joined with Roman virility of thought:

> And through the trumpet of a child of Rome
> Rang the pure music of the flutes of Greece.

Classic grandeur and breadth, classic purity and severity of form, distinguish all his best writing. There is a classic dignity about his life also, marred, however, by fierce intractability of temper, sudden and disastrous explosions of feeling, and entire want of judgment in all the practical affairs of life. No man was readier in uttering hasty judgments, or more reluctant to modify them when the facts were obviously against him. He has in turn described the French, the Welsh, and the Italians as the most corrupt and worthless of mankind. Where he hated he found no epithet too odious for the object of his hatred, where he loved no praise too extreme. The story of his life is a long history of collisions with authority, with neighbours, with friends, with circumstances, often as intensely amusing to the onlooker as they were painful to himself. There is much in his life which is ludicrous and astonishing; perhaps it is little wonder that the mass of men, ever more ready to gloat over a frailty than to detect a virtue, should have remembered his faults and forgotten his greatness.

Precipitancy of judgment and heat of temper are responsible for all the errors of Landor's life. To recount these errors is neither wise, necessary, nor generous. One thing, however, is noticeable, that in every case the difficulties which he created in himself arose from a sort of undisciplined magnanimity of nature, a belief in impracticable ideals, a radical inability to adapt himself to the common convictions of life. He sinned against himself in a hundred instances, but against others never. His generosity was extreme and incessant. In his enormous agricultural experiments at Llanthony he squandered seventy thousand pounds in five years. In later life he denuded himself of almost all that he possessed in favour of a wife who had embittered his existence, and whom he had twice left. Frugality was a virtue of which he had never heard, common-sense a word of which he did not know the meaning. If he has never yet quite come by his own in literary fame, it is because the same wilfulness and impracticability characterised his genius. The last thought that would ever occur to him was what the public was likely to read ; or, if such a suggestion had been made to him, it is quite certain that he would have instantly chosen a form of writing diametrically opposed to public taste. He planned his literary life much as he planned his gigantic agricultural schemes at Llanthony, without the least reference to the practical conditions of success. His only vice was an indomitable pride. His crown of virtue was magnanimity. In both these qualities he was made more pagan than modern, and deserved his title of Roman. We may pity, love, admire, judge him—each is possible, and does not exclude the other—but no one can get at close quarters with him without perceiving that Landor's nature was wrought out of the rarest and purest material, and that numerous as the flaws are, none of them go very deep, or seriously impair the general impressiveness of the whole.

Landor's literary career began with poetry, and to the close of his long life he wrote poetry, often of the very highest order. It has always seemed to me that the poetry of Landor has been quite unjustly neglected, and even the best critics have paid far too little attention to it. Of course he was not a great poet in the sense in which Wordsworth or Shelley is great, and the reasons of his inferiority are obvious. Both Wordsworth and Shelley had a message to deliver; Landor had none. It was not that he did not feel earnestly and even violently on a variety of subjects, but a certain underlying contempt of his fellow-men robbed him of that sympathy which made anything like a coherent and vital message possible. Again, he had little power of impregnating his poetry with that intimate personal passion which gives poignancy or sweetness to the work of his great contemporaries. He was too reticent, too proud, too self-contained to unveil his heart with the freedom of a Byron or a Shelley. Byron and Shelley intrusted their closest secrets to mankind, and their poetry is a long series of personal confessions. Nothing happened to them, no movement of heart or mind, that has not something corresponding to it in their verse, and consequently they never fail to excite our sympathies, and compel our interest. Even of Wordsworth, a man of much colder temperament, this is true: in all his more vital poetry we share the secrets of his personality. Landor permits no such intrusion. He is shy as a girl over the ardours of his own heart. He addresses us from a standpoint at once remote and detached, and only in rare moments descends from his pinnacle and stands among us. And, as compared with the greatest poets—and it is with these only he deserves to be compared —he fails in execution. He lacks the unfaltering felicity of the perfectly developed artistic

sense. A line or a passage full of gravity and music
is often succeeded by halting and inefficient workmanship, as though his inspiration had suddenly
failed him, or he had tired in his flight. Few poets
have ever soared higher, but, strong as his wing is, it
soon droops. It is not that he is incapable of doing
better, but he is too careless to attempt it, at least
continuously ; and so it may be said that never was
great poetry with greater faults.

But, at its best, Landor's poetry is great poetry,
and he who has not justly estimated the poetry of
Landor is incapable of forming a true estimate of
his genius. He possesses wonderful lucidity, simplicity, and charm, together with great gravity and
depth of feeling, and a peculiar power of intense
imagination. Nothing more perfect of its kind was
ever written than the eight lines on *Rose Aylmer*—
lines which Lamb was never tired of reciting :

> Ah what avails the sceptred race,
>   Ah what the form divine !
> What every virtue, every grace !
>   Rose Aylmer, all were thine.
> Rose Aylmer, whom these wakeful eyes
>   May weep, but never see,
> A night of memories and sighs
>   I consecrate to thee.

Such a poem recalls the sweetness and simplicity of
Wordsworth's lines to *Lucy Gray*, but it possesses also
a certain classic austerity which even Wordsworth
rarely attained. In another kind of poetry, aiming
at larger and epic effect, there is little that surpasses
the closing passages of the poem called *Regeneration*.
Landor was always a close student of Milton, whom
he honoured as the greatest of men, and in this

poem he comes very near Milton in the solemn march
of his blank verse. Such lines as these:

> Let all that Elis ever saw, give way,
> All that Olympian Jove e'er smiled upon :
> The Marathonian columns never told
> A tale more glorious, never Salamis,
> Nor, faithful in the centre of the false,
> Platea, nor Anthela, from whose mount
> Benignant Ceres wards the blessed Laws,
> And sees the Amphictyon dip his weary foot
> In the warm streamlet of the strait below,—

recall not only the pomp of Milton's lines, but also
his classicism. But much as Landor admired Milton,
he was no copyist. He has a grave, sweet concord
of his own, composed of the simplest chords. No
passage of his poetry is better known, and none is
more perfect, than his famous description of the sea-
shell in *Gebir*:

> But I have sinuous shells of pearly hue
> Within, and they that lustre have imbibed
> In the sun's palace-porch, where, when unyoked
> His chariot-wheel stands midway in the wave :
> Shake one, and it awakens ; then apply
> Its polisht lips to your attentive ear,
> And it remembers its august abodes,
> And murmurs as the ocean murmurs there.

Byron took the same image, and spoiled it ; Wordsworth certainly did not improve it when he turned it
to moral uses in the *Excursion*. These are, of course,
but random samples of Landor's poetry, taken from
an opulent and various storehouse. No single poem
can rightly illustrate his power ; yet, if one needs
must be chosen which displays his rarest qualities in
their most perfect combination, there is none so
distinctive as the following brief idyll from his

Hellenics. Notice how grave and simple is the movement of the verse, how the full tragedy is exquisitely indicated rather than described (a constant habit with Landor in all his dramatic writing), the abruptness of the close, with the brief phrase, ''twas not hers,' which tells everything, and leaves an ineffaceable impression of a mourning too profound for words.   It is the husband who speaks :

> 'Artemidora ! Gods invisible,
> While thou art lying faint along the couch,
> Have tied the sandal to thy slender feet
> And stand beside thee, ready to convey
> Thy weary steps where other rivers flow.
> Refreshing shades will waft thy weariness
> Away, and voices like thine own come nigh,
> Soliciting, nor vainly, thy embrace.'
>   Artemidora sigh'd, and would have prest
> The hand now pressing hers, but was too weak.
> Iris stood over her dark hair unseen
> While thus Elpenor spake.   He lookt into
> Eyes that had given light and life erewhile
> To those above them, those now dim with tears
> And watchfulness.   Again he spake of joy
> Eternal.   At that word, that sad word, *joy,*
> Faithful and fond her bosom heaved once more :
> Her head fell back : and now a loud deep sob
> Swell'd through the darken'd chamber ; 'twas
>   not hers.

What can be more perfect than this?   What more tender?   Infelicitous as Landor's own domestic life was, yet no one has spoken of love with such condensed passion, no one has described its inmost workings with a touch so sure and subtle.   To him we owe many an apophthegm on love—such, for instance, as this : 'The happiest of pillows is not that which Love first presses, it is that which Death has frowned on and passed over.' Landor's tenderness is the rare tenderness of the strong man, than which none is more moving, and in this poem we have its most exquisite expression. Such a lucid gem of poetry ought to be sufficient to convince even the most sceptical that in point of quality Landor's best poetry is worthy to be ranked with the greatest of the nineteenth century.

It was not until Landor had come to the confines of mid-life that he finally adopted the form of literary expression best suited to his genius. At forty-six much of his life had been futile and disappointing. Admirable as his poetry was, yet it was obvious that it would never be popular. Great as were his personal gifts and qualities, it was equally obvious that they were counterbalanced by serious and irritating defects. He had behaved alternately as a schoolboy and a sage. His love of combat had carried him into indiscretions which had seriously alienated those who were most ready to honour him. He had revenged fancied slights by ferocious lampoons. He had run through his fortune, was embarrassed in circumstances, and was an exile in Pisa. Olympian methods of conduct suit ill with sedate English conventions, as he had discovered to his cost. Through all this turmoil—lampoons on fools, law-suits with neighbours, collisions with authorities, volunteer soldiery in Spain, and what not—the main element of Landor's life, however, had suffered no change: he had never ceased to be a scholar. The range of his reading, always extraordinary, had widened with the steady growth of his mind. There was scarcely a great writer of antiquity with whom he was not intimately acquainted, nor a great historical personage of any period, the motives of whose conduct and the nature of whose action he had not thoroughly sifted. History was for him the story of great men at work. His temperament was the temperament of the hero-worshipper. He tells us that the great figures of the past affected his sympathies, as though he had known them intimately. They were the friends of his solitude, and almost the only friends he had. In his long country walks, and in his nights of study, he fell into the way of holding conversations with them as if they were real; he found a keen joy in dramatising some well-known act of their lives, some tragic or happy crisis in their careers. His published dramas, abounding as they did in fine passages, nevertheless lacked that true creative touch which gives to figures of the imagination a local habitation and a name. But in past history there were crowds of figures ready to his hand: why not dramatise these? Twenty years earlier he had sketched a dialogue between Burke and Grenville, and his mind now returned to this novel form of composition. He left Pisa in 1821, moving to Florence, where for the next five years he resided in the Medici Palace, and later on at the Villa Castiglione. No sooner had he settled in Florence than this idea of dramatic dialogues with the great personages of the past took entire possession of his mind, and the result was the *Imaginary Conversations*, which are the finest fruit of his genius, and his enduring monument.

It would be quite vain to introduce these great pieces of literature to those who have neither the aptitudes nor the instincts of culture. They are

above all things the work of· a scholar, and Landor
neither expected nor desired that they should appeal
to the great mass of readers. This is, of course, a
serious disqualification. Men of a genius as great
as, or greater than Landor's, have contrived to write
in such a way as to interest all classes of readers.
That peculiar breadth of touch which distinguishes
the greatest masters of literature was not Landor's
at any time, and he was much too proud and self-
contained to consider for an instant what would be
likely to prove popular with the public. He wrote
to please himself, and this is the source of both his
strength and his weakness. Shakespeare himself
had no more vivid insight into the play of human
motive and the complicated issues of human passion,
but Shakespeare was forced by the traditions of the
stage to express himself in popular forms. If we
can conceive of Shakespeare as a solitary scholar,
free from all exigency of popular appeal as a means
of earning money, writing in his closet simply to
please himself, we may conceive him writing dramatic
dialogues after Landor's fashion. Nor is it in the
least exaggerated praise to say that it is hard to
think of any one else who could have rivalled the
best of these *Imaginary Conversations.* But fortunately for us Shakespeare was forced to please others
as well as himself. He selected such stories as those
of Antony and Cleopatra, Cæsar and Brutus, Othello
and Desdemona, as much from a sense of their
popular significance as of their philosophic importance. Landor selects his themes without the least
regard to popular significance. Hence one cannot
but feel that he is at a disadvantage. The writer,
not less than the actor, is one who lives to please, and

must please to live. And yet it must be remembered that it needs but a very little accommodation on our part to Landor's point of view to find in these matchless dialogues one of the richest inheritances of the human mind. The more cultured a man is, the more will he appreciate them ; but, after all, it is only the absolutely uncultured who will take no interest in them. Granted that we know who his personages are, that we have some elementary knowledge of the part they played in life, and we at once catch the spirit of the dialogue. The case is almost parallel with that of Carlyle's *French Revolution*: some preliminary knowledge is demanded of us simply because much is taken for granted. In each instance it needs some *effort* to master the method of the writer, but when once the effort is made, the reward is out of all proportion to the exertion.

The quality which strikes one most in these *Imaginary Conversations* is the enormous variety of Landor's power. They range through the whole realm of human history, and there is no part of that history which he has not thoroughly comprehended. Everywhere there is adequate knowledge and often profound scholarship ; everywhere there is also strenuous thinking, and a marvellous energy of conception and expression. It must not be supposed, however, that Landor ever aimed at exact history. He once said that he usually had one history which he read, and another which he invented. His method is essentially dramatic. He was not concerned with the actual things which his personages are reported to have said, but with the things which they might be imagined as saying. In all the more than two hundred dialogues of Landor, it is difficult to recall an instance in which he puts into the mouth of the speaker anything which history reports him as saying. He even took care never to consult history when he had once begun to write upon some historic personage. His immense reading and exact scholarship enabled him to dispense with such aids to knowledge. Before he wrote, he had arrived at a fundamental conception of the character of his protagonist; he then let him think and speak in the way in which he might be supposed to have thought and spoken in the actual crisis depicted. An excellent example of this method is the conversation between Essex and Spenser. There is no record of any interview between Essex and Spenser, when the latter fled from Ireland after the burning of his house and the destruction of his property; but it is likely enough, and indeed certain, that some such interview did occur. Landor brings the two men face to face in a scene that Shakespeare would not have disowned. By a variety of exquisite dramatic touches the scene grows in poignancy, until at last Spenser breaks forth in uncontrollable agony, and horrifies Essex with the news that not only his house, but his child is burned. The impression made upon the mind is one of absolute truth, which is the highest excellence of dramatic art. Cæsar did not make the speeches which Shakespeare puts into his lips, but he might have made them. They are justified by his character, and that is the main thing. So with Landor: Pericles, Sophocles, Cicero, Cecil, Elizabeth, Milton, Marvel—all hold his brief stage in turn, but each is distinctly individual, each speaks in his own accent, each says the things which from our knowledge of history he may be supposed as saying, if ever Pericles discussed art with Sophocles under the shadow of the Acropolis, or Milton discussed tragedy with Marvel in the scant seclusion of Bunhill Fields.

The *Imaginary Conversations* do not, however, all range themselves under the plain category of the dramatic. Some are philosophic, some are critical, though even in these the dramatic instinct is always present. One of the most terrible of all the dramatic pieces is Landor's dialogue between Peter the Great and his son Alexis. In reading this dialogue one can well believe that Landor often wrote in a passion of tears and frenzy. The timid, gentle, kindly son, condemned to death by his own father, and saying— 'My father truly says I am not courageous ; but the death that leads me to my God shall never terrify me,' touches a rare height of nobility ; the brutality of Peter, shaking off the entire remembrance of the scene the moment it is over, and calling loudly for brandy, bacon, and some pickled sturgeon, and some krout and caviare, and good strong cheese, is rendered with a savage intensity almost peculiar to the lesser Elizabethan dramatists, a Marlowe, a Webster, or a Ford. One can only marvel, in the presence of work so great as this, what the readers of England have been about for the last fifty years that they have paid so little attention to it. But in another mood, the purely critical, Landor is almost as impressive. Here, of course, personal likes and dislikes come into play, and Landor was not the man to conceal them ; but his criticism is never less than acute and luminous. Nothing finer in this way is to be found than the conversation between Petrarca and Boccaccio on Dante's *Paolo and Francesca.* The whole story of the unhappy lovers is told in six lines, but, says Landor, 'What a sweet aspiration in each cæsura of the verse! three love-sighs fixed and incorporate. Then when she hath said,

> "*La bocca lui baciò tutto tremante,*"

she stops: she would avert the eyes of Dante from her; he looks for the sequel: she thinks he looks severely; she says,

> "*Galeotto* is the name of the book,"

fancying by this timorous little flight she has drawn him far enough from the nest of her young loves.

> "*Galeotto* is the name of the book."
> "What matters that?"
> "And of the writer?"
> "Or that either."

At last she disarms him: but how?

> "*That* day we read no more."

'Such a depth of intuitive judgment, such a delicacy of perception, exists not in any other work of human genius: and from an author who, on almost all occasions, in this part of his work, betrays a deplorable want of it.'

Landor's opinion of Dante was not high, and he even went so far as to say that the *Inferno* was the most immoral and impious book that was ever written; but the most admiring critic of Dante may rest satisfied with such a piece of criticism as this.

Strong and even violent as Landor often was in antipathy and opinion, he never failed to see the excellency of really fine work. A fine strenuous sincerity breathes throughout his work of this kind, which is full of invigoration; and in this particular criticism we may justly ascribe to him the merits he ascribed to Dante, great 'depth of intuitive judgment' and 'delicacy of perception.'

Another kind of writing in which Landor excelled may be best described as 'fantasy.' Perhaps the noblest specimens of this work are the *Dream of Boccaccio* and the *Dream of Petrarca*. Each is distinguished by peculiar delicacy of sentiment, beauty of cadence, and grace of imagination. They illustrate also in a very striking manner the thorough paganism of Landor's mind. His theme is love and death; it is treated after the fashion of the greatest of antique poets; and here, if anywhere, we most distinctly hear the music of 'the flutes of Greece.' Surely Death was never described with more solemn pregnancy of phrase, with more beauty and serenity too, than in this passage: 'I cannot tell how I knew him, but I knew him to be the genius of Death. Breathless as I was at beholding him, I soon became familiar with his features. First they seemed only calm; presently they became contemplative, and lastly, beautiful; those of the Graces themselves are less regular, less harmonious, less composed. Love glanced at him unsteadily, with a countenance in which there was somewhat of anxiety, somewhat of disdain, and cried, "Go away! Go away! Nothing that thou touchest lives."

'"Say rather, child," replied the advancing form, and advancing grew loftier and statelier, "say rather that nothing of beautiful or glorious lives its own true life until my wing has passed over it." ' In the *Dream of Boccaccio* the allegory is of equal loveliness, and the imagery is equally grave and solemn, but there is a warmer glow. When was the charm and spirit of Italian scenery so admirably rendered and imparted as in this brief passage :

' I dreamt ; and suddenly sprang forth before me many groves and palaces and gardens, and their statues and their avenues, and their labyrinths of alaternus and bay, and alcoves of citron, and watchful loopholes in the retirements of impenetrable pomegranates. Farther off, just below where the fountain slipt away from its marble hall and guardian gods, arose, from their beds of moss and drosera and darkest grass, the sisterhood of oleanders, fond of tantalising with their bosomed flowers and their moist and pouting blossoms the little shy rivulet, and of covering its face with all the colours of the dawn. My dream expanded and moved forward. I trod again the dust of Posilippo, soft as the feathers in the wings of Sleep.'

But quotation does little to help us in understanding the beauty of such works as this. One striking peculiarity of Landor's style at all times is that it seldom yields the full secret of its charm at a first reading. There is perfect ease and lucidity in all his prose, but also a sense of impenetrable depth. And nowhere are these characteristics so fully felt as in those passages of his writings where he indulges in allegory—the finest passages in all his writings, and unequalled by anything else of the same kind in the whole realm of English literature.

' He who is within two paces of the ninetieth year

may sit down and make no excuses,' wrote Landor. 'He must be unpopular, he never tried to be much otherwise; he never contended with a contemporary, but walked alone on the far eastern uplands, meditating and remembering.' In this confession, almost the last of many such, Landor does much to anticipate the judgment of posterity. He was by nature solitary, and spent his life in meditating and remembering. He was by nature impatient of the modern world, and took refuge in an older world. For these reasons, as he well knew, he could never be popular. But on a certain class of mind Landor will always exercise an undeniable fascination, and even those least amenable to his charm can scarcely regard his *Imaginary Conversations* with anything but reverence, as one of the most wonderful achievements of the human intellect. The dialogue is in itself a somewhat repellent and cumbrous literary form, and occasionally even Landor succumbs beneath its heaviness, and drifts away into tedious disquisition. But for the most part he puts so much movement, so much intensity and fire into his dialogues, that they are quite as easily read as the dramas of Shakespeare. And in the best of them what moderation and composure breathe, what clear serenity of intellectual view, what a spirit of force and beauty : what a closely-packed wisdom is there, and what dauntless energy of thought. A great thinker, in the sense of a systematic thinker, Landor was not, but few writers have ever uttered so many noble thoughts upon so many themes. And they are often clothed in a sort of splendour, which is so peculiarly his own, that it can only be called Landorian. Pregnant epigram, massive strength, vivid imagination characterise all his best work. His sentences, often abrupt, are always clear and decisive ; and when he chooses, they rise by easy stages into pomp and stateliness, into exquisite and haunting cadences, into a full harmonious roll, as of a great organ. If he spoke of his work with a superb self-confidence, he was justified in doing so. He presents almost a solitary instance of a man's own judgment of his work being more accurate and just than the judgment of his wisest contemporaries. Some day, perhaps, unless the sense of what is truly great in literature wholly declines among his countrymen, Landor's claim to fame will be fully met; even now, those who know most about the matter will cheerfully indorse his proud challenge: 'What I write is not written on slate, and no finger, not of Time himself, who dips it in the clouds of years, can efface it.'

CHAPTER X

THOMAS DE QUINCEY

[Born in Manchester, August 15, 1785. *Confessions of an Opium-eater* appeared in the *London Magazine*, 1821. Settled in Edinburgh, 1828. Contributed to *Blackwood's*, *The Quarterly Review*, *Tait's Magazine*, *Hogg's Instructor*. Published *The Logic of Political Economy*, 1844. Died in Edinburgh, December 8, 1859. Collected edition of his writings, edited by David Masson, in 14 vols. Published by A. & C. Black, 1893.]

THE fame of De Quincey rests upon one hundred and fifty magazine articles. Late in life he meditated a new *History of England*, in twelve volumes, but this, like many other projects of his, came to nothing. It was not that he was incapable of industry, for a more prolific writer never lived, but that his mind lacked the consecutive purpose and aim which is necessary for literary tasks of magnitude. The circumstances of his life were also against him. Almost all that he wrote was produced under dire pressure, and it can scarcely be expected that his work should be free from the haste and over-emphasis which are the common vices of the magazine article. In ordinary circumstances such work would be ephemeral; in De Quincey's case the faults of his writing are forgotten in the contemplation of a style so eloquent, an invention so rich, an imagination so intense, that none can doubt his right to be called one of the

140

greatest masters of English which the century has produced.

It is with a curious mixture of pity, wonder, and affection that the reader will regard De Quincey as he is revealed in his writings and the story of his life. Never was man so incurably wayward, or so entirely helpless in the worldly management of his affairs. A plain record of his habits would appear too whimsical and fantastic for the broadest farce. For no reason whatever he slunk furtively from lodging to lodging, as though he were a hunted criminal. He believed himself to be in the direst poverty, and went from friend to friend humbly soliciting the loan of seven-and-sixpence, when he had in his pocket a banker's draft for fifty pounds, which he did not know how to convert into cash. Beggars, loafers, and wastrels of every description found in him an easy prey. Lodging-house keepers stole his papers, and sold them back to him at exorbitant ransom; they made him believe himself culpable of faults which he had never even imagined; when every other method of fraud failed, they invented a death in the family, and extorted supposititious funeral expenses from him. In the days when his fame was most brilliant in Edinburgh society, he lived in obscurity, and looked like a beggar. His most intimate friends never knew where to find him. When he had completely filled the room in which he happened to be living with an illimitable confusion of papers—'Snowed himself up,' as he called it—his practice was to disappear, and begin the same process somewhere else. The only way to get him to a dinner-party was to send an able-bodied man to find him and bring him by force. Occasionally he revenged himself by making a stay of several weeks, so that the difficulty of getting him into a friend's house was forgotten in the more appalling difficulty of how to get him out again. At one time he took sanctuary in Holyrood, believing himself in instant peril of arrest for debt; as a matter of fact, his debts were inconsiderable, and large sums were due to him, which he had either received and mislaid, or had never applied for. He had no idea whatever of the value of his own work. When he is over sixty, with an established reputation, he goes to editorial and publishing offices, meekly hawking his articles, as though he were an emulous amateur. Thus, with a genius of the rarest order, a secure reputation, and a ready market for his work, De Quincey reproduced the traditions, and lived after the fashion, of the most obscure Grub Street hack of Johnson's day, and for no apparent reason except that this was the sort of life which he preferred.

For much of this extraordinary eccentricity of habit no doubt opium was responsible. It is now certain that he suffered from gastrodynia, an obscure form of internal inflammation, which produces the acutest physical misery. For this malady he found opium a specific. Solid food of any kind was abhorrent to him, and could only be taken in the smallest quantities. Opium gave him instant relief; and, as he soon found, had a remarkable effect upon the mind. The sordid realities of existence dissolved into rose-tinted clouds; squalor became splendour, life a dream, the world a gorgeous insubstantial pageant. The barriers of Time and space, those landmarks and anchorages of the finite, themselves disappeared, and the mind recovered the temporary freedom of the infinite.   Obviously, for most men such an emancipation would be likely to involve the dissolution of virtue and the moral sense ; with De Quincey it meant simply the severance from the conventional.   The opium-dreams of De Quincey were not sensual but spiritual.   They had the singular effect of greatly stimulating both the intellectual and the moral powers.   What they dissolved was the material, the commonplace, the ordinary aspects of life.   Hence the unconscious incongruity and even absurdity of his habits.   If he was entirely ignorant of the value of money, and even of its use ; if he turned night into day, prowled round the bridges of Edinburgh when all slept but he, clothed himself in the first chance garments that came to hand, appeared at dinner-parties in a finely-selected assortment of rags, wandered lonely as a cloud among the throngs of his fellow-men, and behaved generally as no other man would have cared or dared to behave, it was because the ordinary world of humdrum civilised customs did not exist for him.   He was under no obligation to live after the manner of a world whose very existence was only real to him at intervals.   He claimed to be judged by standards very different from those which we should apply to our ordinary fellow-mortals.   And, to the great credit of all who knew him with any intimacy, he was so judged.   He was loved and esteemed by some of the best men and women of his time. They laughed perhaps at his grotesque childlike unfamiliarity with the commonest matters of practical life, but they knew him as wise, tender, and patient, they listened with delight to his conversation, they shielded him as far as they were able from the inconveniences of his conduct, they honoured him alike as mystic and man.

Even if De Quincey had never come under the thrall of opium, it is doubtful if he ever could have behaved like an ordinary mortal. There are some natures constitutionally incapable of conventional behaviour. A drop of wild blood has been mixed with the sober sequences of pedigree: the nomad is resurgent in them, the Ishmaelite, the restless tenant of some forgotten primeval world. Such a nature was Thoreau's; George Borrow showed the same characteristics, and so, from the first, did De Quincey. Civilisation is, in essence, an attempt to tame nature, and one of its most palpable results is the attenuation of vigorous individualities. But even in the oldest civilisations from time to time men are born who refuse to come under the yoke. They prefer strenuous liberty to bondage with ease. They are irresistibly attracted by the life of the open road, the hard adventurous life of the wanderer who has never seen a tax-gatherer nor paid a rate. Perhaps of all mortals they are the happiest, because they have the fewest wants and the sources of their happiness are the easiest of access. Pity is wasted on them: they have their own methods of delight, of which the dull plodding citizen knows nothing; and even amid the real hardships of their lot, they retain much of the irresponsible joyousness of the bird or of the child.

With all his fits of profound melancholy, De Quincey thus lived a happy life by living it in his own way. One can hardly pity the emancipated schoolboy wandering at large through Wales, sleeping on bare hillsides, the debtor of a casual charity, and hard put to it at times to find bread. Nor can one altogether pity the youth sucked into the vortex of London life, familiar with 'stony-hearted Oxford Street,' and the brother of its sad sisterhoods. He possessed the temperament which idealises all things, so that all he saw was seen in vast misty outlines, a cloudy phantasmagoria—to use a favourite word of his own—painted on the palimpsest of his brain. Even in his sensations of suffering there was something peculiar, poignant, and intense, which brought them subtly near to delight, in the same way in which extreme cold becomes impregnated with the sensation of heat. Most men who had endured the rough handling which De Quincey endured in youth, would have been glad to forget it all as a bad dream; if they had reflected on it at intervals it would have been with disgust or shame. To speak of such things by way of literary performance, would have seemed an outrage on the modesty of nature; especially when the narrative involved the confession of a habit so enslaving as the opium habit, which very early became an integral factor of De Quincey's life. But De Quincey felt no shame in such confessions, because he idealised all his experiences. He tells us with perfect calmness of all the sordid miseries he endured, and of his growing, and at last abject, enslavement to opium, because he realised these things only from their subjective side. He speaks as a child might speak, with astounding frankness, yet with complete innocence. There is hardly a more curious phenomenon in literary history than this. Were his *Confessions of an Opium-eater* entirely destitute of style, yet it would remain one of the most remarkable human documents in existence; when there is added to its extraordinary subject matter a style never surpassed in eloquence or imaginative richness, it is not difficult to understand how De Quincey has come to occupy the place of a classic.

De Quincey is at his best in the *Confessions* and parts of the *Suspiria*, because in these writings he found the fullest opportunity for the display of emotion and imagination. By nature and instinct he was a poet; by which I mean that his apprehension of things was essentially poetic. There are indeed passages in the *Confessions* which are so exquisitely modulated that they may be described as lyric, and they produce the kind of æsthetic pleasure which is peculiar to great poetry. Take the well-known passage in which he speaks of the tumultuous horror and ecstasy of his dreams, full of the oppression of inexpiable guilt, dominated by the sense of 'mysterious eclipse,' penetrated by a strange 'music of preparation and awakening surprise. . . . Then, like a chorus, the passion deepened. Some greater interest was at stake, some mightier cause than ever yet the sword had pleaded, or trumpet had proclaimed. Then came sudden alarms, hurryings to and fro: trepidations of innumerable fugitives, I knew not whether from the good cause or the bad; darkness and lights; tempest and human faces; and at last, with the sense that all was lost, female forms and the features that were worth all the world to me; and but a moment allowed—and clasped hands with heart-breaking partings, and then—everlasting farewells! and with a sigh, such as the caves of Hell sighed when the incestuous mother uttered the abhorred name of Death, the sound was reverberated

—everlasting farewells! and again, and yet again reverberated everlasting farewells! And I awoke in struggles, and cried aloud, "I will sleep no more!"' Here we have an accumulation of images, each essentially poetic. This power of cumulative imagery is peculiar to De Quincey. When his mind is strung to intensity he seems to receive a multitude of almost simultaneous impressions; he communicates to us the sense of indescribable commotion; there is a rush and tumult in his rhetoric which is thrilling and overpowering; yet, perhaps, not so much a movement as of a pageant that rolls past us, as of something that soars over us, splendour capping splendour, till wonder holds us breathless. It is like his dream of the delirious Piranesi and his staircase; aerial flights of stairs open one above the other, till the abyss swallows all. And in passages like these the method as well as the matter comes nearer poetry than prose. Modulations, melodies, and rhythmic effects unknown to prose surprise the ear; in substance and expression they are poetry.

How far what is sometimes called 'prose-poetry' is a legitimate form of literary art, is a question that might be endlessly debated. Most critics insist that the demarcation between prose and poetry is sharp and decisive, that the properties of the one are not the properties of the other, and that by mingling the two we do but succeed in begetting a Eurasian form of literature, to which little credit attaches. But such a rigid distinction can scarcely be maintained. The great Elizabethan writers perpetually introduce into prose the modulations of poetry. In the preface to Raleigh's *History of the World* are many examples of this practice; it is found in Milton's prose writings, in Sir Thomas Browne's *Urn Burial*, and in the pure melodious prose of the English Bible. Every one recalls Milton's superb description of the English nation: 'Methinks I see in my mind a noble and puissant nation, rousing herself like a strong man after sleep, and shaking her invincible locks; methinks I see her as an eagle mewing her mighty youth, and kindling her undazzled eyes at the full midday beam; purging and unscaling her long-abused sight at the fountain itself of heavenly radiance; while the whole noise of timorous and flocking birds, with these also who love the twilight, flutter about amazed at what she means.' Or take, again, a well-known passage from Sir Thomas Browne's *Urn Burial*, wherein he speaks of the bones of the dead as having 'rested quietly under the drums and tramplings of three conquests.' Every one feels at once that these splendid bursts of rhetoric do not justly belong to the realm of prose. De Quincey called them 'impassioned prose,' and impassioned prose insensibly fuses itself into poetry. In other words, prose at a certain height or heat of passion becomes rhythmic, and passes into a series of 'complex harmonies,' common to true poetry, but unusual in prose writing. To write thus is certainly not to beget a bastard or Eurasian form of literature. The form is legitimate enough, but it is rare because it demands in the prose-writer all the gift and temperament of the poet. De Quincey was perfectly right when he described the *Confessions* and the *Suspiria* as 'modes of impassioned prose'; the only mistake he made was in supposing that he was the inventor of the art, or, to quote his own words, 'that such modes range themselves under no precedent that I am aware of in literature.' There were many precedents: Raleigh, Milton, and Sir Thomas Browne had all preceded him in the art. The only difference is, that what these older writers did occasionally he did habitually, and what passed without comment in their days seemed a novelty, and even an anomaly, when introduced into the sober literature of the nineteenth century. Granted the poetic temperament and genius in a writer, and it matters very little what vehicle of literary performance he may select; the temperament will overmaster the vehicle, turning it to new uses, and securing by it, or in spite of it, new effects. If De Quincey wrote what has been called prose-poetry, it was simply because he was a poet engaged in writing prose.

Naturally, De Quincey did not always keep, or seek to keep, the level of impassioned prose. To tell the truth, few writers have mixed more chaff with their fine wheat. The dominant vice of his writing is diffusion. His thought is seldom compact. He indulges in endless parentheses and qualifications: goes off at a tangent on any idea that interests him for the moment, and is at times prolix and tedious to the last degree. It was an admirable idea on the part of Hogg to collect De Quincey's writings, but it is quite possible that De Quincey would have stood higher in general estimation if Hogg had stuck to his original plan of publishing only six volumes of *Selections*. A man who writes one hundred and fifty magazine articles obviously writes often on subjects which do not greatly interest him. Moreover, few writers resist the temptation of writing carelessly on ephemeral subjects, because they regard their work as being ephemeral also. Thus De Quincey's inaccuracies are many. In his essay on Wordsworth, he quotes five passages of his *Prelude* from memory, and of the five only one is correct. On any matter where truth is in controversy, De Quincey is the unsafest possible exponent of the facts of the case. Often, also, his extremely fine analytical faculty is put to very poor tasks of mere logic-chopping. When he attempts humour, he nearly always fails. Pathos of the sombre and melancholy kind he could always command, but humour eluded him. In fact, what one misses in De Quincey is the note of his really great mind. An ingenious and subtle mind he had; an imagination of singular intensity and power; but that massiveness of nature which gives to the work of the greatest men a certain cohesive and inherent force and dignity, is not found in De Quincey.

Yet in many respects, dreamer as he was, he was very shrewd, and had the keenest eye. Probably the best, because the most lifelike, picture ever painted of Wordsworth is De Quincey's. It is not altogether flattering, and possibly on some minor points it is not accurate. But when he tells us that Wordsworth was 'too much enamoured of an ascetic harsh sublimity'; that he was extremely self-centred and, therefore, in small ways selfish; that there was little benignity about him; that in person he was not impressive, his head being commonplace and his appearance almost mean, he gives us a vivid and true account, in which every detail has been carefully studied. It is not surprising that the picture gave great offence to Wordsworth, but Wordsworth might have remembered that De Quincey was not writing captiously, but in a spirit of the utmost loyalty and admiration. He appreciated Wordsworth's poetry when few others did so, and never failed to champion his cause. He had known what it was actually to tremble in the presence of Wordsworth; he had met him first with such an intensity of expectation that 'had Charlemagne and all his peerage been behind me, or Cæsar and his equipage, or Death on his pale horse, I should have forgotten them.' Even when he is criticising the physical shortcomings of Wordsworth, he is at pains to tell us that his facial likeness to Milton was astounding, and that in certain moments of conversation he saw in Wordsworth's eyes an expression the most solemn and spiritual that he had ever seen, 'a light which seemed to come from unfathomed depths, truly a light that never was on land or sea.' Such an essay as this suggests that De Quincey had the makings of a first-rate biographer in him, if inclination and opportunity had coincided.

Authors who leap into sudden fame through some personal cause often have to pay the penalty of being ranked after death as much below their rightful place, as in life they were elevated above it. This is, in part, true of De Quincey. From the moment that the *Confessions of an English Opium-eater* saw the light, De Quincey was famous. His matter and style were new and entrancing, the story deeply suggestive and affecting. But in later generations the story is familiar, and its novelty is discounted. Thus it happens that we judge him by a colder light, and are insensible to the glamour that once clothed his name. The dispassionate critic sweeps aside as entirely irrelevant to the case the fact that De Quincey drank laudanum by the wine-glass. Johnson was a voracious eater; Shelley lived on vegetables; Keats peppered his tongue, that his palate might be more sensitive to the coolness of a fine wine; but such habits and eccentricities are best forgotten when we discuss questions of literature. The case of De Quincey, in regard to opium-eating, is analogous to the case of a painter who has no hands, and has learned to paint with his toes. Many estimable artists might paint as well with their hands, but it is natural that the man who paints with his toes should be much more talked of, and attract a quite disproportionate share of fame. The wonder is not that the thing is done well, but that it is done at all.

It is clear that the personal elements in De Quincey's living fame have not helped him with posterity, beyond giving a peculiar interest to his history. But when every sort of deduction is made, few persons will doubt that De Quincey's fame is legitimate, and that his place as a literary artist is secure. As a literary artist; for his contribution to the history of human thought, or to the growth of philosophy, is inconsiderable. Nor are his critical judgments of any great value. He had the insight to discern the greatness of Wordsworth, it is true; but, on the other hand, he derided Locke, called Johnson mendacious and dishonest, spoke of Goethe's *Wilhelm Meister* as nonsense, rated Horace Walpole about Voltaire as a memoir writer, and had no words strong enough to express his contempt and detestation of Rousseau. His real strength lay not in any power of original thought, or any gift of luminous criticism, but in that narrow realm of letters which may be designated literary phantasy. Here the literary artist appears; the man of rare delicacy of ear and exquisite sense of words who, by means of language, secures effects that can be best described as musical. He himself makes no secret of his method: he explains that he laboured to attain 'the evasion of cacophony,' and that his ear could not endure 'a sentence ending with two consecutive trochees.' And the result is often very beautiful: the best passages of De Quincey have never been surpassed for sustained splendour of language, exquisite balance and modulation, and rhythmical charm. No doubt one might tire of such a style in a compendious work of history, but in the brief essays of De Quincey it is the most seductive and impressive of styles. The man who wore pure cloth of gold by way of ordinary apparel would be a ridiculous object, but there are occasions when it may be worn with fine effect. In this respect De Quincey stands related to the great masters of a soberer prose, much as Poe does to the great poets. Poe performs the most astounding jugglery with words, and with results so inimitable that none can deny his rank among the true poets of the world. But no one would dream of comparing Poe with Wordsworth; nor would one compare De Quincey with Milton; although in their own way Poe and De Quincey are as deserving of praise as Wordsworth and Milton. But it is the way of the literary artist, as distinguished from the great seer or the profound thinker. In those steadfast qualities of character, which, after all, constitute the immovable basis of great fame—that interior force of soul and personality which make Milton and Wordsworth living and abiding influences—De Quincey was as deficient as Poe ; but, like Poe, he was one of the greatest of literary artists, loving and using his art for its own sake in the main, and it is as a literary artist of extraordinary accomplishment that De Quincey will be remembered.

CHAPTER XI

CHARLES LAMB

[Born in The Temple, London, February 10, 1775. Educated at
Christ's Hospital, which he left in November 1789. Obtained a
clerkship in the India House, 1792. *Blank Verse*, by Charles
Lloyd and Charles Lamb, 1798; *Rosamund Gray*, 1798; *John
Woodvil, a Drama*, 1802; *Tales from Shakespeare*, 1807; *Essays
by Elia*, begun in *London Magazine*, 1820; Collected Edition,
1823; *Last Essays of Elia*, 1833. Died at Enfield, 29th December 1834.]

THE art of essay-writing which De Quincey perfected
in one form, was carried to a yet rarer perfection by
Charles Lamb. In his hands it became a vehicle of
the brightest banter, of the most intimate personal
confession, and of a peculiarly humane and tender
wisdom. Lamb is frankly an egoist, as was Montaigne, but of a much more genial temper. There is
a gentleness in his irony and a sweetness in his
humour which no one else has attained : they spring
from his width of sympathy and entire humility.
He is odd and delights in oddity; loves paradox,
revels in perversity, and pushes both to the point of
' delicate absurdity'; eccentricity of any kind attracts
him, conventionality repels; he has no scorn of human
weakness, no respect for any species of respectability;
his wit is a very Ariel in its lightsomeness, a Puck in
its love of frolic; and yet withal, a serious wisdom
dwells within his more fantastic mood, and he jests

as one who hears behind his laughter ' the still, sad music of humanity.'

Of no man is it truer that you must either greatly love him or dislike him. The man of grave temper will probably dislike him, finding little in him but frivolity ; the man whose mind is not too stiff to unbend, and whose temper still retains a certain buoyancy of childhood, will find him the most delightful of companions. A great deal has been made of the peculiarly harsh criticism which Carlyle passed on Lamb, but it is quite easy to see how matters stood between them. Carlyle could appreciate humour, but it was of the ' pawky' kind common to his countrymen, or of the saturnine kind peculiar to Swift. Lamb's humour was of the grotesque order, and Carlyle mistook it for buffoonery. To Carlyle he was a foolish imp, grimacing and dancing before the veiled solemnities of life—' contemptibly small,' ' a sorry phenomenon,' ' an adept in ghastly make-believe wit.' And no doubt in the presence of Carlyle, Lamb showed at his worst. One of his closest friends and most ardent admirers, Mr. Patmore, has told us that in unsympathetic society Lamb always showed badly, and ' the first impression he made on ordinary people was always unfavourable, sometimes to a violent and repulsive degree.' Lamb had a love of shocking people who were antipathetic to him. The presence of a very solemn person provoked him to impish perversity of temper and absurdity of conduct. Probably Carlyle affected him in this way. For once the insight of Carlyle failed him, and he did not perceive the real genius of Lamb, and not so much as guessed that out of pure mischief Lamb was deluding him by a pretence of folly, and all the while quietly deriding him for his Scotch obtuseness.

If Lamb sometimes behaved in a way scarcely compatible with common sense, or even sanity, his temperament and history should be remembered. No man ever carried a heavier burden through life. Every one knows the pathetic story of his sister's mania, and the cloud which it threw over both lives. It is not always recollected that Lamb himself had at one time been confined in an asylum. With him the attack soon passed and never returned, but the taint was in him. Those who loved him knew this, and knew how to make allowance for his oddities. Haydon, the painter, recounts an inimitable scene, in which Lamb showed himself in his most irresponsible humour. It was at what Haydon calls ' The immortal dinner,' held in his studio on December 28, 1817. Wordsworth and Keats were present, and Lamb led the fun. ' Now, you old Lake poet, you rascally poet,' he cried, ' why do you call Voltaire dull ? ' Suddenly there intruded on the company a certain Comptroller of Stamps, of abnormal stupidity, who tried to make himself agreeable by asking Wordsworth if he did not think Milton a great genius. He followed this up by a similar question about Newton, whereupon Lamb rose, in a spirit of the wildest drollery, called for a candle, and insisted upon examining ' the phreno-logical development ' of the unfortunate comptroller. The comptroller, nothing abashed, put his question afresh ; Lamb immediately began to sing—

> ' Diddle, diddle dumpling, my son John,
> Went to bed with his breeches on.'

' My dear Charles ! ' said Wordsworth, but Lamb only chanted the absurd ditty the louder. ' Do let me have another look at that gentleman's organs,' he cried. Keats and Haydon, properly scandalised, or pretending to be so, hurried Lamb into the painting room, from which, amid peals of laughter, the voice of Lamb could still be heard, importunate— 'Allow me to see his organs once more.' Here is drollery, with just a touch of madness in it, quite scandalous to respectability, and a stranger entirely ignorant of Lamb, who only saw him once, and in such a mood as this, might be pardoned if he called Lamb's wit diluted insanity. But Wordsworth clearly was not scandalised, grave as he was ; he knew Lamb too well. It might be said of Lamb, as of Abraham Lincoln, 'laughter was his vent'; if he had not laughed, he would have died of a frenzied brain or of a broken heart. With Lamb the maddest mood of frolic was a rebound from the blackest mood of melancholia ; a fact which Carlyle, who did know Lamb's history, might have remembered before he used the phrase 'diluted insanity,' which in view of that sad history is nothing less than brutal.

The oddity of Lamb's behaviour owed something, no doubt, to his habits as well as his temperament. That Lamb was an habitual drunkard is an absurd charge, over which no serious critic will pause for a moment. But that he was convivial in his habits, often beyond the degree of strict sobriety, cannot be doubted. Even his sister, with all her reverence for him, speaks of him as coming home 'very smoky and drinky.' He himself, in the piece of pathetic banter in which he describes 'his late friend Elia, admits that his habits were scarcely such as respectable persons would approve. He uses one phrase, in apology for Elia's habit of smoking, which may cover other habits also, when he speaks of tobacco as 'a solvent of speech.' The fact was that Lamb was intensely shy, and had the shy man's morbid self-consciousness and sensitive dread of society. Speech, in any case difficult to him, was rendered doubly difficult by his stammer. One can readily understand that to such a man stimulants proved a 'solvent of speech.' They served to unlock, as Mr. Patmore puts it, 'the poor casket in which the rich thoughts of Charles Lamb were shut up.' Moreover, in the early part of the nineteenth century, convivial habits pervaded society in a degree now entirely unknown. The earlier novels of Dickens made much of conviviality; occasional inebriety is nowhere treated as a serious offence, whereas anything in the nature of total abstinence is held up to ridicule. The part that the brandy-bottle plays in *The Pickwick Papers* is enormous, and the social historian of the future will find quite enough in Dickens alone to suggest the hard-drinking habits of the period. Of course, this is no adequate excuse for Lamb, but it is at least an extenuation, since men must be judged, if they are judged fairly, not only by fixed standards of ethics, but by the nature of their times. Lamb in these matters was certainly no worse, probably, indeed, very much more strict, than the average writer of his days.

The charm of Lamb to those who knew him best lay in his infinite kindliness of heart, and the singular acuteness of his wit. No one could turn a phrase with more rapid felicity, frame a happier repartee, sum up in a stroke of wit so profound a criticism of literature or life. 'An archangel, a little damaged,' —such is his trenchant description of Coleridge

'Charles, did you ever hear me preach?' asked Coleridge once. 'I never heard you do anything else,' answered Lamb. 'If dirt were trumps, what a hand you would have,' he once said to an unsavoury card-player. He can even joke on his own misfortunes——'the wind is tempered to the shorn Lambs'—a peculiarly happy use of quotation, an art in which he excelled. It is the same in his *Essays*; a wit that surprises and delights us meets us on every page. The oddity of a man or of a situation is hit off in a phrase, as when he says of his landlord at Enfield, that he has retired on forty pounds a year *and one anecdote*. It was as impossible for Lamb to resist the temptation of poking fun as for Coleridge to overcome his habit of preaching. One wet night, after supping with Coleridge, he takes the coach for Holborn at the foot of Highgate Hill. As it is starting, a flurried female thrusts her head in at the door and asks, 'Are you all full inside?' 'I am,' says Lamb, with an ecstatic smile—'it was the last piece of pudding that did it.' Of his witty use of quotation none is cleverer than his remark to a young barrister who had just received his first brief—'I suppose you said to it, "Thou great First Cause, least understood."' The tragic nature of his own life not only made him welcome laughter as a relief, but led him to recognise in laughter a divine gift. One of his complaints against the Elizabethan dramatists is that they purposely dwelt upon the harsh and painful facts of life, and were 'economists only in delight.' Lamb knew more than enough of the pain of life, but he was no economist in delight. His is the spirit of genuine mirth springing from an acute knowledge of human nature, but always restrained from bitterness by a recognition of man's inherent nobility. No one who ever saw the foibles and errors of human nature so clearly has spoken of them so tenderly ; it is not his 'to torture and wound us abundantly,' as Ford and Webster do ; rather there is in him that unfailing 'sweetness and good-naturedness' which he attributes to Shakespeare.

Lamb's discovery of his own genius was as nearly accidental as might be. He was long enough at the Christ's Hospital to imbibe a passion for literature and form a close friendship with Coleridge. When he left the school it became necessary for him at once to earn his bread. No obliging friends stepped in, as in the case of Coleridge, to secure for him by their generosity 'shelter to grow ripe and leisure to grow wise.' His father was in ill-health, his brother John had sailed off on his own course, determined to make the most of his own life, and the family came near to depending on Lamb for bread. What better could be desired than the common shift of the hard-driven, middle-class Londoner—a clerkship? So to his clerking Lamb went, stifling any disappointment he felt as he best could, and uttering no complaint. The entire burden of the family soon rested on his young shoulders. Then poverty suddenly joined itself to tragedy ; no less dreadful spectres than madness and murder became his familiars. As one reads the story, the wonder grows that Lamb ever gathered strength to lift up his head again. Once, and once only, does a cry of despair escape him : 'I am completely shipwrecked,' he writes, 'my head is quite bad. I almost wish that Mary were dead.' But in Lamb there was a quiet indomitable magnanimity which the greatest might envy. He recognised at once that the supreme practical duty of his life henceforth was to care for his sister. Mary Lamb was a remarkable woman. She had early learned to love the older literature, and she had much of her brother's fine critical gift. Her mental malady was intermittent, allowing long periods of perfect lucidity. Its signs were well defined, and at the first approach of danger there was but one course —instant return to the asylum. On these terms the brother and sister found life possible; but who can estimate the horror of anxiety which hung over it, the sense of calamity not yet placated, perhaps to prove implacable to the end? Was ever literary life lived before under such conditions? Is there in the invention of the greatest dramatic genius any situation more terrible, any picture more pathetic than that of Charles and Mary Lamb walking through the meadows in the morning sunlight, hand-in-hand, bathed in tears, toward the asylum, where, from time to time, Mary Lamb became a voluntary prisoner?

Possibly, however, the conditions of such a life helped to turn it inward, and contributed more than we know to the development of Lamb's genius. Lamb knew what the 'city of the mind' meant. In one of his earlier letters he uses a phrase that reveals much; he says that he and his sister were *marked*. Interpreted into gross fact this means that he found the outer life unfriendly to him. There were sudden exits from lodgings, quests for new lodgings; a man of odd habits, a woman liable to fits of insanity were not likely to be welcome guests among landladies. There were, no doubt, coarse words, coarse actions; things said and done that wounded the fugitives to the quick. To think on such things only—that way madness lay. It was absolutely necessary, as a mere term on which life could be held at all, to get outside one's self. And so Lamb retired into the city of the mind: dwelt with delight in the seclusions of the older literature; knew his Thomas Browne, his Donne, his Cowley, his Burton well; fed his mind with their wisdom and their quaintness, and forgot the outer world. It is sometimes complained that Lamb cares nothing for Nature. This is not quite true, for his essays show us that he found great pleasure in scenery of a quiet pastoral type; but it is so far true that Lamb was pre-eminently a citizen. Solitary Nature was much too solitary for a mind smitten with such incurable grief as Lamb's. But London, with its incessant pageant, its curious, endless, shifting spectacle, was curative to him. He could lose himself in it. It afforded him precisely what he needed—an opportunity for constant observation, a drama that excited him, and dispelled his gloom. Skiddaw he once saw and climbed, but his heart was in London—'London, whose dirtiest and drab-frequented alleys I would not exchange for Skiddaw, Helvellyn, James, Walter, and the Parson into the bargain. O! her lamps of a night! her rich goldsmiths, print-shops, toy-shops, mercers, hardware men, pastry-cooks, St. Paul's Churchyard, the Strand, Exeter Change, Charing Cross, with the man upon a black horse. All the streets and pavements are pure gold, I warrant you. At least, I know an alchemy that turns her mud into that metal —a mind that loves to be at home in crowds.' Thus, with his books and the streets, Lamb contrived to touch happiness, and found in them the magic which at last set free his genius.

But the process was slow. There are records of jokes written for the papers at the munificent rate of sixpence apiece. Comparative affluence is reached with two guineas a week from the *Post*. Many experiments in authorship are tried, among them a farce hissed off the stage on the first night, Lamb himself joining vigorously in damning it. His little tale of *Rosamund Gray* brought him some reputation. Shelley was much impressed by it, and said of it, 'How much knowledge of the sweetest and deepest part of our nature is in it! When I think of such a mind as Lamb's, when I see how unnoticed remain things of such exquisite and complete perfection, what should I hope for myself, if I had not higher objects in view than fame?' Brief as this criticism is, yet it is remarkable how unerringly Shelley discerns the true nature of Lamb's genius. It is precisely in knowledge of the deepest and sweetest part of our nature that Lamb excels, and what he knew he was able to communicate in an art of unrivalled delicacy. Already in some of his verses, for example, the lines beginning,

'When maidens such as Hester die,'

this rare delicacy of touch had been very marked. At last the opportunity of a wider use for his gift came. In January 1820, *The London Magazine* was founded, and in the August number the first *Essay of Elia* appeared. Lamb was now forty-five. His gift had taken long to ripen ; he now found himself, and in the essay discovered the one form of literary expression adequate to his genius.

With the nature of these *Essays* all students of literature are familiar. A man of genius who has lived through such a life as Lamb's does not come to forty-five without learning many hard lessons. By this time he will be gently detached from the world, purged of the yeasty vanity of youth, softened in spirit toward all men—that is, if his heart be good—philosophic in temper, apt in reminiscence, mellow in judgment. From one point of view, Lamb recalls Thomas à Kempis. Each has passed his life in a cloister, the one in a cloister of literature, the other of religion; each speaks with the same far-away cadence in the voice, the same instinct of felicity, the same tempered, peaceful, almost happy sadness. Lamb in mediæval times might very well have been a monk sworn to scholarship; Thomas à Kempis in the rough tumult of modern London might very well have taken refuge in the Temple—does he not confess that he was never happier than 'in a nook with a book'? It is the entire unworldliness of Lamb that does as much to fascinate us as anything. He speaks as one who has long ago seen through the sham of the world, yet is preserved by his own sweetness of nature from the least touch of cynicism. The way in which he speaks of his brother John is typical. The most casuistic of advocates could not disguise the gross selfishness of John Lamb. His brother knew all that well enough, but he does not choose to speak of it. He paints John Lamb faithfully: jovial, smiling, prosperous; going up Piccadilly 'chanting,' with his Hobbima under his arm, quite forgetful of poor Mary, convinced that it is his destiny to enjoy life as it is the destiny of Charles to endure it; but there is not one word of complaint, of ill-nature, of envy. The irony is so gentle that its sting is drawn; it is almost wistful. And it is in the same spirit that Lamb regards life at large. There are no swelling words about the inhumanity of man to man, the cruel disparities of the human lot, the hope of future recompense. The head is bowed to the yoke in perfect meekness. Thus things are; why quarrel with them? Nay, more; who would have them different? John proceeds westward to Pall Mall 'chanting a tune,' while I proceed in my opposite direction 'tuneless'—opposite, indeed, yet not unhappy. It is a thing to smile at after all; clearly, also, it were wise to smile, since no angry tirade can alter it. So Elia passes to his toil with the wise smile upon his lips, making us feel that the true happiness remains with him, as it did long since with the old monk who has taught us to expect little of the world since the world has little to give, but to seek our wealth within.

Upon the whole, it may be said that a more religious-minded man than Lamb has not left his mark on English literature. Not, of course, that he has anything to do with creeds, dogmas, or churches; to these he is absolutely indifferent. It is rather in the width of his charity, his sense of pity, his fine feeling about things that his religion lies. He never writes so beautifully as when his theme is the affections. Places he has loved, people he has known, things made sweet and familiar by memory—with what exquisite tenderness does he speak on such matters! There is deep essential reverence underlying his most extravagant badinage. Jest he must, but never at sacred things. One slight story sums up this trait. A discussion arose one night in which the names of Shakespeare and Christ were coupled, and the disputants seemed not to recognise the gulf that lay between the two. Lamb restored the lost equipoise of comparison with a single observation. 'If Shakespeare entered the room, we should all rise,' said he. 'If Jesus Christ entered the room, we should all kneel.'

Humour since Lamb's day has more and more tended to pure extravagance. Even in Dickens, the greatest of all English humorists, this decadence is very plain. Dick Swiveller is humorous, Sairey Gamp is humorous, but Pecksniff is farcical. In the one case you have a character sketched humorously, but yet quite truly; in the other, you have a farcical exaggeration of defects, which is quite untrue to life. And it is the fashion of Pecksniff which has prevailed in later humour. In almost all that passes for humour nowadays, there is really little else than broad farce. Lamb's is a much more delicate and subtle art. Probably the reader accustomed to a coarser draught will find Lamb's humour almost insipid. His art is so artless, so pellucid, so effortless, that its rarity of quality is not perceived. But it is this peculiar delicacy of touch that makes Lamb's art original, and gives it its most enduring charm. If any fault may be charged upon it, it is that it smacks sometimes of affectation. Lamb is nothing if not bookish. Loving writers like Sir Thomas Browne and Burton as he did, it is not surprising that he fell into their conceits and reproduced their quaintness. But he did not imitate them; rather, his whole mind was so saturated with them, that he could not help expressing himself in their manner. But even when these admissions are made, Lamb's style was distinctively his own. The odd turns of expression, the sudden flash of the felicitous epithet, owe something to a profound study of the older writers; but the spirit and manner are distinctive. As regards our appreciation of these peculiarities of style, it is a question of palate. If the ordinary reader finds them tedious and affected there is nothing more to be said. There will always be some—let us hope many—who will love him; and those who love him at all will love him much.

Lamb's writings differ widely in quality, though it is scarcely possible to speak of good and bad as it is with most authors. There are degrees of excellence, but no positively inferior work. His best essays are his most intimate; these partake of the nature of confessions, and thus belong to the rarest form of literature. In his lightest vein of pure drollery there is nothing to surpass the *Dissertation upon Roast Pig*. It must also be remembered that Lamb was one of the finest critics whom English literature has produced. He was among the first to recognise Wordsworth, and it was solely through his fine discrimination that a taste for the older dramatic writers was revived. Few people read Isaac Walton till Lamb praised him, and such books as Burton's *Anatomy of Melancholy* owe much of their present popularity among students of literature to him. A student, a philosopher, a thinker; a man of original mind and great critical discernment; a poet of great sweetness within his own range; a most human-hearted man, sorely tried, but never soured by adversity; humble, magnanimous, charitable in all his thoughts and acts—one of the most quaint and lovable figures in all English literature—such was Charles Lamb.

CHAPTER XII

THOMAS CARLYLE

[Born at Ecclefechan, December 4th, 1795. Entered Edinburgh
University, 1809. Published *Life of Schiller*, 1825. Married Jane
Welsh, October 1826. Contributed to *Edinburgh Review, Westminster, Foreign Quarterly*, etc., 1828-33, when *Sartor Resartus*
was published in *Fraser's Magazine. French Revolution*, 1837.
Past and Present, 1843. *Latter-Day Pamphlets*, 1850. *Cromwell's Letters and Speeches*, 1845. *History of Frederick the Great*,
begun 1858, completed 1865. Elected Lord Rector of Edinburgh
University, 1865. Died at 5 Cheyne Row, Chelsea, February 5th,
1881.]

WITH the name of Thomas Carlyle we become
conscious of a changed atmosphere in literature.
Taking him for all in all, he is the most representative, and by far the greatest, man of genius of the
nineteenth century. The four notes of genius are
originality, fertility, coherence, and articulation. He
is so far original in style and method that there is
no one with whom we can justly compare him. He
followed no master, and acknowledged none; his
angle of vision on all questions was his own, and
what he saw he expressed in a fashion which decorous
literary persons of the old order felt to be dazzlingly
perverse, startling, eruptive, and even outrageous.
His mind was also one of the most fertile of minds;
not so much in the matter of industrious production
as in the much rarer function of begetting great

seminal ideas, which reproduced themselves over the entire area of modern literature. Coherence marks these ideas, for the main principles of his philosophy are so simple and so definite, that from his earliest writings to his last there is perfect unity. Lastly, in the matter of articulation or expression, he is supreme. He enlarged the potentialities of language, as every great literary artist does, and in precision, splendour, and suggestiveness of phrase stands unapproached.

But Carlyle was much more even than a great man of genius, or a great writer. He never conceived himself, nor did any one who knew him intimately conceive him, as having found a sufficing expression of himself in his writings. He knew himself, and was felt by others, to be a great spiritual force. Criticism has had much to say upon the strangeness and mass of his genius; it has hardly yet apprehended aright his prophetic force. That he brought into English literature much that is startling and brilliant in style is the least part of the matter; he brought also a flaming vehemence of thought, passion, and conviction, which is unique. Goethe, with his piercing insight, was the first to recognise the true nature of the man. He discovered Carlyle long before England had heard of him, when he was simply an unknown and eccentric young Scotsman, who found astonishing difficulty in earning daily bread. The great German incontinently brushed aside, as of relative unimportance, all questions about his genius, and touched the true core of the man and his message, when he said that Carlyle was 'a new moral force, the extent and effects of which it is impossible to predict.' In other words, Goethe recognised the main fact about him, which was that by nature, temperament, and vocation, he was a prophet.

If Carlyle had been asked to state what he understood by the word 'prophet,' he would have laid emphasis upon two things: clearness and vividness of vision in the apprehension of truth, and resolute sincerity in acting on it. Carlyle held that there is within every man something akin to the Dæmon of Socrates—intuition, spiritual apprehension, a living monitor and guide; and that the man who obeys this inward voice knows by a species of celestial divination where his path lies, and what his true work is. In nothing does the essentially prophetic nature of Carlyle appear more plainly than in these qualities. During the first forty years of his life, forty years spent in the desert of the sorest discipline a man could suffer, there was no moment when he might not have instantly improved his position by a little judicious compromise. But all compromise he regarded with scornful anger. He might have entered the Church, and his spiritual gifts were vastly in excess of those of thousands who find in the pulpit an honourable opportunity of utterance. He might have obtained a professorship in one or other of the Scotch seats of learning, if he had cared to trim his course to suit the winds and tides of the ordinary conventions. He might at any moment have earned an excellent competence by his pen, if he had consented to modify the ruggedness of his style and the violence of his opinions to the standards of the review editors and their readers. But in either of these courses he recognised a fatal peril to his sincerity. Poor as he was, he would not budge an inch. He was fastidious to what seemed to men like Jeffrey an absolutely absurd degree over the honour of his independence. He would make no hair's-breadth advance to meet the world; the world must come over to him, bag and baggage. He acted with implicit obedience on his intuition. He had the prophet's stern simplicity of habit. He cared nothing for comfort or success; and when at last success came, his Spartan simplicity of life suffered no change. If ever man in modern days knew what the burden of prophecy meant, what it is to be impelled to utterance by an imperious instinct for truth, and to be straitened in spirit till the message was spoken, that man was Carlyle. It was in this respect that he differed as much from the ordinary man of letters as Isaiah in his most impassioned moments from the common sermon-writer. The pulpit, the bar, the professor's chair were not for him; therefore he seized upon pen and paper as the only means left of uttering himself to his age. He was perfectly sincere in despising even this as a medium for his spiritual activities. He despised writing as a profession, because he found that when men began to write for bread they became poor creatures, and if they had any real message in them they stifled it to win praise or money. To both praise and money he was contemptuously in-different. His only passion was a passion for truth, and to speak this with the least possible of those literary flourishes which capture popularity was his meat and drink.

Further than this, Carlyle was both poet and humorist. He could not indeed write verse. He was never able to master the technicalities of the art of metre. He was as little able to write a novel,

which next to verse affords a medium for the man
of constructive poetic genius. He tried both arts,
with rare and partial success in the first, and abject
failure in the second. Goethe, who is the only man
who could be spoken of even in a partial sense as
Carlyle's master, had a serene equipoise of faculty,
a fine and supreme artistic sense, which enabled
him to succeed equally in poetry, drama, fiction, or
philosophy. Carlyle's genius was as remarkable as
Goethe's, but its powers lay apart in streaming
fire-masses, nebulous and chaotic, and were not
co-ordinated into perfect harmony by that æsthetic
sense which was Goethe's highest gift. But fundamentally he was a poet, and among the greatest of
poets. He saw everything through the medium of
an intense and searching imagination. No one could
describe the impression which his *French Revolution*
produces on the mind better than he himself has
done, when he says, 'Nor do I mean to investigate
much more about it, but to splash down what I
know in large masses of colours, that it may look
like a smoke and flame conflagration in the distance,
which it is.' He cannot even walk in Regent Street
without exclaiming, 'To me, through these thin cob-
webs, Death and Eternity sate glaring.' All his
personal sensations are magnified into the same
gigantic proportions, now lurid, now grotesque, by
the same atmosphere of imagination through which
they are perceived. His sensitiveness is extreme,
poignant, even terrible. When he talks of immensities and eternities, he uses no mere stock phrases;
he hears the rushing of the fire-streams, and the rolling
worlds overhead, as he hears the dark streams flow-
ing under foot, bearing man and all his brave arrays

down to 'Tartarus, and the pale kingdoms of Dis.'
When he speaks of himself as feeling 'spectral,' he
simply expresses that sense of spiritual loneliness,
detachment, and mystery, out of which the deepest
poetry of the world has come.   To judge such a
man by ordinary prosaic standards is impossible.
He is of imagination all compact, and his writings
can only be rightly regarded as the work of a poet,
who has the true spirit of the seer, but is incapable
of the orthodox forms of poetry.

It is perhaps even more essential to remember
that Carlyle was a humorist of the first order.   On
the one side of his genius he approaches Burns ; on
the other, Swift.   He shares with Burns a rugged
independence of nature, native pride, a sense of the
elemental in human life, a power of poignant realism,
a rare depth and delicacy of sentiment ; he shares also
with him the rollicking, broad, not always decorous,
humour of the Olympian peasant, racy of the soil.
Carlyle's account of Carnot suddenly leaving the
dinner-table 'driven by a necessity, needing of all
things paper,' is a sample of what I mean ; the humour
of the peasant, half-grim, half-boisterous, of which
Burns has given imperishable examples in *Tam o'
Shanter* and *Holy Willie's Prayer.*   But there was also
mingled in Carlyle's humour a strain of something
darker and more subtle, akin to the saturnine humour
of Swift.   He has much of that intense and scathing
scorn, that sardonic and bitter penetration which
made, and still preserves, the name of Swift as a
name of terror.   To be sure, we do not find that
depth of silent ferocity in Carlyle which alarms and
appals us in Swift.   Swift often thought and wrote
like a mere savage, smarting with the torture of some

lacerating, cureless pain. He is at heart a hater of his kind, who spits in the face of its most familiar nobilities, out of mere exasperated truculence. There is something abominable and insane in the humour of Swift, with only a rare touch of redeeming geniality. But Carlyle's humour, in all its sardonic force, still preserves an element of geniality. He loves the grotesque and the absurd for their own sakes. He cannot long restrain himself from laughter, good, wholesome, volleying laughter, directed as often against himself as others. Gifts of insight, passion, eloquence, and imagination he had in plenty; but the greatest and rarest of all his gifts was humour.

Those who knew Carlyle most intimately have all recognised this wonderful gift of humour which was his. It was said of him by his friends that when he laughed it was Homeric laughter—the laughter of the whole soul and body in complete abandonment of mirth. This deep, wholesome laughter reverberates through his writings. No man is quicker to catch a humorous point, or to make it. A collection of Carlyle's best stories, phrases, and bits of personal description, would make one of the most humorous books in the language. He makes sly fun of himself, of his poverty, of the unconscious oddities of the obscurest people, and equally of the greatest. His raillery is incessant, his eye for the comic of supreme vigilance. Of the obscenity of Swift there is no trace; it was not in Carlyle to cherish unwholesome thoughts. But in the strange mingling of the wildest fun with the most penetrating thought, of sardonic bitterness with the mellowest laughter, of the most daring and incisive irony with deep philosophy and serious feeling, there is much that recalls Swift, and suggests his finest qualities. With Swift the bitterness closed down like a cloud, and extinguished the humour, with the result of that tragic madness which still moves the pity of the world. With Carlyle the humour was always in excess of the bitterness, and supplied that element of saving health which kept his genius fresh and wholesome amid many perils not less real than those which destroyed Swift.

There is one respect in which it is especially necessary to recollect this element of humour in Carlyle, if we are to judge him correctly, because most of the harsh and unfair judgments passed upon him have directly resulted from its neglect. It must be remembered that Mrs. Carlyle had many qualities in common with her husband, and not the least of these was a similar power of irony and humour. She was accustomed to speak of Carlyle in a fashion of the freest banter. When his lectures were first announced in London there was much speculation among his friends whether he would remember to begin orthodoxly with 'Ladies and gentlemen,' to which Mrs. Carlyle replied that it was far more likely he would begin with 'Fool creatures come hither for diversion.' Her satiric comment on the success of the business was that at last the public had apparently decided that he was a man of genius, and 'worth being kept alive at a moderate rate.' Is it not conceivable to a person of even moderate intelligence that the conversation of two persons so witty, keen-tongued, and given to satiric burlesque and banter as the Carlyles, was in no sense to be taken literally? Is it not further conceivable that many things which look only bitter when put into print, had a very different effect and intention when uttered in the gay repartee of familiar conversation? The fact is that the Carlyles habitually addressed one another with irony. It is no uncommon thing between intimates: it is rather a sign of the security of the affection which unites them. But if, by some unhappy accident, a third person who has no sense of humour hears this gay clash of keen words, and puts them down in dull print, and goes on to point out in his dull fashion that they do not sound affectionate, and are phrases by no means in common use among excellent married persons of average intellects, it is easy to see that the worst sort of mischief may readily be wrought. Thus, for example, when Mrs. Carlyle lay ill with a nervous trouble which made it impossible for her to close her mouth, Carlyle, who knew nothing of this peculiarity of her disease, stood solemnly at the foot of her bed one day, and said: 'Jane, ye'd be in a far more composed state of mind if ye'd close your mouth.' This story is told, forsooth, as an illustration of the harshness of Carlyle to his wife. So far was Mrs. Carlyle from interpreting it in any such way, that she tells it herself with inimitable glee, and is keen to describe its ludicrous aspect. And, as in this instance, so in a hundred more that might be analysed, humour was a dominant quality in all the conversations of Carlyle, and in almost equal degree of his wife's also; and it is only by recollecting this that it is possible to judge rightly a married life which was passed in an atmosphere and under conditions peculiarly its own.

It is necessary to dwell on this matter with more fulness than it deserves, because nothing has so

greatly injured Carlyle's reputation and influence as
the reported infelicities of his domestic life. All
these reports depend on the testimony of one or two
witnesses, whose word is worthless. Fortunately for
us the real truth is preserved, not in the chance
impressions of friends or guests who saw the Carlyles
from the outside, but in the mutual correspondence
of husband and wife, in their journals, and in their
intimate confessions to others through a long range
of years. There have been many exquisite love-
letters written by literary men, but there are none to
surpass Carlyle's letters to his wife. No woman was
ever loved more deeply : had not the love on both
sides been real and vital there would have been no
tragedy to record. It was simply because these two
were so much to each other that the slightest varia-
tion of temperature in their affection was so keenly
and instantaneously felt by each. The real source
of their difficulties was that they were too much
alike in temper, in methods of thought, and in
intellectual outlook. There was about each that
difficult Scottish reticence which sealed the lips and
forbade speech even when the heart was fullest.
The moment they are separated the love-letters flow
in a continuous stream : love-letters, as I have said,
which are the tenderest in the language so far as
Carlyle is concerned, and which never lost their
warmth through all the years of a long married life.
On paper the heart opens itself; face to face they
cannot speak. As they recede from one another
each grows in luminous charm, and faults are forgotten, and passion is intensified ; as they come
back from these constant separations the glow fades
into the light of common day, and neither has the

tact or grace to retain it. Each is exquisitely, even poignantly sensitive, and gives and suffers wounds which are totally unsuspected by the other. The heart is always at boiling-point; the nerves are always quivering; there are no cool grey reaches of mere pleasant comradeship between them. It is not difficult to understand that in such a marriage there were hours of the deepest blackness; but there were also seasons of such light and radiance as are never found in duller lives.

But there was another cause of bitterness, which Carlyle has touched with the utmost delicacy and insight when he writes (Aug. 24, 1836): 'Oh, my poor bairn, be not faithless, but believing! Do not fling life away as insupportable, despicable; but let us work it out, and rest it out together, like a true *two*, though under some obstructions.' One would have supposed that Carlyle would have written 'a true *one*'; but that he had ceased to hope for. Mrs. Carlyle's nature was of a stubbornness as invincible as his own, and was as deeply independent and original. It galled her to shine only in Carlyle's light. She had a literary faculty, in its way as remarkable as her husband's, and she felt that it was obscured by his more massive genius. She was not the sort of woman to find her life in the life of any man; she craved a separate platform. What Carlyle could do to soften and ease matters he did. He absolutely refused all invitations to great houses where his wife was not as welcome as himself. He sincerely believed her to be the cleverest and best of women, who deserved distinction for her own sake. But it was all of no avail. She allowed herself to become frantic with jealousy, and absolutely without cause. Her tongue could be as satiric, as undiscriminating, as his. For the most part she used that potent instrument, as Dr. Garnet says (a little unjustly, I think), 'to narrow his sympathies, edge his sarcasms, intensify his negations, and foster his disdain for whatever would not run in his own groove.' When it was turned against him one can imagine the result. That which strikes one most in reading the story is that all the bitterness between them might have been avoided by a little tact, a little common sense. But in these qualities each was deficient. Each was accustomed to see life through the atmosphere of an imagination which exaggerated into grotesqueness or tragedy the simplest things. Each felt the least jar upon the nerves as a veritable agony. Life was unquestionably hard enough for them in any case, but this intense sensitiveness made it tenfold harder.

Yet, when all these admissions are made, we should take an altogether wrong impression if we supposed that these disagreements were normal and continuous. Not merely does Mrs. Carlyle's real love for Carlyle come out in so many direct and positive expressions, but it is admirably reflected in her humour. There may be wit, but there cannot be humour, without love, and the way in which she permits her bright and vivacious humour to play round him in her letters reveals not merely her genius but her heart. He is her 'poor Babe of Genius.' 'Between two and three o'clock is a very placid hour with the creature.' 'He never complains of serious things, but if his finger is cut, one must hold it and another get plaister.' On the New Year morning of 1863, Carlyle no sooner gets up than he discovers 'that his salvation, here and hereafter, depended on having "immediately, without a moment's delay," a beggarly pair of old cloth boots that the street-sweeper would hardly have thanked him for, "lined with flannel, and new bound, and repaired generally."' 'Nothing in the shape of illness ever alarms Mr. C. but that of not eating one's regular meals.' She relates with positive glee, and in the spirit of the brightest banter, innumerable episodes in which 'the creature' performs some eccentric part; and often enough, as Mr. Moncure Conway has told us, these little pieces of inimitable farce were performed in Carlyle's presence, and to his own infinite amusement. There is always a certain *soupçon* of bitterness in the banter, but it is a pleasant and not a corrosive bitter. She knew exactly where the trouble was between them; she knew that when Carlyle was exhausted with his immense labours, and she worn to the nerve with neuralgia, sleeplessness, and domestic worries, each was apt to rub the other the wrong way, and to magnify unintended slights into mischievous offences. She knew it, and was sorry for it, and would have avoided it if she could. 'Alas, dear!' she writes, 'I am very sorry for you. You, as well as I, are too vivid; to you as well as me has a skin been given much too thin for the rough purposes of human life —God knows how gladly I would be sweet-tempered, and cheerful-hearted, and all that sort of thing, for your single sake, if my temper were not soured and my heart saddened beyond my power to mend them.' But though she could be neither sweet-tempered nor cheerful, she was always brave, bright, and sensitive to the humorous aspect of things. Upon the whole, one may doubt if any braver woman ever lived: Joan of Arc in her glittering armour was no more of a heroine than Mrs. Carlyle in that small dominion at Cheyne Row, in her endless strifes with servants and mechanics, her resolute sorties on the wolf of poverty that for so many years growled at the door, and her desperate ingenuities to make the path easy for her poor 'Babe of Genius.'

The actual amount of physical and nervous suffering which Mrs. Carlyle endured during these years, and especially towards the end, exceeds the total of the worst agony of those we call martyrs. What sadder or more poignant cries have ever been wrung from a human spirit than these? 'Oh, my own darling, God have pity on us! Ever since the day after you left, whatever flattering accounts may have been sent you, the truth is I have been wretched—perfectly wretched day and night, with that horrible malady. So, God help me, for on earth is no help!' 'Oh, my dear, I think how near my mother I am!' [She was then staying at Holm Hill, not far from where her mother was buried.] 'How still I should be, laid beside her! But I wish to live for you, if only I could live out of torment. . . . I seem already to belong to the passed-away as much as to the present; nay, more. God bless you on your solitary way! . . . Oh, my dear, I am very weary. My agony has lasted long. I am tempted to take a long cry over myself—and no good will come of that.' She expresses her sorrow for 'the terrible, half-insane sensitiveness which drove me on to bothering you. Oh, if God would only lift my trouble off me so far that I could bear it all in silence, and not add to the troubles of others! . . .

I am very stupid and low. God can raise me up again : but will He ? My dear, when I have been giving directions about the house, then a feeling like a great black wave will roll over my breast, and I say to myself, whatever pains be taken to gratify me, shall I ever more have a day of ease, of painlessness, or a night of sweet rest in that house, or in any other house, but the dark narrow one where I shall arrive at last ? Oh, dear ! you cannot help me, though you would ! Nobody can help me ! Only God : and can I wonder if God take no heed of me, when I have all my life taken so little heed of Him ? ' Nor are the replies of Carlyle less pathetic. ' My thoughts,' says he, ' are a prayer for my poor little life-partner, who has fallen lame beside me, after travelling so many steep and thorny ways. . . . My poor little friend of friends ! she has fallen wounded to the ground, and I am alone— alone ! ' In her worst agonies she turns to her husband always with cries for consolation, and says : ' I cannot tell how gentle and good Mr. Carlyle is. He is busy as ever, but he studies my comfort and peace as he never did before.' At the same time he is taking sorrowful note of the fact that she is more careful of his comforts than in her busiest days of health. Is there anywhere in literature a more pathetic page than this ? Can there be any clearer testimony to the reality and depth of that love which bound these two sorely-tried souls together, or to the error of the general assumption that their marriage was a foolish and unhappy one ?

Pages might be written on such a theme, but all that can be said profitably is said when we are asked to recollect the extreme and almost morbid sensitiveness of both Carlyle and his wife, their common love of irony, their common practice of humorous exaggeration on all subjects, but especially those in which their own personalities were involved, and the strain upon nerve and temper which was imposed by years of unintermittent labour and vain struggle. One thing is at least clear, that in their more serious misunderstandings they were neither in thought nor deed unfaithful to one another, and never ceased to love each other with absorbing passion. Of the dull, truculent, selfish brutality of temper attributed to Carlyle by some writers, he was utterly incapable, for he was the most magnanimous of men. ' I could not help,' says Emerson, on recalling his memorable visit to Carlyle at Craigenputtock, 'congratulating him upon his treasure of a wife.' Others who visited the Carlyles during this same period, when life was hardest with them, have borne witness that they lived with one another upon delightful terms. Surely, if some bitter words escaped them in the long struggle, it is a matter not for wonder but forgiveness ; surely also some allowance can be made for a man of genius staggering beneath a burden almost too great to be borne, and for a woman broken in health by a most distressing malady, each of them, as Mrs. Carlyle confessed, 'too vivid,' and 'with a skin much too thin for the rough purposes of human life.' When the unwholesome love of scandal, aroused by the passion which mean natures find in discovering the faults of the great, subsides, no doubt the true facts will be seen in their right perspective, and blame will be exchanged for pity, censure for a comprehending charity.

In the meantime we may remember that those

who knew Carlyle the best speak most warmly of the magnanimity of his character.

The impression which Carlyle made upon his contemporaries is the best comment on his character. The most serious men of his time recognised him as a modern John the Baptist, and even a worldly ecclesiastic like Bishop Wilberforce described him as 'a most eminently religious man.' Charles Kingsley honoured him as his master, and has drawn an admirable portrait of him as Saunders Mackaye in *Alton Locke*, of which description Carlyle characteristically said that it was a 'wonderfully splendid and coherent piece of Scotch bravura.' His gospel is contained in *Sartor Resartus*, of which it has been pertinently said that it 'will be read as a gospel or not at all.' A calm and penetrative critic like James Martineau witnesses to the same overwhelming religious force in Carlyle when he speaks of his writings as a 'pentecostal power on the sentiments of Englishmen.' On the truly poetic nature of his genius all the great critics have long ago agreed. How could it be otherwise in regard of writings whose every second paragraph kindles into the finest imaginative fire? His power of imagery is Dantesque; his range is truly epic; the very phrases of his diaries and letters are steeped in poetry, as when he speaks of John Sterling's last 'verses, written for myself alone, as in star-fire and immortal tears.' The testimonies to his power of humour, so far as his conversations are concerned, are much too numerous for recapitulation. His own definition of humour was 'a genial sympathy with the under side'; and this vivid sympathy expressed itself in his use of ludicrous and extraordinary metaphor, and in his 'delicate sense of absurdity.' His most volcanic denunciations usually 'ended in a laugh, the heartiest in the world, at his own ferocity. Those who have not heard that laugh,' says Mr. Allingham, 'will never know what Carlyle's talk was.' Prophet, poet, and humorist—so stands Carlyle before the world, a man roughly hewn out of the primeval earth, conceived in the womb of labour and hardship, yet touched with immortal fire, fashioned in the rarest mould of greatness, tenderness, and heroism ; clearly the most massive, impressive, and fascinating figure in nineteenth-century literature. It remains for us to see what his writings teach us, and what is taught yet more forcibly by the epic of his life.

CHAPTER XIII

CARLYLE'S TEACHING

MAURICE once said of himself that he only had three or four things to say, and he felt it necessary to go on saying them over and over again. The same criticism might be passed upon Carlyle. No great writer has repeated himself with such freedom and emphasis. It therefore becomes a comparatively easy task to discern the main lines of his teaching. In whatever he wrote, whether history or essay, private journals or biography, these main lines of thought perpetually appear, like auriferous strata, pushing themselves up through the soil, and indicating the nature of his thinking.

The remark of Bishop Wilberforce, that Carlyle was an eminently religious man, gives us the true starting-point for any honest understanding of his teaching. Mr. Froude has spoken of him as a Calvinist without the theology, and in the main this is true. Every one knows the striking passage in which Carlyle tells us how Irving drew from him the confession that he was no longer able to see the truths of religion from the orthodox standpoint. Upon analysis this will be found to mean that he had definitely rejected the supernatural. He once said that nothing could be more certain than that the miracles, as they were related in the Gospels, did

197

not and could not have occurred. For the Church, as such, he had small respect, because it seemed to him to be mainly given over to a hollow recitation of formulæ which it had really ceased to believe, and which no rational man ever would believe again with genuine sincerity. He regarded the efforts of Maurice to frame a rational basis for belief in the supernatural as the endless spinning of a rope of sand. He once pointed to Dean Stanley, and said with cutting sarcasm, 'There goes Stanley knocking holes in the bottom of the Church of England.' But, on the other hand, he had more than sarcasm, he had an absolutely savage contempt for anything approaching atheism. Of Mill he spoke with bitter and habitual ridicule, although he recognised in him the finest friendliness of nature; of Darwin 'as though he had robbed him.' He dismissed the discoveries of Darwin with the scathing phrase, 'Gorilla damnifications of humanity.' He speaks of his 'whole softened heart' going out anew in childlike utterance of the great prayer, 'Our Father, who art in heaven.' While he cannot believe the Gospel miracles, he nevertheless teaches that the world itself is nothing less than one vast standing miracle. No saint or prophet ever spoke with a surer faith of that great Yonder, to which he believes his father is gathered, and where he and all whom he loves will some day be reunited in some new intimacy of infinite love. He scruples even to use the name of God, inventing paraphrases of it because he feels it is too great and holy for common utterance. A profound belief in Providence governed all his estimates of life, and prayer was with him a habit and an urgent duty, since it was the lifting up of the heart to the Infinite above, which answered to the Infinite within.

Now nothing can well appear more contradictory than these statements, and they can only be harmonised by the recollection of one fact—viz. that in Carlyle emotion outran reason, and what was impossible to the pure intellect was constantly accepted on the testimony of his spiritual intuitions. The merely theological conclusions of Calvin he absolutely rejected, but the essence of Calvinism ran like a subtle spirit, through his whole nature. What he really aimed at was to show that religion rested on no external evidences at all, but on the indubitable intuitions of the human soul. He would not even take the trouble to set about proving that there was a God : he would have agreed with Addison that the man who said that he did not believe in a God was an impudent liar and knew it. He was angrily contemptuous of Renan's *Life of Jesus*, although Renan probably said nothing more than he himself believed ; but he felt a reverence for Christ which revolted from Renan's method of statement, and he said that his life of Christ was something that never ought to be written at all. Thus it becomes more necessary with Carlyle than with any other writer of our time to distinguish sharply between his opinions and his convictions. In point of fact he wrote on religion, as on all other subjects, from the standpoint of the poet rather than of the scholar or the philosopher. Driven back upon his defences, Calvin himself could not have spoken with more lucidity and passion of his primary religious beliefs than Carlyle. The Shorter Catechism had passed into the very blood and marrow of his

nature.   In the bare house at Ecclefechan the
Cottar's Saturday Night was a veritable fact, and
from the Puritan mould of his childhood he never
escaped.   He never wished to do so.   He sought
rather to distil the finer essences of Calvinism
afresh, and in a great measure he did so.   His real
creed was Calvinism shorn of its logic and inter-
penetrated with emotion.   He translated it into
poetry and touched it with the iridescent glow and
colour of transcendentalism.   He separated what
he considered its accidental and formal elements
from the essential, and to those essential and imperishable elements he gave a new authority and
currency by the impact of his own astonishing
genius.

What were these elements?   As restated by
Carlyle, they were belief in God as the certainty
of certainties on which all human life is built: of
a God working in history, and revealing Himself in
no mere collection of books, but in all events: of all
work as perenially noble and beautiful, because it
was God's appointed task: of duty and morality as
the only real prerogatives of man: of sincerity and
honesty as the chief achievements which God demanded of man, and the irreducible minimum of
any honourable human life.   The world was no
mere mill, turning its wheels mechanically in the
Time-floods, without any Overseer, but a Divinely
appointed world, and to know that was the chief
element of all knowledge.   Man was not a mechanism but an organism; not a 'patent digesting
machine,' but a divinely-fashioned creature.   The
everlasting Yea was to admit this; the everlasting
No to deny it.   'On the roaring billows of Time

thou art not engulfed, but borne aloft into the azure of Eternity. Love not pleasure: love God. This is the everlasting Yea, wherein all contradiction is solved, wherein whoso walks and works it is well with him. Even to the greatest that has felt such moment, is it not miraculous and God-announcing, even as under simpler figures to the simplest and the least. The mad primeval Discord is hushed; the rudely jumbled conflicting elements bind themselves into separate firmaments; deep, silent rock-foundations are built beneath; and the skyey vault with its everlasting luminaries above; instead of a dark, wasteful Chaos, we have a blooming, fertile, heaven-encompassed World.'

To believe this, according to Carlyle, implied a species of conversion, and of his own conversion, when these things suddenly became real to him one night in Leith Walk, he has left as circumstantial an account as we have of the conversion of Luther or Wesley. What it implies is, in effect, a certain reconciliation to God, to the world, and to one's self. Carlyle's intense sympathy with Cromwell, which has made him his best biographer, arises from the fact that he found in Cromwell an echo of his own thoughts, and a picture of his own experiences. When Cromwell said, 'What are all events but God working?' we readily feel that the very accent of the thought is Carlyle's. When Cromwell steadies his trembling hand and says, 'A governor should die working,' he expresses Carlyle's gospel of work in its finest form. When Cromwell talks of dwelling in Kedar and Meshech where no water is, and of passing through strange hours of blackness and darkness, he is talking entirely after the manner of

Carlyle. After that memorable experience in Leith Walk, Carlyle tells us, his mood was no longer despondence, but valorous defiance. The world, at least, had no further power to hurt or hinder him: is he not now sure that he lives and moves at the bidding of a Divine Taskmaster? Long afterwards, when his first draft of the *French Revolution* was burned, this faith in the mystery of God's ordering was his one source of solace. 'It is as if my invisible Schoolmaster had torn my copy-book when I showed it, and said, "No, boy! thou must write it better." What can I, sorrowing, do but obey—obey and think it the best? To work again; and oh! may God be with me, for this earth is not friendly. On in His name! I was the nearest being *happy* sometimes these last few days that I have been for months!' To be reconciled to himself meant in such circumstances that he was willing to work, even if nothing came of his work, since work in itself was the appointed duty and true glory of man. 'Produce! Produce! were it but the pitifullest infinitesimal fraction of a product, produce it, in God's name. 'Tis the utmost thou hast in thee: out with it, then. Up! up! Whatsoever thy hand findeth to do, do it with thy whole might. Work while it is called to-day; for the Night cometh wherein no man can work.' Not, perhaps, a hopeful or a cheering creed this; but at all events a strenuous and a noble one. Such as it is, it contains the substance of Carlyle's contribution to religious thought. And we may profitably remember that the true effect and grandeur of a creed is not to be measured by its dimensions but by its intensity. We do not need large creeds for high lives, but we do need deep convictions, and Carlyle believed his creed and lived by it with passionate sincerity.

I have said that this is not a hopeful creed, nor was Carlyle ever a hopeful prophet. He called himself a Radical of the quiet order, but he had none of the hopefulness of Radicalism, nor was it in him to be quiet on any subject that interested him. There is a good deal of truth in the ironical remark of Maurice, that Carlyle believed in a God who left off governing the world at the death of Oliver Cromwell. He saw nothing in modern progress that justified its boasts, and it must be owned that his social forecasts have been all too amply fulfilled. The hopefulness of Emerson positively angered him. He took him round London, showing him the worst of its many abominations, asking after each had been duly objurgated, 'Do you believe in the devil now?' His very reverence for work led him to reverence any sort of great worker, irrespective of the positive results of his energy. It led him into the mistake of glorifying Frederick the Great. It led him into the still greater error of defending Dr. Francia, the Dictator of Paraguay. So far as the first article of the Radical faith goes, a belief in the people and the wisdom of majorities, he was a hardened unbeliever. Yet it was not because he did not sympathise with the people. His rapid and brilliant etchings of labouring folk—the poor drudge, son of a race of drudges, with bowed shoulders and broken finger-nails, whom he sees in Bruges; the poor Irishman 'in Piccadilly, blue-visaged, thatched in rags, a blue child on each arm: hunger-driven, wide-mouthed, seeking whom he may devour'—are full of tenderness and compassion. He never forgot that he himself was the child of labouring folk, and he spoke for his order. But he had no mind to hand over the government of the nation to the drudges. His theory of government was government by great men, by which he meant strong men. History was to him at bottom the story of great men at work. He believed in individualism to the last degree when government was in question. If a man had the power to rule, it was his right to be a ruler, and those who had not the power should be glad and thankful to obey. If they would not obey, the one remedy was the Napoleonic 'whiff of grape-shot,' or something akin to it, and in this case Might was the divinest Right.

Yet this is very far from being all Carlyle's political gospel. He advocated emigration, and by systematic emigration a dimly formulated scheme of imperial federation, long before these things were discussed by politicians. His denunciations of competition really paved the way for the great schemes of co-operation which have since been effected. More or less he believed that the great remedy for poverty was to get back to the land. 'Captains of industry' was his suggestive phrase, by which he indicated the organisation of labour. His appeals to the aristocracy to be a true aristocracy of work, alive to their social duties, and justly powerful because nobly wise, were certainly not unregarded. Much that we call socialism to-day had its real origin in the writings of Carlyle. The condition of the people was with him a burning and tremendous question. It was not within the range of his powers to suggest much in the way of practical measures; his genius was not constructive. The function of the prophet has always been rather to expose an evil than to provide a remedy. It must be admitted that Carlyle's denunciations are more convincing than his remedies. But they had one effect whose magnitude is immeasurable : they roused the minds of all thinking men throughout England to the real state of affairs, and created the new paths of social reform. The blazing vehemence of his style, the intense vividness of his pictures, could not fail to arrest attention. He shattered for ever the hypocrisy that went by the name of ' unexampled prosperity.' He forced men to think. In depicting the social England of his time he 'splashed' great masses of colour on his canvas, as he did in describing the French Revolution, and all earnest men were astonished into attention. The result has been, as Dr. Garnett puts it, that ' opinion has in the main followed the track pointed out by Carlyle's luminous finger'; and a completer testimony to his political prescience could not be desired.

Much must be allowed for Carlyle's love of paradox in the statement of these truths. Fundamentally, it is the exaggeration of the humorist who, in his habitual ironies, is half-conscious that he caricatures himself as well as his opponents. No doubt it would have been very helpful to persons of slow understanding if he had always spoken with logical gravity, and had strictly defined and stated what he meant. But then he would have been as dull as they are. The half-dozen truths which he had to teach are as common as copy-book headlines, and as depressing Put in plain and exact English, they are things which everybody knows, and is willing to accept theoretically, however little he is disposed to act upon them. The supreme merit of Carlyle is that he sets these commonplaces on fire by his vehemence, and vitalises them by his humour. It is the humour of Carlyle that keeps his writings fresh. His nicknames stick when his argument is forgotten. In his hands political economy itself ceases to be a dismal science, and becomes a manual of witty metaphors. This is so great an achievement that we may readily forgive his frequent inconsequence, and what is worse, his unfairness and exaggeration of statement.

To this it may be added that, where Carlyle was convinced of any unfairness of statement, or unneedful acerbity of temper, no one showed a quicker or nobler magnanimity in apology. His bark was always worse than his bite. We read his ferocious attacks on opponents, or his satiric descriptions of persons, in cool blood, and do not hear that genial laugh which wound up many similar vituperations in his conversation, and drew their sting. For all his angry counsel to whip drones and shoot rogues, Mrs. Carlyle tells us that when she read aloud to him the account of the execution of the assassin Buranelli, 'tears rolled down Carlyle's cheeks—he who talks of shooting Irishmen who will not work.' He was lamentably wrong in his judgment of the great issues involved in the American Civil War; but when, years afterwards, Mrs. Charles Lowell, whose son had fallen in the war, visited him, he took her by her hand, and said, even with tears, 'I doubt I have been mistaken.' Amid all his bright derision and savage mockery, no one can fail to see that he sought for and loved truth alone. That was, and will always remain, his crowning honour. He sought it, and was loyal to it, when he turned sadly from the ministry for which he was destined, when he went into the wilderness of Craigenputtock, when he was content to be ostracised by Jeffrey and his clique as an intellectual Ishmael, when he finally came to London and took up his real life-work, content to starve, if needs be, but resolved to speak or write no word that should win him bread or fame at the price of insincerity. And in the hearts of thousands of men, and among them the best and ablest of his time, he begot the same temper. Kingsley, Sterling, Ruskin, and a score of others gathered to his standard, not to name the throng of humbler disciples in every walk of life who caught the inspiration of his passion, and re-interpreted his thoughts. This was the work he did for England; amid manifold shams and hypocrisies he stood fast by the truth, for it was to bear witness to the truth that he was born, and came into the world.

CHAPTER XIV

CARLYLE : CHARACTERISTICS

'NOTHING seems hid from those wonderful eyes of yours; those devouring eyes; those thirsty eyes; those portrait-eating, portrait-painting eyes of thine,' wrote Emerson to Carlyle in one of his early letters. These phrases of Emerson are not less striking than true, and they convey to us much of Carlyle's secret as an artist. Whatever may be said about certain infelicities of style which persons of conventional judgment lay to his charge, there can be no doubt that Carlyle is a consummate artist, with a power of vivid expression unmatched in English literature. There is, indeed, something almost terrible in his power of vision. Nothing escapes him. If he visits a strange town or village, crosses the Irish sea with a rough group of 'unhappy creatures,' talks with a labourer at Craigenputtock, spends an hour with Leigh Hunt or Coleridge, meets Lamb, Fraser, Irving, Murray—the result is the same, a powerful etching, done with the fewest strokes, but omitting nothing of either pathos or folly, absurdity or weakness. A rarer gift—let us also say a more perilous gift—than this could not be; perilous because from its inconsiderate display upon those who stood nearest to him, Carlyle's reputation has suffered most. But it is a supreme gift, and that which more than any other constitutes the great artist. It is by virtue of this extraordinary vigour of intellectual vision, and artistic sensitiveness, that Carlyle has written books which not merely reflect life, but are life itself, and move us as only the greatest masters of the creative imagination can move us.

After all, the man of letters must expect fame for his literary qualities, rather than for his message. It is possible enough that his message may be out-dated ; but the quality of a man's literary gift is not subject to permutation. The message of Carlyle we have considered: let us finally ask, what original combination of gifts does he possess as a man of letters ?

First of all, and chiefly, is this supreme artistic faculty. His dramatic instinct is perfect, his eye for the fine points and grouping of his picture inevitably right. It is this gift which is so conspicuous in the *French Revolution*, and makes it a great epic, a series of astonishing *tableaux vivants*, rather than a prose history. But the gift is his in whatever he touches, and it imparts the glow of genius to his least considered writings. There is not another modern writer of English who has produced so much of which so little can be spared. Not even Ruskin has a truer eye for colour and effect in Nature, nor can Ruskin paint Nature with a more impassioned sense of fellowship in the mysteries and glories of the outward world. Could the view from Highgate be painted in any finer fashion than this, with clearer austerity of phrase, and yet with a certain noble largeness of effect too: 'Waving, blooming country of the brightest green ; dotted all over with handsome villas, handsome groves; crossed by roads and human traffic, here inaudible or heard only as a musical hum; and behind all swam, under *olive-tinted haze*, the illimitable limitary ocean of London?' Or what picture of a Scotch spring can be more accurately perfect than this: 'The hills stand snow-powdered, pale, bright. The black hailstorm awakens in them, rushes down like a black, swift ocean-tide, valley answering valley; and again the sun blinks out, and the poor sower is casting his grain into the furrow, hopeful he that the Zodiacs and far heavenly Horologes have not faltered?' Or who that has read it, will not recall the passage in which he speaks of riding past the old churchyard at midnight, the huge elm darkly branched against the clear sky, and one star bright above it, and the sense that God was over all? It is in such passages that the deep poetry of Carlyle's soul utters itself most freely. And these fine moments abound in all his writings. He has no need to save up his happy inspirations for future use, after the fashion of lesser men. His is the freest and most prodigal of hands; and nowhere outside the great poets, and very rarely within them, can there be found depictions of Nature at once so simple, adequate, and perfect.

The same faculty manifests itself even more re-markably in his sketches of persons. Without an effort, by the mere instantaneous flash of a word, the photograph stands complete. Sometimes the process is slightly more elaborate, but it is always characterised by the same intensity and rapidity of execution. As pieces of description, which sum up with a strange daring and completeness not merely the outward appearance of men, but their spiritual

significance also, what can compare with these :—
Coleridge, 'a steam-engine of a hundred horse
power, with the boiler burst'; Tennyson, 'a fine,
large-featured, dim-eyed, bronze-coloured, shaggy-
headed man is Alfred: dusty, smoky, free and easy,
who swims outwardly and inwardly with great composure in an inarticulate element of tranquil chaos
and tobacco-smoke'; Mazzini, a 'swift, yet still,
Ligurian figure ; merciful and fierce ; true as steel,
the word and thought of him limpid as water, by
nature a little lyrical poet.' It often happens, indeed,
that there is none of the geniality of these descriptions of Tennyson and Mazzini in Carlyle's later
pictures of some of his contemporaries. There is
something even savage and terrible in his sketch of
Charles Lamb, and his description of Mill—'wither-
ing or withered ; his eyes go twinkling and jerking
with wild lights and twitches, his head is bald, his
face brown and dry—poor fellow after all.' It must
be remembered, however, that this picture of Mill
occurs in a letter never meant for publication, and it
never ought to have been published. Yet there is
no doubting either its truth or power as a piece of
art. The lines are etched in with a heavy and
savage hand, but undoubtedly by the hand of a
master. In this peculiar power of portraiture by
means of terse and vivid phrases, Tacitus is the
only writer with whom Carlyle can be compared,
and Carlyle is in every way his master.

The artistic sense which makes him so superb
a phrase-maker in describing men serves him in
another form when he comes to the criticism of
their works. One secret of his method is to convey
his impression in some strange and yet felicitous

metaphor, rather than by any mere collocation of qualities. Thus, when he says of Emerson's style that it has 'brevity, simplicity, softness, homely grace, with such a penetrating meaning, soft enough, but irresistible, going down to the depths and up to the heights, as silent electricity goes,' we feel that there is nothing more to be said. It is the last phrase, the metaphor of 'silent electricity,' which completes and fixes the whole impression. Reams of essays on Emerson would tell us nothing more than Carlyle has already told us in this one abrupt, yet half-rhythmic sentence. And it is so with all his criticism. He has an inevitable instinct for the right word, the one fine and accurate phrase which expresses what is the dominant quality of a writer. Thus, when he speaks of Gibbon, he has nothing to say about the pomp and roll of his style; he puts his finger at once upon that which is of vastly higher significance—'his winged sarcasms, so quiet, and yet so conclusively transpiercing, and killing dead.' Some allowance must, of course, be made for personal likings and prejudices, especially in a man so liable to impulse as Carlyle. Many of his judgments upon his contemporaries are not only ill-natured, but they are ignorant. When he personally disliked a man, he made no effort to understand his writings, and refused him even courtesy, as in the case of Newman, whose brain he said was probably about the size of a moderate rabbit's. But these grotesque injustices occur for the most part in conversation, or in private letters, where he felt himself free to talk much as Dr. Johnson did, with small regard to anything but his own enjoyment in expressing his mind. When he sat down to any deliberate piece of criticism, the case was wholly altered. He then brought all his great powers of insight, sympathy, and vividness to bear upon his author. He permitted no prejudice to keep him from expressing what he felt to be the essential truth about the man and his work. The result is that his essays on authors—for example those on Johnson and Burns—are in themselves imperishable pieces of literature. They convey to the mind a clearer image of the man, both physical and spiritual, than can be found anywhere else. They are sufficient to prove that in the domain of criticism, it is a case of Carlyle first and the rest nowhere.

As compared with other writers of history, essay, and biography, the power of Carlyle comes out in two ways. The first is a superior sincerity. He will have the truth, the whole truth, and nothing but the truth about his hero. Thus, for example, no one could have been more antipathetic to him than Voltaire. He disliked his writings, and perhaps resented still more his light and airy mockery, his power of riding on the wave, of utilising popularity, of dancing through life with inimitable gaiety, scattering scathing jests as he went. But he could recognise that Voltaire was after all a sort of prophet, and honest to the bone. At all events, he had stood upon the side of unpopular justice, and had a passion for right. Macaulay, when he speaks of Voltaire, sees none of these things. He writes a bitter and clever verse about him, and dismisses the subject. Carlyle, with a far more intense passion for religion, and a stronger detestation of Voltaire's temper toward it, than Macaulay could ever have felt, has a searching sincerity of insight which discovers at once the true spiritual calibre of the man. Considering what Carlyle's own beliefs were, and what his usual temper was toward those who differed from him, his essay on Voltaire is one of the most conspicuous triumphs of sincerity which literature affords.

The other direction in which the power of Carlyle appears is his insight. Here, again, one cannot but compare Macaulay at the risk of repeating what has been already said. Macaulay steps before the court amid rounds of applause, with instructions to smash his opponent's case. The audience is not disappointed. As a rule he fulfils their utmost hopes. He marshals his case with the consummate ability of a great advocate. In nothing that he has written is he so much in his element as in his demolition of poor Robert Montgomery, who, it must be owned, richly deserved all he got. His notion of describing a man is the special pleader's notion—to accumulate various ascertainable details about him. He can pack a paragraph with interesting trivialities about a man's appetite, his clothes, his habits, his pleasures, and his vices. If he is not a Whig, a great deal more will be said of his vices than of anything else. But Macaulay never, by any chance, gives us the full-length portrait of a man, and Carlyle does. He arranges the wig, the clothes, the gloves he wore when he went to court, and all the other useful accessories of the studio, but he does not paint the man. Carlyle will take as deliberate and patient care as Macaulay to gather details, but he knows that they are only details. What he wants, and will have, if it be discoverable, is the spiritual truth about the man. He constructs his history and biography from the inside, not the outside. He sees, and boldly fingers, the 'very pulse of the machine.' He analyses and combines spiritual elements with an alchemy whose secret no other shares. The result is that when Carlyle has finished such a work as his *Cromwell*, there is nothing more to be said. 'Here,' he says, 'is the veracious man, warts and all. Take him or leave him as you will, but you can't make him different.' Nor can we. Nothing that has been written on Cromwell since Carlyle wrote has had the slightest effect on public opinion, at least by way of modifying Carlyle's verdict. But there is scarcely a great passage in Macaulay which is not capable of another version, and Mr. Gladstone has even gone so far as to speak of Macaulay's mind as hermetically sealed to truths which he did not wish to know. In matters of private judgment Carlyle could often be both unjust and ungenerous, but no such charge can be made against his writings. As historian, biographer, and essayist, his power of insight is so acute that it often seems almost magical, and it never fails to discover and attest the truth, so far as the absolute truth can be known, about any great actor or maker of the past.

Of the peculiarity of Carlyle's dialect much has been written, but only a word need be spoken here. It used to be the custom to accuse him of Germanising the English tongue, and Wordsworth once said that he was a pest to the language. But what was supposed to be a German discoloration was really a Scotch. He simply talked all through his life the strong Doric he had learned as a boy at Ecclefechan. His father had the same faculty of flashing and rugged phrase: Carlyle inherited it.

It is true that, when he began to write, he wrote precisely and smoothly. Precisely, indeed, he always wrote: no slipshod sentences ever escaped him, and his hastiest note is finished with as jealous an attention to phrase as though it were meant for the press, and intended as a hostage for immortality. But as his own poetic power grew, he felt the need for a larger form, and he found it in the expressive language of his boyhood. Thinking always as an idealist, he was more and more constrained to write as a realist, and smoothness and polish of phrase is inconsistent with a realism so vigorous as his. In prose he does pretty much what Browning does in poetry, except that with all his ruggedness he is never obscure. Burns also wrote smooth English, but not when he felt deeply; then his tongue fell into the deeper harmonies of the mellow Doric. Who does not prefer the latter? Who cannot perceive that *Tam o' Shanter* is worth forty volumes of letters to Clarinda? And difficult and harsh as it may appear at first, till the secret of its rhythm is learned, who does not also feel that, as a vehicle of utterance, the style of *Sartor Resartus* is every way nobler and greater than the polished paragraphs of the *Life of Schiller* and the earlier essays?

Of the many books of Carlyle it is impossible to take detailed notice. The *Miscellaneous Essays*, *Hero-Worship*, and *The French Revolution* will probably remain the most popular. The political writings will be the first to perish in the nature of things. The gospel of Carlyle—that is, the fullest expression of what he regarded as his spiritual message to his times—will be best learned from *Sartor Resartus* and the *Life of Sterling*. Beyond these numerous and various writings there rises the huge bulk of the *History of Frederick the Great*, which in many ways is his greatest work. Emerson said that it was the wittiest book ever written, and as a series of scenes, inimitably staged, and ranging through every latitude of emotion, there is nothing comparable with it. The man who could afford but two histories should read Gibbon and Carlyle's *Frederick* : in these the greatest historical genius of our race finds its expression. But when all estimates of his works are weighed and ended, all depreciations of time and opinion allowed for, most people will feel that Carlyle's great legacy to the world is, after all, himself. Next to Dr. Johnson there is no other figure that stands out in English literature with such distinctness and virility. In mere Titanic mass Carlyle, indeed, bulks far larger than the old dictator of eighteenth-century letters. But what is common to both is a fascinating perversity, a brusque and humorous honesty, and above all a certain antique severity and nobleness of nature. Just as we remember and discuss Johnson by his characteristics rather than his writings, so it may be, in a century's time, the figure and actual life of Carlyle will prove more fascinating than anything which he wrote. It may be so, but who can say? The one thing that is clear to us is that he is by far the greatest man of letters of the nineteenth century, the most interesting, noble, and impressive ; and as a spiritual and moral force, there is no other writer who has touched his times so deeply, or deserves more honourable memory.

CHAPTER XV

EMERSON

[Ralph Waldo Emerson, born in Boston, May 25, 1803. Graduated
at Harvard, 1821. Minister of the Second Church, Boston, 1829.
Resigned in 1832. Visited Europe in 1833, an account of his
impressions afterwards appearing in *English Traits*. Settled at
Concord, 1834. *Nature* published, 1836. First series of *Essays*,
1841. Second series, 1844. Died in Concord, April 27, 1882.]

INTIMATELY associated with Carlyle, not alone by
one of the most beautiful of literary friendships, but
by a certain kinship of genius, is Emerson. Emerson
had something of Carlyle's keenness of vision without his melancholy, his humour, or his ruggedness.
He was a seer in the poetic sense rather than the
prophetic; and, as one of his warmest admirers remarked, much more of a seer than a philosopher.
In his famous *Fable for Critics*, Mr. Russell Lowell
institutes an elaborate comparison between Carlyle
and Emerson, the most discerning lines of which are
these :

> 'To compare him with Plato would be vastly fairer,
> Carlyle's the more burly, but E. is the rarer ;
> He sees fewer objects, but clearlier, trulier,
> If C.'s an original, E.'s more peculiar ;
> C.'s the Titan, as shaggy of mind as of limb,
> E.'s the clear-eyed Olympian, rapid and slim.'

An American Plato Emerson was, yet owing
nothing to Plato, for had Plato never lived, Emerson

would have arrived by instinct at a Platonic view of
the universe. His essential difference from Carlyle
lies in the calmness and depth of his inspiration, as
compared with the turbulence and intermittent
vividness of Carlyle's. What Carlyle writes in
lightning, Emerson writes in light. He once
described himself as being somewhat of a Quaker;
clearly he possessed that secret of fine poise and
innermost tranquillity which is peculiar to the best
type of Quaker temperament. In him it amounted
almost to austerity, and yet a thoroughly kindly and
genial austerity. Anger, violence, passion of any
kind he did not know. He stood aloof from the
world, dreamed his dream, and was content. Perhaps
much of his influence arose from this spiritual aloofness. He does not carry the intellect by assault,
but gently interfuses and penetrates it with his
ideas; speaks not loudly but with quiet convincing
power; dazzles us a little, yet with a certain veiled
softness of light; melts our opposition rather than
overcomes it; dissolves our materialism in a subtle
elixir of spirituality; steals into our mind with a
footfall so light our logic does not waken; annexes
and occupies it, making loyal subjects of us before
we know it, and by methods that we have neither
the will nor the means to dispute.

Emerson's life is remarkable for a certain noble
unity. One discovers in it no trace of spiritual conflict, no disruption of thought, none of those acute
hours of conflict which give sudden and new
determination to ideas and conduct. He was born
into culture, the very best of its kind then available.
As a boy he was intensely interested in Montaigne,
and was accustomed to take Pascal's *Pensées* to

church with him.   The first awakenings of his mind
were eagerly watched and sedulously nurtured.   Yet
it does not appear that either his family or his early
friends credited him with genius.   Probably this was
because he was too sensitive and reticent to say
much about the processes of his own mind.   Always
very much of a recluse in his habits, he was a recluse
in mind also.   In later life it was often remarked
that he bore a singular resemblance to Newman; he
resembled Newman also in many qualities of
temperament.   He belonged essentially, as Newman
did, to the great society of the mystics, possessed the
same power of personal charm, had the same air of
austerity touched with suavity, impressed all who
knew him with the same sense of separation from
the common passions of the flesh, and the conventional pursuits of men.   Emerson, bred at Oxford,
can be easily conceived as falling under the fascination of mediæval theology.   Newman, bred in the
brisk intellectual air of New England Unitarianism,
might quite as easily be conceived as drifting into
transcendental conceptions of life and nature.   The
parallel, however, must not be pushed too far.
Emerson had little of Newman's spiritual passionate-
ness—a most important matter.   It would appear
that he never felt at any time that sense of sin which
has been so pregnant and so real to all men of profound religious genius.   Nor had he the least spark
of that divine discontent which all reformers have
known.   Carlyle felt this as a disappointing element
in Emerson's character.   'He seems very content
with life, and takes much satisfaction in the world,'
wrote Carlyle.   'It's a very striking and curious
spectacle to behold a man in these days so con-

fidently cheerful as Emerson.' Yet Carlyle would have been the first to admit that Emerson possessed a quiet intensity of soul, by virtue of which he was an appointed teacher of men.

The first efforts of Emerson as teacher were not very successful. One hears of certain college addresses, which owed their charm, perhaps, to a singularly melodious voice—all the Emersons had beautiful voices—but which wakened no enthusiasm. 'I found it long and dry,' writes Josiah Quincy of one of these dissertations. The real Emerson of this period is found in certain private letters. 'I am seeking to put myself on a footing of old acquaintance with nature, as a poet should '—'a pair of moonlight evenings have screwed up my esteem several pegs higher, by supplying my brain with several bright fragments of thought, and making me dream that mind as well as body respired more freely here.' In these confessions we have the first prelusive notes of a music since familiar. In the natural order of things Emerson should have followed the family tradition, and have found his vocation in the pulpit. He made the experiment as became a dutiful son, but without enthusiasm. If he did not succeed, he did not fail. The experience did him no harm ; it probably taught him something of the art of public address, and gave him a breathing-time. At last a crisis came, if one may dignify by so large a word the equable and gentle process of events which gave Emerson his liberty. Ostensibly the ecclesiastical rock on which Emerson split was the Sacrament. He informed his congregation that he could not regard the Lord's Supper as meant to be a permanent institution, adding, with a touch of brusqueness unusual with him, that even if he did so think he would not adopt it. 'I should choose other ways, which, as more effectual upon me, He would approve more. For I choose that my remembrances of Him should be pleasing, affecting, religious. I will love Him as a glorified friend, after the free way of friendship, and not pay him a stiff sign of respect, as men do to those whom they fear!'

Emerson probably imagined that he could carry his congregation with him in these conclusions. It seems unlikely that he really wished to terminate a career in which he had found a good deal of quiet happiness. Certainly his congregation had no wish that he should leave them. They were as liberal in thought, as devoted to culture, as any congregation could well be, and throughout New England a traditional respect and affection attached to the name of Emerson. But Emerson was not aware that he had outgrown them till this sudden cause of difference arose. When the mind is full of fluid elements of new thought, held in a state of suspension, it needs but a touch to precipitate crystallisation. The question of what the Lord's Supper meant served to bring matters to the test, but any other subject would have served as well. He had spoken truth when he said that he was more of a Quaker than anything else; he found the Quaker in him now quietly protesting against all form, and dreaming of a wider worship. He resigned his pastorate, not without some disappointment at the intractability of his flock, but with not the least trace of soreness or ill-feeling. Three days later, on the Christmas Day of 1832, he sailed for Europe.

The record of this tour, which is perhaps the

most memorable event in Emerson's quiet life, is
full of interest. He described its purpose in a singular
phrase—'To find new affinities between me and my
fellow-men.' The ordinary shrines at which the
tourist worships do not seem greatly to have attracted
him. For art he had the liking of the ordinary
cultivated man, but little real interest. In Rome,
he reflects that the emotion awakened by names of
places, art, and magnificence is, after all, evanescent
and superficial. He remembers at Syracuse the great
names identified with its past history, but he only
warms into real feeling when he speaks of picking
wild-flowers near the fountain of Cyane. Venice
kindles no raptures, Paris repels him by its likeness
to New York. In these confessions one reads the
man. Nature, then and always, held the first place
in Emerson's affections, and next to nature, man in
his spiritual significance. Even the famous men whom
he meets do not seem to have made much impression
on him. Landor, he does not find equal to his
reputation ; Coleridge is disappointing ; Wordsworth,
even more so. He admits the rare elevation of
Wordsworth's mind in its own domain ; but it is
upon the whole 'a narrow and very English mind.'
Newman he did not meet, nor does he seem to have
been aware of the great influence he was beginning
to exert. Carlyle he did meet, discovering his
whereabouts at Craigenputtock with difficulty, and
the meeting was memorable in every way. In Carlyle
he found the true friend of his soul. With the widest
possible difference of temperament, each regarded
the universe much in the same way. The most
remarkable feature of this famous interview was, as
Dr. Garnett remarks, 'the perfectly equal footing of

him whose genius was acknowledged at least by his visitor, and the thinker as yet entirely unknown to fame.' Carlyle at once recognised his worth, found him full of essential sincerity—'the most simple and frank of men'—felt his charm, and foresaw the growth of his genius. The impression made by Carlyle on Emerson was deep and permanent. Fifty years later, when Emerson lay dying, he turned with a smile of affection to Carlyle's portrait hanging on the wall, and said, '*That* is the man, *my* man.'

Carlyle probably gave an impulse of cohesion to Emerson's genius at the precise moment when it was most needed. Hitherto he had written nothing, and although he was not wanting in self-confidence, had no idea of any urgent message which it was laid on him to utter. Carlyle's frank recognition of him as a spiritual and intellectual equal must have had a most stimulating effect upon him. He had left America in a state of ill-health and general despondency, so far as it was in one of so equable a temperament to know despondence. He had buried his young wife after a brief union of but a few months, had severed himself from the ministry for which he had been trained, and, beyond certain vague dreams of literary work, had no very definite aim in life. Carlyle's approval and warm regard helped to reveal him to himself. He went back to America with a new and well-grounded confidence in his own powers. Henceforth he was to become the prophet of spiritual ideas to America, as Carlyle was to England, and in many ways the work of the two men was to intersect.

The centre of all Emerson's system of thought is to be found in the essay which he called *The Over-*

soul. All matter was to him the vesture of the spiritual, or of the universal soul. 'We see the world, he writes, 'piece by piece, as the sun, the moon, the animal, the tree ; but the whole, of which these are the shining parts, is the soul. . . . From within, or from behind, a light shines through us upon things, and makes us aware that we are nothing, but the light is all. What we commonly call man, the eating, drinking, planting, calculating man, does not, as we know him, represent himself, but misrepresents himself. Him we do not respect, but the soul, whose organ he is, would he let it appear through his action, would make our knees bend. When it breathes through his intellect, it is genius ; when it breathes through his will, it is virtue ; when it flows through his affection, it is love. . . . All reform aims, in some one particular, to let the great soul have its way through us.' The same truth is put even more felicitously in his lecture on Montaigne. 'The lesson of life is to believe what the years and the centuries say against the hours. Things seem to tend downward, to justify despondency, to promote rogues, to defeat the just, and by knaves, as by martyrs, the just cause is carried forward. Let a man learn to look for the permanent in the mutable and the fleeting ; let him learn to bear the disappearance of things he was wont to reverence without losing his reverence ; let him learn that he is here, not to work, but to be worked upon ; and though abyss open under abyss, and opinion displace opinion, all are at last contained in the Eternal Cause.' Man is here *to be worked upon*—that is the prevailing note of Emerson's teaching. The greatest man is he who is most fully surrendered to the energy of the universal soul, most plastic to its pressure. All history is the working of the universal soul through man—in essence the conclusion of Cromwell when he asked what were 'events' but 'God working'? So again with genius. Genius is the instrument of the unuttered. It originates nothing, but it perfectly reports messages inaudible to others. The true efficacy of genius lies in what we call its power of intuition ; but what is intuition but the power of arriving at truth by processes which have no connection with logic or external evidence? Milton, praying that the Holy Spirit may brood over his mind and touch it to utterance, comes nearer to expressing the true method of poetry than any other has done. Emerson uses a different terminology, but his meaning is the same. He once told a friend that when he spoke of God he preferred to say *It.* His friend soon discovered, however, that when they spoke of the omnipresence of God they really meant the same thing.   In the same way there is no substantial difference between Milton and Emerson in the definition of genius except in phrase. Where Emerson gave his doctrine new force was in widening its range. Not only in man, not only in history, but in all nature he saw the universal soul moving behind the screen of matter. The same force that was genius in Milton was form in the mountain, beauty in the cloud, fragrance in the flower. Thus, like Spinoza, he was 'God-inebriated,' seeing the whole universe brimming over with God. In God we lived, and moved, and had our being ; and not only we, but every humblest creature under heaven, every dew-drop on the field, every leaf upon the tree, every tiny life hidden in the deep obscurity of sea or forest.

Carlyle has, of course, said much the same thing, but scarcely, I think, with such an accent of experience. Nor is Carlyle consistent in his Pantheism. He was too thoroughly impregnated with the iron atoms of Calvinism to be quite easy in Pantheism. His early training had implanted in him what the Hebrew sage calls 'the fear of the Lord.' He believed, with Emerson, in the Divine Immanence, but after a Hebrew fashion. Emerson's way of putting things did not please Carlyle—'a gymnosophist sitting on a flowery bank,' was his humorously ironic epithet. And many others beside Carlyle felt as if Emerson's essays were simply so much thinly-spun moonlight. After one of his lectures the presiding minister thanked God that they had never heard such transcendental nonsense before, and prayed that they might never hear the like again. Emerson's only comment was that his critic seemed 'a very plain-spoken, conscientious man.' The story does something more than illustrate the magnanimous good temper of Emerson ; it is an illustration of his entire intellectual serenity. He had no doubt whatever that he had read aright the secret of the universe. The entire absence of dubiety in a mind so keen as Emerson's is very remarkable. He announced his conclusions with an air of mild amicable infallibility, which was quite impervious to logic. It is quite characteristic that, while he loved books, and was unhappy when away from them, yet they were his comrades rather than his counsellors. It may be doubted if he ever read a single book which altered by an iota his general ideas. He found his own light sufficient for him. Greatly as he loved Carlyle, he learned nothing new from him, and owed nothing either in style or philosophy to his teachings. In his own quiet way he was the most self-poised of individualists, and the firmest of dogmatists. If this dogmatism does not repel us, it is because it is so manifestly the fruit of experience. He reports upon the universe not from hearsay, but as he himself has found it, and the real power of his essays, especially over young minds, is in their entire sincerity and deliberate egoism.

The secret of the peculiar serenity of Emerson is not merely his Quaker temperament, but his real love of Nature. In a very charming passage he tells us that when he bought his farm at Concord, 'I did not know what a bargain I had in the blue-birds, bobolinks, and thrushes, which were not charged in the bill. As little did I guess what sublime mornings and sunsets I was buying, what reaches of landscape, what fields and lanes for a tramp.' He took an elemental joy in simple things, and dwelt close to the heart of Nature. Much of the sweetness of his own temper was drawn directly from these habits of intercourse with sylvan solitude. With health and a day, he characteristically says, he will make the pomp of empire ridiculous. Great cities did not attract him; the havoc which commercial life made with the mind distressed him. He did not go so far as Thoreau in his doctrines of a return to Nature, but Thoreau was his pupil, and carried Emerson's ideas to a logical conclusion. 'Nature,' he writes, 'stretcheth out her arms to embrace man; only let his thoughts be of equal greatness. A virtuous man is in unison with her works, and makes the central figure of the visible sphere.' Here, at least, was a perfectly intelligible and very practical message. What Wordsworth did by his example and his poetry, Emerson also did in his own way. He furnished his own countrymen with a much-needed illustration of the beauty of plain living and high thinking. He was never wealthy; in his early career he must have been poor. He followed the profession of a public lecturer in a day when it was not the well-paid profession that it now is. His books for many years had an extremely limited circulation. Nor was Concord the place of exquisite loveliness that it appeared in Emerson's eyes; clearly not one of those rare combinations of natural beauty which reconcile a man to poverty, as the daily vision of the Lake District reconciled Wordsworth to a cottage. But it contented Emerson. He lived in it like a sage; wrote about it like a poet. The philosophic axioms of Emerson may lose their force, and be neglected; it is not possible to neglect his poetry. There is a nameless sweetness and freshness in all his writings—a sense of the elemental. And as the general ways of life become more and more artificial, and the general interests of mankind more material, those who feel the unspeakable baseness of our later civilisation will assuredly find themselves turning to Emerson, and in him will find that which revives the sense of beauty, invigorates the virtue, and confers healing and refreshment alike on mind and spirit.

Emerson's style is one of great faults and great beauties. It has sometimes been complained that it is obscure, but this is a contention which cannot be sustained. It would be truer to say that it is fragmentary, and therefore gives the occasional impression of confusion. For this blemish Emerson's habits of composition are to blame. He rarely worked for long in his study; he preferred the solitude of the woods. He was accustomed to keep what he called a 'Thought Book,' and this book accompanied him in his rambles. When an essay was to be written the book was searched for material, and, as Emerson himself said, his gems were strung together like beads on a thread. This frank confession is entirely corroborated by the structure of his essays. There is no gradual unfolding of thesis and argument; the first sentence is a paradox as likely as not. The paragraphs do not grow out of one another, and there is little continuity in the thought. But each paragraph, like the bead upon the string, has a particular lustre and colour of its own. No writer is richer in epigram. Whatever we may think of the particular truth which he is enforcing, the manner in which he utters it arrests us.

His felicity of phrase is as remarkable as Carlyle's felicity of epithet. Such a phrase as 'Hitch your waggon to a star,' has become the brief summary of all that is meant by lofty ideals in practical action. Occasionally, too, there are passages of very rare and noble eloquence. His meaning is never in doubt; so far from being obscure is he, that as a rule he is astonishingly luminous. Upon the whole his style is one of the most stimulating in literature. The worst that can be said of it, that it coruscates a little too much; but those who have suffered much from the dull tediousness of philosophic authors will not count that a fault. A certain vivid nimbleness, sometimes reaching restlessness, is characteristic of the American intellect, and Emerson is distinctively American. But in his case there is so much sound scholarship, such broad sanity and width of view, such innermost serenity of temper, that his nimbleness of mind never declines into a fault. It is what Carlyle called it, 'soft electricity,' bathing great heights and depths of solid experience. It is only a captious criticism which will blame Emerson because he did not possess the gift of stateliness and sobriety which characterises the older prose writers; the outstanding fact is that he invented a style of his own, absolutely fitted to his own mode of thought, thoroughly pungent, individual, and original, and capable of much detached brilliance and real eloquence.

In spirit Emerson was never less than noble, in temper never less than hopeful. Even the great cataclysm of the American War did not for an instant dim his hope. It drew from him one of his noblest verses—

> 'So nigh is grandeur to our dust,
>   So near is God to man,
> When Duty whispers low, *Thou must*,
>   The youth replies, *I can.*'

When it was all over it was his also to say the wisest word about it: 'Everybody has been wrong in his guess, except good women, who never despair of an ideal Right. . . . I shall always respect war hereafter. The waste of life, the dreary havoc of comfort and time, are overpaid by the vistas it opens of Eternal Life, Eternal Law, reconstructing and upholding Society.'

The spirit of his own life cannot be better expressed than in his own fine lines :—

> ' Revere the Maker, fetch thine eye
>   Up to His style, and manners of the sky,

Not of adamant and gold
Built He heaven, stark and cold.

.   .   .   .   .

Built of tears and sacred flames,
And virtue reaching to its aims ;
Built of furtherance and pursuing,
Not of spent deeds, but of doing.
House and tenant go to ground,
Lost in God, in Godhead found.

CHAPTER XVI

JAMES ANTHONY FROUDE

[Born April 13th, 1818.   First two volumes of *History of England, from the Fall of Wolsey to the Defeat of the Spanish Armada*, published 1856 ; completed in 1869.   *Short Studies on Great Subjects*, essays appearing between 1867 and 1882.   *Cæsar; a Sketch*, 1879. *Life of Carlyle*, 4 vols., 1882-84.   *Life of Erasmus*, 1894.   Died Oct. 26, 1894.]

THE tradition of Macaulay was maintained, though upon a much inferior scale, by a writer of great versatility and romantic instinct, James Anthony Froude.   Educated at Westminster School and subsequently at Oxford, the son of an Archdeacon of competent fortune, he may be said to have inherited a certain traditional view of society from which he never wholly freed himself.   His intellect was eager rather than acute ; he knew how to doubt, but not how to doubt men's doubts away ; he could discover a fallacy, but often in exposing it fell into a worse fallacy; great talent he had, and a quite unusual power of stating old positions with freshness and novelty, but the power of original thought, and the serene temerity of genius which thinks for itself, was denied him.   If he was not in the true sense a great writer, it was because he was not in any sense a great man ; yet his work possesses so many high qualities of literature, that it is impossible to deny him rank among the chief writers of the nineteenth century.

His first trial of literature was unfortunate.   At

Oxford he soon came under the influence of Newman, for whom he professed then and always the warmest admiration. Probably the best qualities of his own style—lucidity, ease and eloquence—were derived from Newman. Newman set his promising pupil to work on writing some of the *Lives of the English Saints*, an occupation of which he soon tired. 'St. Patrick I found,' he says, 'once lighted a fire with icicles; changed a Welsh marauder into a wolf, and floated to Ireland on an altar stone. I thought it nonsense. . . . After a short experiment I had to retreat out of my occupation, and let the series go on without me.' He retreated out of the Oxford movement and all vital association with Newman at the same time. The fact appears to be that he had never had any real sympathy with the movement; he was of much too cold a temperament to indorse a propaganda of any sort. At heart he was a trimmer. He wished to combine rationalism with orthodoxy, to maintain a free mind on theological questions, and yet retain a fellowship which implied in its holder assent to a definite creed. His *Nemesis of Faith*, published in 1848, deals with these questions. It is a book long since forgotten, and quite unworthy of revival; but it has a certain biographical interest, especially when we remember that it was the success of this book which first turned the thoughts of Froude towards literature as a profession.

The Nemesis of Faith was in form a novel, and for some time Froude cultivated fiction, but without success. One of his stories, *The Lieutenant's Daughter*, is peculiarly mawkish in sentiment and nauseous in substance. It would not be worth mention but for the circumstance that Froude was twenty-nine

when it was published, an age at which most robust
natures have worked out the fermenting crudities of
youth.   Left to himself it is exceedingly doubtful if
Froude would ever have worked himself free of these
crudities, and have become an efficient man of letters.
His mind was essentially imitative and susceptible,
lacking initiation, but quick to follow a path opened
by another.   Once he had followed the initiative of
Newman, now he was to find a more potent master
in Carlyle.   It is curious to note, however, that he
was much too conventional in mind to discover the
greatness of Carlyle for himself.   Carlyle's *French
Revolution* came in his way, and he read it, wondering
at it, and candidly confessing that, like the rest of
the world, he did not know what to make of it.   It
was John Sterling who first explained to him its
significance, and led him to appreciate, in part at
least, the greatness of Carlyle.   In part only, however ; for as we shall see later, Froude never formed
a just estimate of the man whom he afterwards
calumniated in the most mendacious biography of
modern literature.   But there is no reason to doubt
that his appreciation of Carlyle, as far as it went,
was sincere.   All that Froude became, as man of
letters, was the work of Carlyle.   Many of his original
faults remained to the end, and in increased viru-
lency ; but whatever there was of virtue in the man
and in his writings, he derived it from Carlyle.   Essentially a man who needed a master, who never had,
nor could have, sufficient efficacy of genius to start
an independent course, Froude in the most critical
moment of his life exchanged Newman for Carlyle,
and never did literary man make a more fortunate
or fruitful exchange.

P

In 1856 the first volume of Froude's *History* appeared. How far the views of Carlyle inspired the views of Froude in his treatment of his great theme, it is of course impossible to determine, but it is reasonable to suppose that Froude owed something to Carlyle, and certainly more than he ever acknowledged. One of the regrets of literature must be that Carlyle did not himself deal with the times of Henry VIII. and Elizabeth, instead of giving the best years of his life, and his powers in the very consummation of their strength, to the dreary story of Frederick the Great. The view which Froude took of Henry's character was Carlyle's view, distinctly announced years before the first volume of the *History* was published. 'Henry,' said Carlyle once, in conversation with Sir C. G. Duffy, 'when we come to consider the circumstances he had to deal with, would be seen to be one of the best kings England had ever got. He had the right stuff in him for a king—he knew his own mind; a patient, resolute, decisive man, one could see, who understood what he wanted, which was the first condition of success in any enterprise, and by what method to bring it about. . . . He was a true ruler at the time when the will of the Lord's Anointed counted for something, and it was likely that he did not regard himself as doing wrong in any of those things over which modern sentimentality grew so impatient.' This is the real thesis of Froude's *History*, elaborated with great skill, frequent eloquence, and much vivacious energy. The book is in every respect a brilliant piece of work. In the art of word-painting Froude is a master. When he comes to certain central episodes, such as the story of the Armada, he rises into a species of easy epic power. He marshals his facts with the care of a consummate stage-manager, knows how to give colour and splendour to the page, is never confused or dull, works steadily toward the true dramatic crisis, and invariably leaves us with the impression that the pageant could not have been better staged. Other contemporary historians, such as Freeman and Gardiner, brought to bear upon the problems of history a patient and acute faculty of investigation of which Froude showed hardly a trace ; but in power of easy, picturesque, and dramatic narrative, Froude easily distanced his rivals. His temperament is essentially that of the Romancist. He is always in search of large effects, pictorial situations, sharp and striking contrasts. Thus, whatever may be said as to the truth of his *History*, it is impossible to deny its charm ; history in the accurate sense of the term it may not be, but it is certainly literature.

In his own way, and according to his lights, no doubt Froude tried to write accurate history, and thought that he had done so, but the fact of the matter was that his methods of work were much too hasty and slovenly to attain even moderate accuracy of statement on matters where a great mass of evidence had to be sifted. No one can expect absolute accuracy in a historian, but we have a right to expect the most patient and judicial examination of evidence before conclusions are pronounced. Carlyle possessed in a degree, immeasurably beyond Froude, the art of word-painting, the instinct of pictorial grouping, but he never sacrificed truth to effect. Every student of Carlyle's life knows what incredible pains he took to get at the exact truth about things; and thus it happens that while many other writers have since traversed the ground he took, and the opportunities of historical research have been greatly increased since his day, scarcely one of his facts has been seriously impugned. Brilliant in every way as Carlyle's historical tableaux are, yet they are not less brilliant than veracious, and in this combination of the highest imaginative powers, with an infinite capacity of dull, steady drudgery, of painstaking digging and delving after the least grain of authentic truth, Carlyle is unique.

But this species of laborious industry was not at all in the way of Froude. Carlyle was essentially a student; in the strict sense of the term, Froude was nothing of the kind. He has told us that he consulted 400,000 references in the preparation of the *History*; no doubt he did so, but with what degree of care? Perhaps the question is best answered in a single incident. One of the greatest figures in Elizabethan history is Burleigh, and on one occasion Froude was invited to stay at Hatfield, in order that he might exhaustively examine the great mass of Cecil papers preserved there, and at that time accessible nowhere else. Froude accepted the invitation, and stayed a single day! In the same way the executors of Lord Beaconsfield invited him to examine the papers of the deceased statesman before writing his brief biography, and he was content with what he could discover in a visit extending from Saturday to Monday. If the 400,000 references for the *History* were gone through at this rate, there is not much in the boast which is calculated to assure the reader of the accuracy of the narrative. But all that has been written of Froude since his death goes to prove how rooted and invincible was his incapacity of taking pains. Scholars who read his vivacious sketch of *Cæsar* perceived at once that he had read very few of Cicero's letters, and none of them properly; men of the world, who knew the life and institutions of the West Indies, discovered in the first pages of Froude's *Oceana*, that he had never really seen things for himself, nor had even tried to understand them. A novel may be written without a close examination of facts, so long as it is inherently and artistically probable; but history depends for its value on its truth. Froude wrote history in the spirit of the novelist. As long as things looked artistically probable, he thought little of essential veracity. He was either too indolent, or too prepossessed by certain views which he wished to uphold, or too indifferent to truth, to take ordinary pains to make the structure of his narrative secure against collapse or assault.

But this is not all. Not to examine one's facts is a bad thing, but to pervert them is a still worse. There can be little doubt that the habit of Froude's mind was casuistic; and when you unite gross carelessness with a manifest determination to prove a case at all costs, truth is rapidly reduced to a minus quantity. That Froude purposely or consciously perverted facts seems improbable. The errors of a radically inaccurate mind owe nothing to volition. The man in ordinary life who has never accustomed himself to strict accuracy of statement makes misstatements without the least sense of the gravity of his offence. It would be unjust to accuse him of lying since he is incapable of truth. Every one knows how extremely difficult it is to get some children to tell the exact truth upon a matter of fact; either by excess of imagination or by lack of logical faculty, they invariably and quite unconsciously over-colour or distort anything which they report as fact. The same thing is constantly seen in the witness-box. Men who have looked upon the same occurrence report it from totally divergent standpoints. In such a case no one accuses the witness of direct lying, though you may rightly accuse him of incapacity of truth. It is probable that very few persons ever speak *exact* truth. It is only the highly-trained judicial mind that is capable of seeing things without distortion, and in cases where matters of fact are in dispute, the last word, as in a law-case, is always with the judge, because the judicial mind is a mind disciplined to the highest degree in habits of precision. But Froude's intellect was not judicial: habits of precise thought he had never formed, and consequently the power of precise statement was not possible to him.

These are no doubt grave accusations, but they are capable of ample proof. A capital instance of Froude's habitual inaccuracy is his *Life of Erasmus*. This is one of his most delightful productions, judged merely from the literary standpoint. It has all the romantic *verve* and freshness of a novel, and the picture of Erasmus himself is singularly lifelike. If the book purported to be what Charles Reade's famous novel *The Cloister and the Hearth* is—a romance of the times of Erasmus, it would deserve the highest praise; but as serious history it is open to the gravest criticism. Take, for example, the translations of the letters of Erasmus. No one can read them without becoming conscious of the note of extreme 'modernity' which distinguishes them. Making allowance for theme and matter, they are just such epistles as might have been written by a gay, brilliant, scholarly, cynical man of the world in the close of the nineteenth century. Even the style is modern; the sentences are short, sharp, full of antitheses, so that the ordinary reader with a slight knowledge of the classics will wonder how such a style was possible in a language so ponderous and inflexible as the Latin—especially the Latin of the Middle Ages. The explanation is quite simple; the letters have been rewritten by Froude. Mr. Lilly, himself a competent scholar, says that in these 'translations' he found on every page 'distortions '—more or less gross, sometimes very gross —of Erasmus' meaning; things attributed to him directly contrary to what he really wrote; things of which the Latin presents no trace at all. It is precisely this distortion of meaning of which Froude's critics have complained. Mr. Lilly calls Froude an 'unscrupulous advocate.' It would be nearer the truth to call him an unscrupulous artist.

A work which lies better within the critical competence of the ordinary reader is Froude's biography of Carlyle. In this case the groundwork of fact is within common knowledge. How far Froude misinterpreted Erasmus is a question for scholars; how far he misinterpreted Carlyle is a question which can be referred to many persons who knew Carlyle much more intimately than he did.

There can be no doubt about the verdict. There is scarcely one cardinal fact about Carlyle's life which is rightly stated in Froude's biography. Thus he speaks constantly of Jane Welsh as an heiress; her modest fortune was about £200 per annum, which she did not touch until after her mother's death. He speaks of her marriage with Carlyle as an 'unheard-of *mésalliance*' which was the 'scoff of Edinburgh society': Jane Welsh was unknown in Edinburgh society; her marriage was not discussed in it: she was the daughter of a country doctor, and her only claim to distinction was that she married Carlyle. He speaks of Craigenputtock as a place of dreary banishment, where a delicate woman was tortured by the whims of a brutal husband; the facts are that the Carlyles went to Craigenputtock with the full assent of Mrs. Carlyle's mother, they neither of them regarded it as banishment, they lived upon delightful terms, they thoroughly enjoyed the Craigenputtock life, and never made serious complaint of it. He speaks of the Chelsea life as though its chief characteristic were incessant bickering, varied by hot explosions of anger on the part of Carlyle, all of which was meekly borne by a drudging, patient wife; the fact was that Mrs. Carlyle was the least patient of women, that what Froude took for bickering was merely the exchange of those pleasant ironies and railleries which are not uncommon between brilliant people who love one another, and that, as the published correspondence of husband and wife conclusively proves, no persons ever loved each other more tenderly than these two. He draws a tragic picture of Carlyle's remorse for his wife after her death; the fact is, that the chief passage on which all this fine dramatic situation is based is one in which Carlyle, with that morbid sensitiveness common to bereaved love, searches his memory to discover how he might have behaved more kindly to the dead, and can discover nothing worse than this, that he once did not enter a milliner's shop with her when she went to buy a bonnet, although by her glance he saw that she would have been pleased had he done so! But it is impossible in a paragraph to unravel all the mystifications, refute all the calumnies, correct all the distortions of this most mendacious of biographies. Even in the mere printing of documents and letters the errors are beyond belief. In one letter of Mrs. Carlyle's which describes her life at Craigenputtock, there are eighty errors of the press in fifty-eight lines. Professor Norton, one of the most careful editors of Carlyle's letters, has shown that in a biography of nineteen hundred pages, the errors greatly exceed the number of the pages. Phrases and incidents are constantly mis-reported. The phrase 'gey ill to live wi',' of which so much is made, should be 'gey ill to deal wi'' (mother's allocution to me once, in some un-reasonable *moment* of mine, says Carlyle), and in its authentic form, and with Carlyle's comment, the impression is totally changed. Episodes which were really humorous, and were so felt and described by Carlyle and his wife, are related with intense solemnity as proofs of the foregone conclusion that Carlyle was too dense to apprehend, too insensitive to sympathise with the infirmities of his wife. If the book were a novel, we may say again, as we said of the life of Erasmus, it would be admirable ; but as the serious biography of a very great man it is wholly disgraceful to its author, a monument of slovenly book-making, bad taste, and unconscious mendacity.

Perhaps it would have been better for Froude's

fame if, after all, he had stuck to the romantic novel. But even when all deductions are made—and with no writer of the nineteenth century are the deductions so many and so grave—it must be admitted that Froude's place in literature is considerable. Posterity forgives much to the stylist, and Froude was a stylist. In matters of fact he was slovenly, but rarely so in style. He had a quite genuine sense of the greatness of England, and hence there is sincerity as well as epic beauty and glow in his narratives. Nor was he destitute of convictions; he believed in the fundamentals of Protestantism, and in the main he apprehended them rightly. Of all his writings, the *Short Studies on Great Subjects* is the most popular, and it is a deserved popularity. In the historical, or semi-historical essay, he was at his best. Nothing was more congenial to his art than vignette-painting; brief, vivid, swiftly-etched portraits of men, descriptions of sea-fights, or records of manners. These vignettes, at once delicate and delightful, are apparently produced without effort, and this is one of the chief elements of their charm. In lucidity, ease, life, movement, and a certain unstrained felicity, Froude's style is remarkable, and as long as style is valued, Froude is sure of his audience. If the sole aim of literature were to give pleasure, Froude might claim the highest place among modern writers; but in the species of work which he undertook, truth ranks higher than artistic felicity, and it is his imperfect apprehension of truth which spoils his fame. If we have charity enough to make due allowance for this infirmity, we may still find it possible to rank him, if not with the great writers, yet among the chief; if not among the masters, yet at a great height above the mere professionals ; if not among those who have added something to the world's thought, or invigorated the world's life, yet among those who, by virtue of a fine style, have added something to the treasures of the language, and much to the pleasures of literature.

CHAPTER XVII

JOHN RUSKIN

[Born in London, Feb. 8th, 1819. Took his degree at Oxford, 1842. First volume of *Modern Painters* published, 1843. *Seven Lamps of Architecture*, 1849. *The Stones of Venice*, 1851-53. *The Two Paths*, 1854. The *Elements of Drawing*, 1857. The *Elements of Perspective*, 1859. Among his most popular smaller books are: *The Crown of Wild Olive*, *Sesame and The Lilies*, The *Queen of the Air*, *Ethics of the Dust*, *Until this Last*, which he has called his best work. *Fors Clavigera*, a series of letters, published with index, 1887. Still living at Brantwood, Coniston.]

IT is the prophetic force of Carlyle which is his most remarkable quality, as we have seen, and the secret of his abiding influence: it is also the primal and distinctive gift of Ruskin. In poetry, Wordsworth and Shelley represent this force; in history, Carlyle; in social economics, Ruskin. The prophet is the summed-up soul and conscience of a community, the emblem and the fountain of its moral life. He derives nothing from convention; he speaks out of his own strength and originality of nature, with the vehemence, and even anger, of great convictions, and with an amplitude of utterance which scorns details in its passion for principles. It is above all things his business to *see*; then to speak of what he sees with unfaltering sincerity, addressing himself to his fellows in such a way as to reveal to them their own deficiencies; finally to inspire in them a desire of reformation, and of all noble progress and accomplishment. This has been the lifelong mission of Ruskin.

It has been, however, a mission very much misapprehended. Tolstoi has affirmed that Ruskin is one of the greatest men of the age, and has said that it pained him to notice that English people generally were of a different opinion. The fact of the matter is that England has never quite known how to take Ruskin.

He presents a character of so many subtleties and variations, so tremulously poised between common sense and eccentricity, so clear and firm in outline, yet touched with such deceptive lights and shadows, and capable of such extraordinary transformations, that average opinion has preferred to accept him as a great stylist rather than a great man. He is by turns reactionary and progressive, simple and shrewd, a mystic and a man of practical affairs. He has bewildered men by the very brilliance of his versatility. No sooner has the world owned him as the prince of art-critics than he sets up as the exponent of a new political economy. He will show us how to weave cloth honestly as well as to draw truly; how to build character, as a matter of greater import even than the building of a Venice; and he who is an authority on Botticelli must needs also be an authority on drains. He links together in the strangest fashion the remotest things—philosophy and agriculture, theology and sanitation, the manner of a man's life and the quality of his pictures. It is this very variety and exuberance of mind which has kept the estimate of his genius low among his countrymen.   They have not been able to follow the nimbleness of his thought, and to perceive that, eccentric as it seems, it moves in a precisely ordered orbit.   The last thing that the English reader would say of Ruskin is that he sees life steadily, and he sees it whole; yet that is the very thing that Tolstoi would say of him, and he would add that therein lies his claim to be a great man.

And in such a contention Tolstoi would be right; the cardinal fact about Ruskin is that he sees life steadily and sees it whole.   This is the explanation of the immense variety of theme in his writings; it springs from width of vision.   If he had seen life only in some one special aspect, as, for example, in its relation to art alone, which is commonly supposed to be his one function, the critics would at once have known how to rank him.   There would have been no hesitation as to the place that was his by right.   But when he links art with morality, when he sets himself to the discovery of the principles by which art is great, and finds them to be also the only verified principles by which life is also great, then criticism becomes purblind and embarrassed.   It was prepared to praise the critic of art, but the critic of life is a very different matter.   Hence there arises the natural tendency on the part of the reader to regard the opinions of Ruskin as eccentric, but their expression as perfect—to value him as a master of literary expression, but not as a teacher—to agree, in point of fact, that he is a great writer, but to deny the contention of Tolstoi that he is a great man.   It is only going a step further to say of him, as it was said of Goldsmith, who 'wrote like an angel but talked like poor Poll,' that Ruskin writes nonsense, but writes it beautifully. That this is the general opinion of English readers, no one would venture to say; but having regard to the general praise of the beauty of his style, and the general contempt of the social principles he enunciates, one can see without difficulty what it is Tolstoi meant when he called him a great man, and deplored that his countrymen held a different opinion.

The personal history of Ruskin is the history of his writings. No youth ever began life with less likelihood of prophetic development. He was the petted, if not spoiled, child of wealthy parents. He begins his long use of the pen by the production of merely pretty and conventional poems. He writes with the certainty of parental praise, and without the fear of parental, or any other, criticism. He has absolutely no acquaintance with the hard facts of life, such as drove the iron deep into the soul of Carlyle, and taught him to become both law and impulse to himself. No youth ever stood in greater danger of a life of mere dilettanteism. There was no urgency to win his bread laid upon him, no special preparation for any profession, no diligent training with a view to the toils or the prizes of a career. His chief tastes are, a love of Nature, carefully fed by early and extensive travel; a love of books, developed by the best examples; and a love of art, which his possession of means enabled him to gratify. We do not gather from any record of his early life which we possess any sense of great robustness either of mind or body. His youth was threatened by consumption, and his mind was delicate and sensitive rather than profound or energetic. There is even the trace of effeminacy in in this early Ruskin, the quite natural and innocent effeminacy of a childhood sheltered from the rough winds of life, and of a youth that flowers into manhood, not by the conquest of a barren soil, but by the sedulous assistance of exotic horticulture. As compared with Carlyle, with whom he stands most closely associated, Ruskin grows in a hothouse, while Carlyle is a product of wild moor and bleak hillside. The one is the child of wealth, the other of poverty ; the one has a nature rich and varied, the other remains to the last stern and narrow as the land that bore him. Any more unlikely environment for a prophet than Ruskin's it would be difficult, and perhaps impossible, to imagine.

But one gift Ruskin had—the rare and superb gift of fearless sincerity, and it was this gift that saved him from the perils of dilettanteism and became the dominant force in the shaping of his life and genius. He had also a mind of the keenest analytic quality, and an imagination alike virile and sensitive. It was natural that in such an environment as his, his genius should fix itself first of all upon the study of art. What was art ? Was it merely a pleasant adornment of luxurious life, or was it in itself an expression of life? Was its true aim pleasure or truth ? Ruskin speedily decided that art was serious and not frivolous, that it had a vital connection with national character, and that its one great mission was truth. He began to train himself with infinite industry and assiduity, that he might be in a position to judge of art with justice and knowledge. He resolved to be led by no traditions, but simply to allow his sincerity of temper unimpeded play, and

to abide by the result. The discovery of the germ
in which all his future teaching of art lay was made
almost by accident. He had been taught in sketch-
ing foliage to generalise it, and to arrange it by
arbitrary rules and on an artificial method. One
day he sketched for himself a tree-stem with ivy
leaves upon it, and instantly perceived 'how much
finer it was as a piece of design than any conventional
re-arrangement would be.' All the rules of artificial
art in which he had been trained perished in that
simple discovery. He saw then that the only rule
of any importance to the artist was, ' Be sincere with
Nature, and take her as she is, neither casually
glancing at her " effects," nor dully labouring at her
parts with the intention of improving and blending
them into something better, but taking her all in all.
On the other hand, be sincere with yourself, knowing
what you truly admire and painting that, refusing
the hypocrisy of any "grand style" or "high art,"
just as much as you refuse to pander to vulgar tastes.
And then vital art is produced, and, if the workman
be a man of great powers, great art.' He had found
a domain which hitherto no prophet had claimed
or touched. The mere painting of pictures, which
to men of a narrower mind, a less refined training,
or a more Puritan temper, might have seemed a
superfluity of luxurious life, without relation to the
more serious principles of conduct or the progress of
society, he perceived to be an essential element of
life and an infallible witness to character. He had discovered 'that art, no less than other spheres of life, had
its heroes ; that the mainspring of their energy was
Sincerity, and the burden of their utterance Truth.'
In its moral aspects this principle is but a redis-

covery of the principle of Milton, that a true poet must make his life a poem. It sounds a commonplace, only we have need to remember that nothing is so original as a commonplace when it is genuinely believed. But it was not a commonplace as Ruskin uttered it, either to himself or the world he sought to instruct; so far from this was it, that it was felt to be the enunciation of a new and revolutionary principle. Art was in those days in peril of becoming a mere handicraft. Its rules were as the laws of the Medes and Persians, which altered not. Given so many rules, you produced a picture with the mathematical certainty by which two and two make four. Mediocre pictures were produced in endless progression, each as like to each as though they had been turned out of a factory. The greatest and most inspired artist of his day, Turner, was the object of rancorous ridicule, because he was outraging the pedantic traditions of artificial picture-making. Ruskin recalled men to Nature in art as Wordsworth did in poetry. He laid down the rule that it was the business of the artist to study Nature with humbleness and docility, 'rejecting nothing, selecting nothing, and scorning nothing.' He laid down the yet harder rule that the character of the artist has more to do with the making of his art than the deftness of his hand; that a picture is the record of a soul, as truly as of some fragment of natural phenomena ; the rule of Milton, in fact, that the true poem is the product of the true life, and that great art is impossible to the man of mean soul. On those two principles all the art criticism of Ruskin is based. The principle of the return to Nature made him the champion of Turner against

the world ; and later on, led him to the discovery
of the pre-Raphaelites, and the counsel 'to paint
things as they probably did look and happen, not
as, by the rules of art developed under Raphael,
they might be supposed, gracefully, deliciously, or
sublimely, to have happened.' The principle of
character as the true secret of art led him to the
much wider field of his later literary labours, and
the fulfilment of his true prophetic mission.

I have associated, and in part contrasted, Ruskin
with Carlyle, and it is a contrast which he himself
sanctions, since he has declared that Carlyle was his
master, and that all his thinking has been coloured
by Carlyle's stronger thought. At first sight the
comparison seems unsustained and impossible, for
the differences between the two men are clear to the
most casual observation. The genius of Ruskin is
subtle, while Carlyle lacks subtlety ; the style of
Carlyle is chaotic, while Ruskin's is polished to the
utmost nicety of expression ; Carlyle despised art,
and Ruskin adored it ; Carlyle is above all things a
humorist, while Ruskin has wit and satire, but no
humour. Each has vast powers of pugnacity ; but
Carlyle hurls the thunderbolt, while Ruskin wields
the rapier. One has the energy of a primeval man,
and his limitations ; the other is the fine product of
a special culture. Yet in moral temper they are
alike, and their criticism of life agrees. Each teaches,
as a fundamental truth, that the first duty of man is
to take care of facts, and that principles will take
care of themselves. Each delights in broad and
vivid generalisation. Each is in violent antagonism
to the main trend of the age, and states the ground
of his revolt with violence. It was by the mere

accident of environment that Ruskin spent the first eagerness of his genius on a theme that Carlyle could never regard as serious ; criticism of art was from the very first, with him, criticism of life ; and as his genius grew, art fell behind him, and life became more and more.

How Ruskin has preached the gospel of sincerity with a force inferior only to Carlyle's, and with a penetrating beauty of phrase all his own, we shall see as we turn to his works. In the meantime we should remember that, however wrong-headed he may seem to those who do not agree with him, he has practised his principles, and maintained from first to last an uncompromising sincerity. He championed Turner, and bought his pictures, when Turner was utterly neglected by both the patron and the public. He praised work, and no more laborious life than his has been lived among us. He insists on a mastery of facts, and no artist ever put himself through a more strenuous discipline to facts than Ruskin, before he considered himself competent to pronounce judgment on the humblest picture. He has advocated a wise simplicity of life, and few lives have been more gracefully austere than his. No duty has been too humble, if commended by a sense of right ; no generosity too great, if it served a wise purpose or a public need. It is the least part of his benefactions that of the £200,000 left him by his father every penny has long ago been given away. He has given what is more than money—himself, his genius, sympathy, and service, as a willing sacrifice to his countrymen ; and thus the gospel of sincerity proclaimed in his writings has been made still more beautiful and convincing by his life.

CHAPTER XVIII

THE TEACHING OF RUSKIN

TO arrive at an estimate of Ruskin's temperament is easy; of the nature and scope of his teaching and philosophy much may be said. In his art-criticism we have seen that Ruskin lays down the great principle that sincerity is the main-spring of the artist's energy, and the burden of his message is truth. It may be said that such a definition precisely expresses his own temper. But this is by no means an inclusive definition. He insists also with Keats, that truth is beauty, beauty is truth; and that the true artist, while not ignoring the facts of ugliness, will feel his passion going out perpetually toward the fairest forms and richest aspects of things. And it follows still further that if truth is beauty, then falsehood is ugliness; and wherever there exist things that are repulsive and disgusting, it is because of some outrage on truth, or some fundamental error which an exacter conception of truth would have prevented.

It needs no great wit to see that such a conclusion as this involves every species of social and moral question. Let it be applied in the direction of art itself, and we perceive at once that where we have a weakly sensational or a morally degraded art—where we have even less than this, an art which is not indeed a moral offence, but is artificial and mechanical, destitute of high imagination and feeling, wrong in its ideals and misguided in its methods—it is simply because of a fault or deficiency in the artist. What is that fault? It is lack of truth and nobleness of moral temper. The greatest artists have not always been good or religious men, but they have been noble-minded men. Their more perfect vision of beauty is the natural result of their profounder love of truth. The lower school of Dutch art is denounced by Ruskin on this very ground; it lacks beauty entirely because the artists lacked the fine sense of truth. They can paint the coarse revels of the tavern with a certain gross realism, but if they had been less of tavern roysterers themselves, they would have had higher visions of truth, and so would have painted things that were beautiful instead of things that are repulsive. It was because they had no thoughts that gave them any noble pleasure, that they relied on sensation rather than imagination for the materials of their art. On the other hand, the great Italian masters were men of a noble moral temper; they saw the higher aspects of truth, and for that reason they also reached a peculiarly noble ideal of beauty. Bad art therefore means either a bad age or an ignobly-minded artist; or it may mean both—an age that is itself too gross to attain any high vision of truth, or to desire it, and an artist who is the product of his age, and acts in conformity with it.

Under one of Fra Angelico's pictures is inscribed the sentence, *Painted at rest, praying.* Those who look at the picture are scarcely in need of such an explanation. There is an infinite peace and spiritual fervour in the picture; it seems to have captured in its rich colour a radiance that is not of this world, and it is the expression not merely of the great technical qualities of the artist, but also of the devoutness of his soul, and the virile purity and reach of his imagination. And this is not an inapt illustration of the truth that Ruskin enforces continually in his art-teaching. To produce a great picture, it is necessary not merely for the artist to prepare his canvas, but to prepare himself. If a picture is not great, it is because the artist lacks moral and spiritual fibre; and no knowledge of technique, or laborious dexterity of hand, can cover this deficiency. Beauty of a mechanical or tumultuous kind there may be, but never the highest form of beauty without the noblest passion for truth.

Let this principle be applied to the general aspects of national life, and it is equally penetrative and infallible. Let it be assumed that English cities of the manufacturing type are squalid and repulsive; that they have no fine order or regulated beauty of arrangement; that they have no noble public buildings; or, if they have them, they are hidden away behind grimy ranges of mean tenements, so that their total effect cannot be realised or discovered; and it will be found that this outward ugliness is the natural witness to a general contempt of truth. It is generally assumed that Ruskin's violently expressed censure of the ignoble grime of manufacturing towns springs from a violent hatred of manufacture. On the contrary, he himself has established manufactures, and praises with Carlyle the great 'captains of industry.' But what he says is, that there is no natural association between manufacture and ugliness, and there need be none.

If there be a notorious violation of beauty, it is because there has been a notorious contempt for truth. What truth? The truth that man lives not by bread alone ; that the soul has claims as well as the stomach ; that to make money is in itself the ignoblest of pursuits, and that where money is made by the sacrifice of men, it is more wicked than war, because more deliberately cruel. If there had been any due and real sense of the claims of the soul, as infinitely superior to the claims of the stomach, England would not have permitted her manufactures to thrive by the destruction of all that refines and ennobles those by whose toil this enormous wealth is created. If English cities are ugly, if there is not one of them, nor all together, capable of giving so much delight to the eye as the meanest mediæval Italian town could furnish, it is because we have been too absorbed in the ignoble haste to be rich to care for anything but the condition of our bank-books. It is not manufactures that are wrong, but the spirit in which they are conducted. Those who administer them have notoriously departed from truth in the essential methods of their administration. They have not sought to provide an honest article for an honest wage. They have had no pride in their work, but only a base pleasure in its rewards. They have not asked, 'Is this thing that I have made as sound and efficient a thing as it is possible for me to produce?' but 'Have I produced something that will pay, and something calculated cunningly to deceive the eye, so that I may obtain a larger payment for it than I have justly earned or have any right to expect?' No wonder manufacturing towns are ugly and squalid when they are governed and created by men of this spirit ; how could you reasonably expect them to be beautiful? There has been a contempt for truth, and there is a corresponding contempt for beauty. Before England can be a land of beautiful cities, it must be renewed in its ideals, and must regain that reverence for truth which it has lost.

The only final strength is rightness, says Ruskin ; and excellence, whether of art or of character, can only be achieved by an unswerving fidelity to right. A contempt of beauty means more than a lack of æsthetic taste in a man's nature : it means necessarily a contempt of right, since beauty is the concrete final expression of rightness. Venice rose from the sea in stern yet exquisite grandeur of form, because the race that laid its stones deep in the shallow waters of the lagoons were for centuries a great and noble race, disciplined into strenuous hardihood by the nature of their perilous position, virtuous by their passion for liberty, great in soul by their reverence for truth. The period of their decline is marked in the corruption of their architecture, and the dream of beauty lessens as the people wax debased. It is useless, says Ruskin, to ask for men like Tintoret or churches like St. Mark's in a day when manufacture prospers by jugglery, and trade is an organised deceit ; we ask for the blossom on the tree, forgetting that its stem is cut, and its root withered. You will get sound workmanship in no department of life, when honesty and truth have ceased to command respect ; and since beauty is rightness, you will not get beauty either. The jerry-builder is simply the natural and inevitable product of an avaricious and corrupt age. He is the parasite of a decaying civilisation, at once springing from the decay and propagating it. Had Venice been built by men whose one passion was money, and whose one evil gift was a minute and absolute mastery of the art of cheating, we should have had a stucco St. Mark's, which long ago had sunk unregretted in the tides from which it rose. An unstable people does not build stable and enduring works, but after its kind unstable erections, only meant to last as long as money can be made by them. The age of cathedral building was naturally the age when belief in God was an intelligible factor in human conduct, and when the imaginations of men were fed by solemn and eternal visions of truth. But when *we* build churches we build them by contract, accepting the lowest tender, and we are utterly indifferent to the quality of the work, so long as we get something showy for our money. All the bad building that goes on in our civic centres is therefore, like the bad art of our time, simply the outward witness to an inward corruption of the conscience. There is only one remedy, says Ruskin : ' No religion that ever was preached on this earth of God's rounding, will proclaim any salvation to sellers of bad goods. If the Ghost that is in you, whatever the essence of it, leaves your hand a juggler's and your heart a cheat's, it is not a Holy Ghost, be assured of that. And for the rest, all political economy, as well as all higher virtue, depends first on sound work.'

To obtain, therefore, fine art or noble architecture, according to the gospel of Ruskin, means an entire reorganisation of commerce, and a renewal of the whole nation in righteousness. And this means a renewal in honesty, a word whose meaning is almost

lost in the dim-sightedness bred of universal chicanery
and fraud. Thus, by what is after all no feat of
intellectual acrobatics, but a calmly reasoned and
intelligent process, Ruskin passes from the considera-
tion of the ethics of art and architecture to the
creation of a new and radical political economy.

What, then, is the chief burden of Ruskin's ethical
and social teaching? He lays down, first of all, the
absolute duty of work, and of work which, as far as
possible, absorbs the full interest, and excites the inven-
tive faculty of the worker. The great evil of modern
civilisation is 'not that men are ill fed, but that they
have no pleasure in the work by which they make
their bread, and therefore look to wealth as the only
means of pleasure.' Now the workmen who built
St. Mark's, or any great English cathedral, were,
beyond doubt, far worse fed than our modern workmen ; but their work was a pleasure to them, because
they put into it such intelligence of soul as they
possessed, and therefore it is good and stable work.
The general thirst for wealth really means, therefore,
a distaste for honest labour, and the resolve to escape
labour by the readiest means in our power. But
why has the workman no pleasure in his work ?
Partly because we have destroyed the possibility of
pleasure by what we call 'division of labour, and
so rendered the exercise of thought and intelligence
unnecessary. 'It is not, truly speaking, the labour
which is divided, but the men : divided into mere
segments of men—broken into small fragments and
crumbs of life ; so that all the little piece of intelligence that is left in a man is not enough to make a
pin or a nail, but exhausts itself in making the point
of a pin or the head of a nail.' This is really the

ground of Ruskin's antagonism to machine-made goods, and his strong preference for goods made by hand; the latter are the product of intelligence, and work that has pleasure in its act, and the former are not; the one work develops men, the other divides and enslaves them.

He then gives his standard of wages in three principles, which to all men of just and honourable minds will appear self-evident and imperative. First, men should be paid for the actual work done; secondly, 'a man should in justice be paid for difficult or dangerous work proportionately more than for easy and safe work, supposing the other conditions of the work similar:' thirdly, 'if a man does a given quantity of work for me, I am bound in justice to do, or procure to be done, a precisely equal quantity of work for him; and just trade in labour is the exchange of equivalent quantities of labour of different kinds.' Thus the employer of labour is himself a labourer, giving, in exchange for work done for him, another kind of work done for those who serve under him. The factory worker is not 'a hand,' but a man, and it is the bounden duty of his employer to see that he has a fair share of food, and warmth and comfort, and a reasonable opportunity of attending to the wants of his mind, and the culture of his soul. His claim is not, and never can be, settled adequately by any award of money; his employer is also responsible for the nature of his life. If the individual employer is too callous or indifferent to attend to these responsibilities, then it is the business of the State to step in, and force upon the avaricious and foolish master the instant attendance to his duties. Indeed, in almost all that concerns trade, Ruskin advocates what we understand as State-Socialism. He would have either the trade-guild or the State fix a standard of excellence for all manufactured articles. The public would soon discover that it was all the better off by buying a sound article, and the craze for mere cheapness would die with the discovery that the cheap thing is, in the long-run, the dearest, being worthless at any price. Moreover, such a wise interference by the State, if all States would unite in its enforcement, would, in the end, kill the demon of competition, which is the curse of commerce. 'The primal and eternal law of vital commerce shall be of all men understood; namely, that every nation is fitted by its character, and the nature of its territories, for some particular employments or manufactures; and that it is the true interest of every other nation to encourage it in such speciality, and by no means to interfere with, but in all ways forward and protect its efforts, ceasing all rivalship with it, so soon as it is strong enough to occupy its proper place.' The one necessary principle for all honourable and efficient trade is thus seen to be co-operation. First of all, between the employers and the employed, each honestly working to serve the public by the production of the best possible article; and then between nations, each separate people producing what it can produce best, for the general international good.

It will, of course, be said, that under such a system as this no large fortunes could be made; but equally it is true that nine-tenths of our want and misery would disappear, the other tenth being that caused by vice and improvidence, which no State can remove, so long as man has the right to ruin himself. The question is, how are large fortunes made, and by what methods, under the existing system? Ruskin replies that such fortunes as are the prizes of commerce can only be made in one of three ways: (1) By obtaining command over the labour of multitudes of other men, and taxing it for our own profit. (2) By treasure-trove, as of mines, useful vegetable products, and the like—in circumstances putting them under our own exclusive control. (3) By speculation (commercial gambling). Ruskin categories these three methods under the scathing title of 'The nature of theft by unjust profits,' and, after explaining by what means such dishonest acquisition is accomplished, asks us to 'consider further, how many of the carriages that glitter in our streets are driven, and how many of the stately houses that gleam among our English fields are inhabited, by this kind of thief!' His remedy for the first kind of theft is, as we have seen, a just system of co-operation; and while no remedy is stated for the second, yet the plain suggestion is the nationalisation of mines and mineral treasure generally, as the property of the State, to be administered for the good of all. Of the third form of theft his words are unmistakably stern and incisive; 'for in all cases of profit derived from speculation, at best, what one man gains another loses; and the net result to the State is zero (pecuniarily), with the loss of time and ingenuity spent in the transaction; beside the disadvantage involved in the discouragement of the losing party, and the corrupted moral natures of both.'

And, beyond all this, Ruskin teaches that great fortunes are rarely a blessing to their possessors, and the truly fortunate man is he whose wealth is in the limitation of his lower desires, and the extension of his higher aspirations. The gospel of plain living and high thinking is after all a possible gospel, within the reach of all. The love of money is the root of all the evil in our modern life. It is right that work should be honestly remunerated; but if we love the fee more than the work, then fee is our master, 'and the lord of fee, who is the devil.' The true advancement of men must begin in the heart and conscience, and it is because England has grown in wealth, but not in character, that we have side by side the prodigality of the rich and the want of the poor; and, having regard to the first alone, persuade ourselves that we live in an era of unexampled prosperity, and are blind to the realities of un-exampled corruption and materialism. We have yet to learn the art of wise and noble living; and 'what is chiefly needed in England at the present day is to show the quantity of pleasure that may be obtained by a consistent, well-administered com-petence, modest, confessed, and laborious. We need examples of people who, leaving Heaven to decide whether they are to rise in the world, decide for themselves whether they will be happy in it, and have resolved to seek, not greater wealth, but simpler pleasure; not higher fortune, but deeper felicity; making the first of possessions self-possession; and honouring themselves in the harmless pride and calm pursuits of peace.' These are truly prophetic words, and contain, not only the counsel of a great thinker, but of a true patriot.

CHAPTER XIX

RUSKIN'S IDEAL OF WOMEN

No summary of Ruskin's teaching would be complete without reference to the more poetical side of his genius; and since it is necessary to quote some concrete example, we can scarcely find a better than that section of his writings which deals specifically with the place assigned to woman in his new Utopia. For him, as for all really great writers and thinkers, woman has held a high place, and been a commanding influence. But one can no more describe in a sentence what is Ruskin's ideal woman, than what is his ideal of art, for in all his writing he is as we have seen, alternately reactionary and progressive, and at all times a mystic, whose perceptions are coloured by a singularly grave and noble imagination. That he would not accept all the theories of female emancipation which are current to-day is clear from the most casual acquaintance with his drift of thought, and in this he may be deemed reactionary. But the reaction on its rebound really becomes a very large measure of progression. He goes back to the more ancient ideals of womanly modesty, humility, and service, only to link them afresh to all that is highest in the aims of modern life. And nowhere is his mysticism—the mysticism of the lover and the thinker, reverent and sweet and beautiful — more pronounced than in his treatment of woman. In Ruskin himself there is a certain feminine element that perhaps enables him to judge woman with a finer delicacy and more accurate eye than belong to most men; certainly with a graver sympathy and more chivalrous regard.

Every one who has read the lecture on 'Queen's Gardens' in *Sesame and the Lilies* will remember the series of fine passages in which Ruskin points out how reverence for womanhood has been the master-note in the rich music of the greatest poets. We cannot do better than recall these passages if we would understand his own ideal of womanhood. Broadly speaking, he says, Shakespeare has no heroes—he has only heroines. The one entirely heroic figure in the plays—and this is after all but a slight sketch—is Henry the Fifth. And then he continues: 'Coriolanus, Cæsar, Antony, stand in flawed strength, and fall by their vanities; Hamlet is indolent and drowsily speculative; Romeo an impatient boy; the Merchant of Venice languidly submissive to adverse fortune; Kent, in *King Lear*, is entirely noble at heart, but too rough and unpolished to be of true use at the critical time, and he sinks into the office of a servant only. . . . Whereas there is hardly a play that has not a perfect woman in it, steadfast in grave hope and errorless purpose; Cordelia, Desdemona, Isabella, Hermione, Imogen, Queen Catherine, Perdita, Sylvia, Viola, Rosalind, Helena, and last, and perhaps loveliest, Virgilia, are all faultless, conceived in the highest heroic type of humanity.' Of course, the mind will also recall the dread figure of Lady Macbeth, and the revolting hard-heartedness of Regan and Goneril;

R

but these, says Mr. Ruskin, were clearly meant by Shakespeare to be frightful exceptions to the ordinary aspects of life.   And as it was with Shakespeare, so it was with Walter Scott, with Dante, with the great Greeks, and with our own Chaucer and Spenser. Wherever woman is pictured, it is in the bright strength of her truth and purity, her constancy and virtue.   Chaucer writes his *Legend of Good Women*, and Spenser makes it clear to us how easily the best of his faery knights may be deceived and vanquished; 'but the soul of Una is never darkened, and the spear of Britomart is never broken.'   This view of woman is one which Mr. Ruskin indorses and amplifies.   He believes in the old Teutonic reverence for women as the prophets of society, 'as infallibly faithful and wise counsellors, incorruptibly just and pure examples—strong always to sanctify even where they cannot save'; and he shows with completeness of illustration that the greatest men have believed in this ideal of womanhood, and that this belief has shaped and coloured all that is noblest in the poetic literature of the world.

Starting from this noble ideal of what woman may be, Ruskin works out the details of his picture with great art and fidelity.   He will hear of no 'superiority' between the sexes, of no obedience demanded by the one as the prerogative of sex, or rendered by the other as its condition.   Woman was certainly not meant to be the attendant shadow of her lord, serving him with a thoughtless and servile obedience ; for how could he be 'helped effectually by a shadow, or worthily by a slave'?   And as for 'superiority,' in what does superiority lie?   For any true comparison there must be similarity, whereas between man and woman there is eternal dissimilarity. They can be neither equal nor unequal who have wholly different gifts, and are intrusted with widely various functions. 'Each has what the other has not; each completes the other, and is completed by the other; they are in nothing alike, and the happiness and perfection of both depends on each asking and receiving from the other what the other only can give.' Yet however radical are the differences, simply because each is the complement of the other, their cause is one, and the mission and rights of women cannot be separated from the mission and rights of men. This is simply a prose statement of the philosophy which Tennyson has interpreted in memorable verse when he says:

> For woman is not undevelopt man,
> But diverse : could we make her as the man,
> Sweet love were slain ; his bond is this,
> Not like to like, but like in difference.
>
> .   .   .   .   .   .
>
> The woman's cause is man's ; they rise or sink
> Together, dwarfed or godlike, bond or free.

To the more ardent and inconsiderate spirits in the modern revolt of woman, all this may seem somewhat antiquated philosophy nowadays. Those who are loudest in proclaiming the advance of women sometimes talk as if they would be content with no advance that did not submerge man, or which at least surrendered the claim of absolute equality to woman. And such women will probably resent the stress which Ruskin lays upon man's fitness for the world, and woman's fitness for the houschold. They will not care to admit that 'man's power is active, progressive, defensive. He is eminently the doer, the creator, the discoverer, the defender. His intellect is for speculation and invention ; his energy for adventure, for war, for conquest, wherever war is just, wherever conquest necessary. But the woman's power is for rule, not for battle ; and her intellect is not for invention or creation, but for sweet ordering, arrangement, decision.' Yet it may be well even for the most advanced woman to ask whether Tennyson and Ruskin have not the truth with them, and whether she would not lose far more than she could gain by scornfully rejecting the programme each assigns her. For it is in the domain of the emotions that Ruskin makes woman supreme. The man, in his conflict with the world, is sure to be hardened ; but it is his business to guard the woman against this hardening of the heart, and her work is to soften and purify the man by the strength of her emotions and the joy of her affection. The hardening of the heart is a doleful and disastrous process, which we see going on around us every day, and perhaps also perceive within us. We accept the responsibility for training the mind, but we do not think it necessary to train and educate the emotions. More than this, we English people are for the most part ashamed of our emotions, and take a pride in repressing them, so that equally in Europe and America we are regarded as the coldest and most phlegmatic of races. It is, no doubt, not well to wear the heart upon the sleeve, but it is still worse to repress the emotions until they become sterile, and the very power of feeling dies in us. For the Englishman, the home is the one secure asylum where he permits his heart to beat freely, and for that reason we, more than most peoples, should reverence women as the queens of the heart, whose work it is to liberate in the home the emotions that have been repressed in the world. Home is the place of peace, the sanctuary of the heart, the realm wherein the emotions may find free air and unimpeded action ; it is, as Ruskin nobly says, roof and fire, shelter and warmth, shade and light— 'Shade as of the rock in a weary land, and light as of the Pharos in the stormy sea.' And in such a home it is the part of woman to be 'enduringly, incorruptibly good ; instinctively, infallibly wise— wise, not for self-development, but for self-renunci- ation ; wise, not that she may set herself above her husband, but that she may never fail from his side ; wise, not with the narrowness of insolent and love- less pride, but with the passionate gentleness of an infinitely variable, because infinitely applicable, modesty of service — the true changefulness of woman.'

'Wise, not for self-development, but for self- renunciation,' this again will sound like a note of reaction, and will be distasteful to many noble souls who toil heroically for the advance of woman. Yet the whole evil is in the sound—there is no error in the sentiment. If morality is more than culture, if to be is better than to know, if character is a more precious gain than even knowledge, then it is clear that self-renunciation, by which the flower of the soul is brought to fulness, is a nobler gain than self- development, by which the mind is trained to alert activity and the body to athletic vigour. But what Ruskin means by self-development is the develop- ment of selfishness, just as by self-renunciation he

means the subdual of self, and its suppression.
Certainly he does not mean that the weapons of
intellectual growth or physical culture are to be
denied to women. On the contrary, he declares that
the first duty of society to women is 'to secure for
her such physical training and exercise as may con-
firm her health and perfect her beauty,' and again,
that 'all such knowledge should be given her as may
enable her to understand, and even to aid, the work
of man.' In this latter respect Ruskin may be
claimed as one of the pioneers of the higher education of women. In 1864, when these words were
uttered, there were not many men who ventured
to claim a perfect equality of education for men
and women ; but this Ruskin does with passionate
pleading, nor is there any passage of satire in his
writings more telling than that in which he contrasts
the education afforded to a boy with that thought
sufficient for a girl. He says that at least you show
some respect for the tutor of your son, and you teach
your son to respect him. You do not treat the
Dean of Christ Church or the Master of Trinity as
your inferiors. But you intrust the entire formation
of a girl's 'character, moral and intellectual, to a
person whom you let your servants treat with less
respect than they do your housekeeper (as if the
soul of your child were a less charge than jam and
groceries), and whom you yourself think you confer
an honour upon by letting her sometimes sit in
the drawing-room in the evening.' Mr. Ruskin's
ideal woman is clearly no creature of unfurnished
mind, meek with the meekness of ignorance, sub-
servient with the humility of self-distrust; she is
the highest product of both physical and mental

culture, and is fitted to sit with man in equal comradeship—

> Full-summed in all their powers,
> Dispensing harvest, sowing the To-Be.

Ruskin's ideal of woman includes, therefore, a
very full trust in those moral instincts which he
regards as her highest gift, and in the unimpeded
exercise of which he discerns her noblest power.
He claims for her the largest liberty, because she is
far less likely than man to abuse her liberty. He
goes so far as to declare that nature in her is to be
trusted far more than in men to do its own work,
and to do it beautifully and beneficently. The boy
may be chiselled into shape, but the girl must take
her own way, and will grow as a flower grows. The
boy needs discipline before he will learn what is good
for him ; but the girl, if she trust her instincts, will
be infallibly guided to what is good around her without any, save the slightest, pressure from extraneous
authority. Thus Mr. Ruskin advocates in a well-
known passage the wisdom of letting a girl pretty
much alone in the choice of her reading, so long
as the mere ephemeral 'package of the circulating
library, wet with the last and lightest spray of the
fountain of folly,' is kept out of her way. 'Turn her
loose into the old library,' he says, 'and let her alone.
She will find what is good for her, and you cannot.
. . . Let her loose in the library, I say, as you do a
fawn in a field. It knows the bad weeds twenty
times better than you, and the good ones too, and
will eat some bitter and prickly ones, good for it,
which you had not the slightest thought were good.'
This is an heroic form of education, indeed, but in
Ruskin's view it is the best form, simply because

he has unbounded faith in the wise intuition and invincible purity of true womanhood. He believes with George Meredith that woman lies nearer to the heart of Nature than man, and is a creature of altogether surer and wiser instinct. There is a sweet, old-fashioned chivalry in this doctrine, of which we hear little to-day. It is characteristic of the man. Simple himself as a child, pure and sweet-natured as a child, he feels something of that reverent worship for woman which was the soul of ancient chivalry ; and no woman can read his writings without a fresh and happy sense of her own endowments, and a new and high ideal of how these can be best applied for the service of the world.

We are all hot for emancipation to-day. Ruskin bids us inquire what such emancipation really means. He reminds us that womanhood may be emancipated in so rough and wrong a fashion that the bloom of virgin grace may be wasted in the process, and the true charm of womanhood may perish. An emancipation which corrupts the delicacy of the soul, or dulls the sensitiveness of the emotions, is a fatal error, for which no gain of worldly shrewdness or mental acumen can be any just or appreciable recompense. It is in her power of sympathy, of kindness, of all fine and tender feeling, that woman's true strength lies, and any diminution here is not only to her a fatal detriment, but it is a boundless loss inflicted on society. To learn to feel, or to keep in unspent freshness the power to feel, is for woman of far greater moment than to learn to know, or to learn to achieve some poor battle in the clamorous strifes of a callous world. There is a higher thing than to speak with tongues, or to know all mysteries, and that is to love with the love that thinketh no evil, that rejoiceth in the truth, that beareth all things, believeth all things, hopeth all things, endureth all things. This is the essence of Ruskin's ideal womanhood. Nothing that ought to be shared with man will he deny her, but he insists that there are many things she need not wish to share, because she is the mistress of a larger wealth which is hidden in her own soul. To know how to love truly, to feed the sacred flame of love which is the glory of the world, to soften the asperities of life with her charity, and to brighten its joys by her diviner force of feeling, this is the true programme of true womanhood, and there is no noble-natured woman who will not grant that it is a high and noble ideal.

CHAPTER XX

JOHN RUSKIN : CHARACTERISTICS

So far I have endeavoured to furnish rather an indication to Ruskin's system of thought than an analysis of it, because no analysis is worth much that is not complete, and a complete analysis needs not a chapter or a paper, but a book. It is to be hoped that some day an industrious student will prepare a Ruskin Primer, in which his intricate and elaborate teaching may be set forth with clearness, order, and precision. I do not for a moment mean to suggest that there is any essential lack of either order or precision, for no writer of English has ever expressed himself with more lucidity. But he is the frankest and most versatile of writers, and his teachings need collection and collation, because they are spread over too vast an area for the ordinary reader to traverse. The truth possesses him ; he does not possess the truth ; and it often happens, as we have seen, that when we least expect it, he turns with the nimbleness of genius from the subject in hand to one that seems only remotely related to it, and plunges without warning from pure art-criticism into social science. And because he is the frankest of men, he has never taken the trouble to reconcile his teachings, and systematise them. He has even defended his contradictions on the ground that no teacher who is himself growing in a knowledge of truth can fail to contradict himself, since such contradictions are the essential conditions of growth. The sterile mind never contradicts itself, because it has become petrified ; but the living mind, which is vehement in its pursuit of truth, will inevitably discover that what seemed truth in youth is but half-truth or even falsehood in age, and that as larger horizons open, a perpetual readjustment of vision is needed. Thus, of the religious truths which he learned in childhood, he has said : ' Whatever I know or feel now of the justice of God, the nobleness of man, or the beauty of nature, I knew and felt then, nor less strongly ; but these firm faiths were confused by the continual discovery, day by day, of error or limitations in the doctrines I had been taught, and follies or inconsistencies in their teachers.'

To the sympathetic student of Ruskin, this perfect candour is not the least part of his charm. There is something of the sweetness and frankness of the child in his temper—the inspired child, who announces not opinions but certainties, with the untroubled positiveness of one who sees only one necessary truth at a time, and utters it with a total disregard of conventions. And yet this positiveness is not offensive, but persuasive, because it is united with the most gracious humility of spirit. Ruskin has never hesitated to confess himself wrong or mistaken, and has made ungrudging amends for any unintended injustice of criticism. The later editions of *Modern Painters* contain many generous modifications of early judgment, which he has since discovered to be erroneous. To a lady who once told him that she had discovered in ten minutes what he meant by the supremacy of Boticelli, he made the scathing reply: 'In ten minutes, did you say? I took twenty years to discover it.' Thoroughness is the very essence of his method, as frankness is of his temper. No writer of our day has been more entirely loyal to facts. But simply because his mind has never ceased to grow, because he has never put away from him the docile temper of the learner, his writings reflect the variations and vital changes of his growth, and by so much lose effect as scientific treatises, and have the rarer charm of personal confessions.

Opinions will no doubt differ as to the value of Ruskin's contribution to the fund of human thought; there can scarcely be a question as to his supremacy as a great writer.

The great writers, who command not a transient fame but age-long reverence, have usually proved their greatness in one or more of three ways—their writings are personal confessions, that is, they are the intimate and enduring records of the individual soul; they possess the secret of style, by which we mean they are written in such a form that they illustrate, in a supreme degree, the art and mastery of language; or they express moral truths of eternal value and infinite moment. In what degree does Ruskin fulfil these conditions?

In the first place, there is no modern writer of English who has more clearly reflected the movements and intentions of his own soul in his writings. We know, without any formal biography, what manner of man he is. We are able to mark every pulsation of his thought, as we watch the wind-ripple or the cloud-shadow on a clear lake. He leaves us in no doubt as to the processes of his intellectual life. We see his childhood, nurtured in loyal love of truth and honour, stimulated in a sense of beauty by familiarity with nature, and in a sense of literature by systematic absorption of the English Bible; a childhood sheltered, yet not secluded; sedulously fostered, yet not pushed forward into unwise precocity; thoughtful and calm, yet in no wise lacking the innocent carelessness and joyous interests of childhood. We see his youth and early manhood with equal clearness of vision, and mark the growth of his mind in his mingled reverence and antagonism for Aristotle, his fruitful study of Locke and Hooker, and his abiding discipleship of Plato. And from the moment that he takes pen in hand, all his sensations, opinions, prejudices, aspirations, and ideals find the sincerest record. He conceals nothing, because he is too generously frank to learn or covet the art of concealment. He uses words, not to conceal thought, but to express it. He takes the world into his complete confidence, without the reticence that springs from self-love, or the timidity that springs from self-distrust. There is not a page which he has written that is not alive with personal feeling, and is not in this respect a frank confession of the interests and purposes of a living soul. There are very few writers, indeed, who have dared so much. The great majority of books leave on the mind no impression whatever of the personality of the author. But wherever a writer does make his book a human document, a truthful and sincere delineation of a soul in its quest of truth, a mind in its search for knowledge, a life in its painful adjustment to the facts and problems of the world, we have a book that lives, and which conquers time. There is no theme that so deeply interests man—as man. Ruskin creates this keen interest in himself, as distinct from the natural interest in his teaching. In the art of personal revelation—that rare art which has given immortality to the writing of Montaigne, and Goethe, and Rousseau—Ruskin stands among the first of moderns.

For whatever reasons, then, Ruskin may be studied in the future, it is at least certain that the personal element in his writings will exercise a permanent charm upon the minds of all who brood over 'the abysmal deeps of personality,' and are fascinated in tracing the curious elements and accidents by which the strange structure of individuality is built up. We have learned in these later days, more completely than in any other, that to perfectly understand the writings of a man it is necessary that we should know all we can about the man himself, and hence the enormous growth of biography. We know that all great writing has its origin in personal feeling and experience, and that which moves us most, does so because it is the passionate voice of an emotion which long since shook the heart or shaped the life of the writer. We read our Burns and Byron, our Shelley and Wordsworth, with a constant recollection of each poet's life and history ; but the knowledge of that history is not derived from any formal biography, so much as from the vital and unconscious record which is embalmed in the writings themselves. It is this personal element that maintains in undiminished freshness and vitality of charm writings such as these ; and while men use many books for their knowledge, and praise many books for their wisdom, they love only those books which speak to the soul, because they have been spoken from the soul. And the writing of Ruskin belongs to this rare order.

Throughout the many hundreds of pages that he has written, there is scarcely one that has not the strong vibration of personal feeling in it, or that fails to communicate that glow of feeling to the reader. His writings are the confessions of a soul in search of truth, and the revelations of a life and character laboriously built up in fidelity to the highest truth that was revealed.

In regard to the second element of great writing—the element of style—it is almost unnecessary to say a word. It was by the charm of his style that Ruskin first captivated the world, and that charm has grown with the growth of his work. It owes something to Locke and Hooker, and still more to Dr. Johnson; but in its flexibility, vivacity, and eloquent grace, it is peculiarly his own, and is surpassed by no dead or living writer of the English language. Its fault is grandiloquence; its virtue is majesty. The long diapason of its antitheses occasionally falls upon the ear with an artificial effect, but even then the ear is not wearied. It is perhaps useless to attempt the definition of style, but a fine style has at least three qualities, without which it cannot be fine; viz., individuality, truth, and beauty. It must be individual, or else it is no style at all, but merely so much writing, unnoticeable in the great mass of printed matter with which the world is littered. It must have truth, by which we mean that it must use language with a precise appreciation of its niceties of meaning; selecting the plain word if it be the fit word, but never the sonorous word for the mere sake of its sound, if it be the unfit; seeking always to express thought in the clearest and exactest manner by employing those words which most entirely convey the meaning of the writer. And finally, it must have beauty, by which we mean that in a fine style there will be an exquisite and intimate knowledge of the subtle modulations of language, so that the sense of beauty is satisfied as well as the sense of truth, and the truth is expressed in the noblest form, and is, as it were, clothed in radiance and music.

There are writers who have one or more of the qualities, but not all; truth but not beauty, beauty but not individuality, individuality but not truth; and by so much they fail to reach the secret of style. A writer of strong individuality will often express himself with truth, but not with beauty; and a writer who has no particular message and no depth of soul, will often attain to such beauty as comes from a sonorous or suggestive use of language, and yet fail to affect us because he is deficient in truth. But to attain a fine style all three of these gifts are needed; and where such a style is reached, a writer passes beyond transient notoriety into the calmer realms of immortal renown. It is therefore no empty compliment to speak of a writer as possessing a great style; it is really equivalent to saying he is a great man, for there is essential truth in the axiom that the style is the man.

That Ruskin fulfils these canons of style more completely than any other writer of our time will be evident to any one who is acquainted with his writings. On the personal element in his work, which is the source of all individuality of style, I have already touched; but it is equally clear that he possesses in an unexampled degree the qualities of truth and beauty. He often becomes almost philological in the minute patience with which he

will take a word, and explain its growth, and
extricate its secrecies and shades of meaning, before
he will use it. No professor or diplomatist could
take more exhaustive care to convey his exact
meaning by the use of words in their exactest sense.
And as regards the sense of beauty, the art of producing fine and modulated music from the various
combinations of language, Ruskin has no peer. But
it is not the charm of beauty only, it is the charm of
truth. Amid all this pomp of language, all this radiance of imagination, and these poignant thrillings of a
sad or noble emotion, there is not one word that does
not perform its duty, and is not the one word perfectly
fitted to produce the effect and express the thought
which the writer would convey to us. In his later
writings Ruskin is much more direct and unadorned
in style, and he has said of his youthful writings
with humorous scorn, ' People used to call me a good
writer then; now they say I cannot write at all,
because, for instance, if I think anybody's house is
on fire, I only say, " Sir, your house is on fire." '
But in his latest, as in his earliest writings, there is
the same charm of style; now direct, pungent, and
simple, now passing without effort into passages of
sustained and sonorous splendour; but always satisfy-
ing the sense of beauty by ' linked sweetness long
drawn out,' and the sense of truth by the precision of
its effects; and, last of all, the soul by the force of
its spiritual fervour and moral earnestness; certainly
one of the noblest styles ever reached, one of the
most varied, and the least capable of imitation.

But it is, after all, in the noblest element of the
great writer—the power of expressing moral truths
—that Ruskin is greatest, and his work is most

S

worthy of renown. No teacher of our generation has uttered truths more pregnant, or has set a higher ideal of life before his countrymen. His own conception and use of life have been noble, and he strikes the keynote of all his teaching when he says, 'Life is real—not evanescent or slight. It does not vanish away; every noble life leaves the fibre of it, for ever, in the work of the world; by so much, evermore, the strength of the human race has gained.' The hope for which he has lived is verily the hope of the kingdom of God—a kingdom visible on the earth in just government and true order, in honest trade and honoured labour, in simplicity of life and fidelity to truth; and thus a kingdom which, having virtue for its foundation, may justly anticipate happiness for its goal. What he has made battle against from youth to age is materialism—materialism in art, in government, in methods of commerce and pro-grammes of life. He has never spent his genius upon an unworthy cause; and while he has not always been able to think hopefully of the world, he has never ceased to preach righteousness in courage-ous scorn of consequence. It would be too much to claim that he has made no mistakes, or that all his views are sound and reasonable; but it may at least be claimed that no teacher has ever more frankly admitted an error when it has been proved an error; and that whether his counsel be reasonable or not, it is always the fruit of a lofty view of life, the only real cause of its impracticability being, as a rule, in the reluctance of the average man to be loyal to self-evident truth and inward conviction. His influence upon the best minds of his generation has been very great; and of this we cannot have a surer witness than the saying of George Eliot, ' I venerate Ruskin as one of the greatest teachers of the age ; ' and the advice of Carlyle to Emerson, ' Do you read Ruskin's *Fors Clavigera?* If you don't, do : I advise you. Also, whatever else he is now writing. There is nothing going on among us so notable to me.' Much of the social movement of our day is the direct fruit of his teaching, while it is the testimony of Sir John Lubbock that he has done far more for science than Goethe, because without making any pretence to profound scientific knowledge, he has used an extraordinary faculty of observation in such a way as to teach people what to observe, and in what spirit to accept the facts of nature without missing the poetry of nature. But all these claims are insignificant beside his supreme claim as a great religious teacher. Religion is, after all, the keynote and inspiration of all his work, and his final message may be stated in his own words : ' All the world is but as one orphanage, so long as its children know not God their Father ; and all wisdom and knowledge is only more bewildered darkness, so long as you have not taught them the fear of the Lord.' It is this religious passion that drew from George Eliot, and commands from us, the testimony, ' He teaches with the inspiration of a Hebrew prophet.'

CHAPTER XXI

JOHN HENRY NEWMAN

[Born in London, 21st February, 1801. Elected Fellow of Oriel College, 1822. First book, *The Arians of the Fourth Century*, published 1833. Published *Tract XC.* in 1841. Resigned the Vicarage of St. Mary's, Oxford, 1843. Received into the Roman Church October 9th 1845. Published *Loss and Gain*, 1848; *Sermons to Mixed Congregations*, 1849; *Callista*, 1855. Wrote *The Dream of Gerontius*, 1865; *Apologia Vitâ Suâ*, 1864-5; *The Grammar of Assent*, 1870. Created Cardinal, May 1879. Died, August 11th, 1890.]

THE life of Newman possesses all the fascination of the enigma. He dominates us by force of a lonely and inscrutable individuality. He is by turns a child and a casuist, a poet and a philosopher; at once simple and profound, direct and subtle. Whatever he thinks or does, and however much we dislike his conclusions or his actions, yet he compels our interest, our deep and unflagging interest. What greater proof can we have of the elemental charm of the man, than that those who hated his ecclesiastical views could rarely bring themselves to speak harshly of him, and that dire as was the blow which he struck at Protestantism, yet all intelligent Protestants regard him with affection? The only other great author one can name as possessing in so high a degree this gift of elemental charm is Shelley. When the worst that can be said has been said about Shelley's errors,

276

still there remains in us a profound love of the man ; he also fascinates us by the compulsion of a lonely and inscrutable individuality.

The parallel might be pushed further. Leopardi, in an admirable phrase, has described Shelley as 'a Titan in a virgin's form.' A certain virginal freshness, the very dew of childhood, never left the nature of Shelley ; yet he was a world-force in the strength of his intellect. The most alluring element in Newman is the same virginal freshness of nature. We become conscious as we read his pages not merely of an exquisite lucidity of style, but of a yet more exquisite purity of emotion in the writer. An angel, writing about the sins and follies of human life, might have written as Newman did ; but it is rarely given to mortal to know life so intimately, and yet survey it from so detached a standpoint. No doubt the real secret of his power over the world was this detachment from the world, for it is ever the unworldly who effect the most enduring conquests of the human heart. And unworldliness is but another name for the temper of the child. Add to this temper great force of intellect, and you have the combination described by Leopardi—'a Titan in a virgin's form.'

The chief characteristic of the man of genius is this peculiar magnetism of person and character. It is this which differentiates him from the man of talent, or the mere accomplished writer. The world desires to know all that can be known about Dickens and Thackeray, but it has not the smallest curiosity about Reade or Trollope ; it seizes eagerly on every scrap of information about Carlyle, but it is absolutely indifferent to the private life of Froude. In the actual battle of the books the victories of talent are often confused with the achievements of genius ; nay, more it happens not seldom that talent is rewarded while genius is neglected. But, however tardy may be the process, genius never fails to come by its own. Books spring out of character ; in Cromwell's phrase, 'the mind is the man.' Provided always that a man of genius has enough literary craft rightly to express his temperament, to give a sincere and vital record of the processes of his own mind, he cannot but compel attention. The interest aroused by his writings is subtly fused into the interest which he exercises as a man. This is pre-eminently the case with Newman. He possessed all the characteristics of the man of genius, and was able to express himself by the vehicle of an almost perfect style.

To narrate the early life of Newman would be equivalent to writing the history of the Oxford movement—a task quite outside the competence of these pages. One or two points only may be noted. When Newman took up his residence in Oxford he found vital religion at its lowest ebb. Those who will take the pains to consult Mr. Mozley's *Reminiscences* will find ample proof of a condition of things wellnigh incredible to us to-day. All sense of the Church as a divine institution had perished, and he who had described a cleric as a man with a divine mission would have been laughed at. The path to preferment in the Church of England was a competent knowledge of Greek. 'Improve your Greek, and do not waste your time in visiting the poor,' was the actual advice given by a respected prelate to his candidates for ordination. The direst threat, according to Mr. Mozley, which could be held over the head of an idle schoolboy was that he would have to be a country curate and keep the accounts of a coal fund. The amount of downright jobbery in the administration of Church patronage was enormous. Naturally it followed that the most incompetent of men held sacred offices, and parishes were neglected. The condition of public worship itself was often scandalous. There was neither order, reverence, nor decency. Services were droned or gabbled through; a stale homily of the baldest and briefest description served for a sermon; magnificent edifices, erected by the piety and genius of former generations, were allowed to fall into shameful disrepair; wherever one turned, in short, there were evidences of moral laxity, spiritual faithlessness, and shameless insincerity and worldliness.

Newman had been trained in Evangelicalism. He tells us that the books which most impressed him in boyhood were the works of Scott, the commentator, Romaine, and Law. These works were standards among the evangelicals, and from them not merely a strict system of theology, but a very high ideal of conduct might be derived. Newman, reading them in the first ardour and fresh sincerity of youth, found them of infinite service. What impressed him most in Scott was 'a bold unworldliness,' what became most cogent to him in the reading of Law's *Serious Call* was the certainty of future rewards and punishments. It was entirely characteristic of Newman from boyhood to old age that all truths, or what he held to be truths, had a strange vividness for him. Dreamy, sensitive, imaginative in the highest and rarest degree, a truth took almost concrete form for him; it dominated him; it was a divine compulsion laid upon his intellect and conscience. This state of mind is recorded in his famous saying that for him there were 'two and two only, supreme and luminously self-evident beings, myself and my Creator.' This is the precise attitude of Calvinism, and in the evangelical ideas of Newman, as in the common evangelical theology of the time, there was a powerful leaven of Calvinism. To a mind occupied and dominated by such a conception as this, unworldliness is a necessity. The world and the lusts of the world fade away into nothingness; worldly success has no allurement, worldly privation no terror; the sublime scenery of eternity is put round human life, the awful and inspiring vision of a world to come attends the lowliest tasks of conduct, and the most coveted rewards of earth become incommensurate beside the supreme felicities of heaven. Such was the actual temper produced in Newman by the study of evangelical theology, but it was very far from being the temper of the average evangelical of his day. The first great shock and disappointment of Newman's religious life was the discovery that the heart had been taken out of Evangelicalism. Here and there, of course, sincere and earnest men were to be found, but with the great majority faith was tepid, and conduct an ingenious compromise between an unworldly creed and a worldly life. It was this discovery which started Newman on his work of religious reformation. He felt that the one thing essential for the nation, and the one object in his own life worth supreme devotion, was to bring men back to a living faith in God and the unseen.

That work, as he understood it, could only be achieved by making the voyage of religious investigation. Mr. R. H. Hutton applies with rare felicity to the thinking aspects of Newman's life the great lines of Wordsworth :

> The intellectual powers through words and things,
> Went sounding on, a dim and perilous way.

New truths, like new worlds, are not found without voyages of discovery. Faith is the last crystallisation of many processes of doubt. A very short residence at Oxford convinced Newman that among all serious and thoughtful men religion had somehow fallen into disrepute. The question was how to deliver religion from this disrepute. There must be somewhere in religion a vital core, an indestructible citadel. Christianity might present a thousand difficulties, but some reconciliation of these difficulties must be possible. For himself, Newman sharply distinguished between difficulties and doubts. 'Ten thousand difficulties do not make one doubt,' he said ; 'difficulty and doubt are incommensurate.' The existence of God, he was wont to say, was at once the most difficult, and yet the most indubitable of truths. Granted that Christianity had difficulties ; the question is, are these difficulties in their total combination such as make valid a general doubt of Christianity ? Or, again, great as are the difficulties of faith, are not the difficulties of disbelief still greater ? Careless students of Newman, and even such a writer as Huxley, have fallen into the error of describing Newman's mind as essentially sceptical. His mind was singularly open, sincere and sympathetic, but in the true sense it was the reverse of sceptical. It was rather an inquiring mind supported by the clearest spiritual intuitions ; and thus, while no man can state an intellectual difficulty with such charity, fairness, and precision, none could show less disposition to linger in the shadows of mere philosophic doubt.

In this brief and inadequate statement we have the real clue to Newman's career. Compromise was the keynote of the Oxford life of his day, and indeed of the life of the English Church as a whole. The popular Oxford creed was that there was 'nothing new, and nothing true, and it didn't matter'; and it was scarcely an irony to describe the prayer of an Oxford don as 'O God, if there be a God, save my soul, if I have a soul.' Newman hated compromise with his whole soul. A thing was either true or false, but it could not be both. He would shrink from the investigation of no real difficulty, but he would not, and could not, leave it in doubt. His mind was essentially dogmatic. 'From the age of fifteen,' he says in the *Apologia*, 'dogma has been the fundamental principle of my religion. I know no other religion; I cannot enter into the idea of any other sort of religion ; religion as a mere sentiment is to me a dream and a mockery. As well can there be filial love without the fact of a father, as devotion without the fact of a Supreme Being.' It was incredible that if there were a Supreme Being who had created man, this Being should have furnished man with nothing better than an enigma to guide him in his passage through the world; still more incredible that if there were a divinely organised Church on earth, it should not be known by certain infallible signs. Where were these signs? And with that question Newman began his journey toward Rome. We may hold what opinions we will about the nature of the logic by which Newman convinced himself that in Catholicism alone was the proper and secure refuge of the soul ; but whatever our opinions we cannot resist the impressiveness of the spectacle which Newman presents of the struggle of a lonely, reserved, sensitive and perfectly sincere soul to find a surer faith its own.

It is this spectacle which is visible in all Newman's writings. With all his reticence, a reticence which almost amounted to shyness, he is the most auto-biographical of writers. When we least expect it, in a sermon or an essay, or even in an historical disquisition, we come upon some enchanting glimpse of himself—something that turns the page into a vivid study of a temperament. With most writers this would be an offence, and in course of time would wear the aspect of artifice ; but in Newman's case all that he wrote is wrought so thoroughly out of himself, is so intimate an expression of his own nature, that it seems perfectly natural and appropriate. Ruskin, in his later writings, has followed the same method ; but Ruskin's style, even at its best, is rarely free from the suspicion of artifice. Sometimes, indeed, we have an uncomfortable sensation that Ruskin writes with a full consciousness of his own eloquence ; it is not in the least that he is insincere, but simply that he is too fully aware of his sincerity. Newman, in his greatest flights of eloquence, and in the passages which most directly call attention to the nature of his own thoughts, experiences and emotions, always leaves us with the sense of something quite spontaneous and natural. Probably the thought of literary fame never once entered into Newman's mind. He was at all times too detached from the world to be unduly sensible of its praise or blame, especially in what he would have regarded as the puerility of literary reputation. In describing the emotions of his boyhood, he once wrote:—'I thought life might be a dream, and I an angel, and all this world a deception, my fellow-angels hiding themselves from me, and deceiving me with the semblance of a material world.' This note of the utter deceptiveness of material things is struck again and again in his writings. It would be hard to parallel among the greatest masters of the English language this description of the world, which occurs in a sermon on *The Mental sufferings of Our Lord in His Passion*:—'Hopes blighted, vows broken, lights quenched, warnings scorned, opportunities lost; the innocent betrayed, the young hardened, the penitent relapsing, the just overcome, the aged falling; the sophistry of misbelief, the wilfulness of passion, the obduracy of pride, the tyranny of habit, the canker of remorse, the wasting power of care, the anguish of shame, the pining of disappointment, the sickness of despair; such cruel, such pitiable spectacles, such heart-rending, revolting, detestable, maddening scenes; nay, the haggard faces, the convulsed lips, the flushed cheek, the dark brow of the willing victims of rebellion, they are all before Him now, they are upon Him and in Him.' And that which most effectually drove Newman out of the English Church was the utter worldliness of its spirit. For him the material world was a dream and an evil dream; but it was only too sadly apparent that for the great mass of those who professed and called themselves Christians, whatever they might say, the material world was the only reality. His test was simple; did average Christians in their daily conduct do anything they would not do, or refrain from doing anything they would do, out of a profound conviction that Christianity was true ; or would they do anything they did not now do, if they were convinced that Christianity was false? His reply was that interest coincided with duty, and thus, whereas the distinct Christian command was that Christians were not to love the world, Christians did love the world, were as eager for its rewards as other people, and practised Christian virtues not out of regard to Christianity, but merely because they were convenient and profitable. And the more he thought on this theme, the clearer became the vision of the Roman communion as one in which self-sacrifice was an authentic fact, and the absolute renunciation of the world a practised law. In a very remarkable sermon at St. Mary's he elaborates this theme with rare felicity. Two years were yet to elapse before his final separation from the English Church, but already he speaks with reverent admiration of the 'humble monks and holy nuns, who have hearts weaned from the world, and wills subdued, and for their meekness meet with insult, and for their purity with slander, and for their gravity with suspicion, and for their courage with cruelty.' When we collate such passages as these, passages which reflect with an exquisite precision Newman's own temperament and habitual thought, we begin to see that it was less the logic of Newman than his temperament which made him a Catholic.

As a sermon-writer Newman has no superior in the English language, either for range or style. He combined in the most felicitous degree two qualities seldom combined, simplicity and profundity. To the philosophic reader probably some of his University sermons will appear the greatest; but, after all, his rarest power lay not in the direction of philosophy, but poetry. It is when he speaks as a poet; when he analyses human motives, lays bare the human heart, cuts through the core of convention to the naked quivering human soul and conscience; when he speaks of death and eternity, of the solemn, tender things of human life, and the more solemn and awful things of the life to come; when he draws broad imaginative pictures of the evil of the world, of the contrasts in human action and destiny, of the felicities or terrors that lie beyond the hour of Judgment, of heroic or saintly episodes in memorable lives, of the different ways in which men regard things, of the littleness and greatness of man, his rare consciousness of, or his habitual indifference to, the splendours of the spiritual universe, and its reality—it is then that he is greatest. In such passages he produces an effect not merely not rivalled, but not attempted by any other. And the effect is greatly heightened by the simplicity of the means employed. Magnificent as this or that passage may appear to us, yet we find, upon examination, that it is composed of the plainest words, and there is not a word that could be bettered, nor one altered, without serious damage both to the sense and melody of the passage. Among his sermons is a very powerful one on *Unreal Words*, in which he argues that words are real things, that insincere language is the expression of an insincere temper, and that 'words have a meaning, whether we mean that meaning or not'; certainly Newman never uses a word without the most scrupulous regard to its real meaning, and hence the convincing sincerity, as well as the literary compactness of his style. Opinions will differ as to whether Newman's greatest sermons are those preached before or after his conversion. The first represent more fully the workings of the intellect and heart, the second the freedom of the imagination and the poetic instinct. If one were called upon to mention any single sermon, which more than any other reveals the poet, perhaps the most striking would be that upon the *Fitness of the Glories of Mary*, with its most solemn and beautiful close :—'But she, the lily of Eden, who had always dwelt out of the sight of man, willingly did she die in the garden's shade; and amid the sweet flowers in which she had lived.' Such sermons delight the mind with an effect more often produced by music than by language; sometimes, indeed, by the highest kind of lyric poetry, but very rarely indeed by prose; and thinking of them, we think less of their substance, than of some rare, almost unnameable quality, subtly akin to both fragrance and melody, which pervades them.

Newman's greatest book is his *Apologia Vitâ Suâ.* Where else can we find such fascinating glimpses of autobiography, such frank confessions, such subtle delineations of motive? Yet the book was the work of accident. Had not Kingsley in an unguarded moment accused Newman of teaching that truth was no virtue, there had been no *Apologia.* Newman retorted with vehement denial, then with one of the most accomplished pieces of witty irony which he ever wrote. But the taunt hurt him more deeply than he was willing to confess; and hence there grew up the idea of stating in precise language what his life had really been, and what were the motives which impelled it. It is by no means a perfect book, and it might easily have been a better book. It bears too visibly the marks of controversy; it was hastily composed; many things which no doubt appeared clear enough to Newman are not stated very clearly, and some links in the logic are missing. It needs some temerity to say this of a book so justly famous, but few dispassionate readers will close the *Apologia* without feeling that occasionally Newman's logic is puzzling, and that as he drew nearer to Rome his attitude of mind became less judicial, and less capable of vindication. But when all such deductions are made, there is no auto-biography in the English language which possesses in so rare a degree the elements of fascination. Nor is there one that contains so many great passages, which seem to touch the very height of literary achievement. Who that has ever read it can forget the passage in which he speaks of the weight of mystery which lies on human life in the contempla-tion of the doctrine of a divine government ?—' The tokens so faint and broken of a superintending design, the blind evolution of what turns out to be great powers or truths, the progress of things as if from unreasoning elements, not towards final causes, the greatness and littleness of man, his far-reaching aims, his short duration, the curtain hung over his futurity, the disappointments of life, the defeat of good, the success of evil, physical pain, mental anguish, the prevalence and intensity of sin, the pervading idolatries, the corruptions, the dreary hopeless irreligion . . . all this is a vision to dizzy and appal ; and inflicts upon the mind the sense of a profound mystery, which is absolutely without human solution!' This is the utterance of a poet, and it is an excellent example of Newman's peculiar eloquence — lofty and yet simple, capable of the largest pictorial effects yet severely reticent, austere and tender, classic and colloquial, delicate and virile, the product of consummate art yet apparently artless —an eloquence which penetrates and overwhelms the mind, and, once heard, leaves behind it echoes which never die away.

Newman, while never attempting to make authorship a profession, or even an aim in life, was nevertheless a prolific author. His books grew out of himself, out of the passing conditions and conflicts of his life; but these conditions were so vividly realised, and these conflicts so numerous, that he was an incessant writer. Books that sprang out of controversy are apt to perish with the controversies which begat them; and no doubt much of Newman's work will from this cause be forgotten. But even in those of his writings least consonant with later thought and taste, there will always be much to repay the student. His purity of style never deserted him, even when his theme was of the driest, and his logic most faulty. His least-known books abound in delightful surprises; not merely in passages of entrancing self-revelation or splendid eloquence, but of incisive wit, of delicate irony, of caustic and overpowering satire. In one department of literature only did he fail: he had no gift for fiction, though many passages in his story of *Callista* have excited the admiration of competent critics. But any failure in the art of fiction is more than compensated by his mastery of poetry. Is there in our English literature any poem of similar aim so powerful and intense as the *Dream of Gerontius*? Assuredly this is one of the great poems of the world, in spirit and substance akin to Goethe's *Faust* and Dante's *Trilogy*, in depth of spiritual insight and emotion superior to the former and the equal of the latter, and in purity of expression comparable with the finest work of the greatest poets. It is also the most characteristic fruit of Newman's genius. For by birth and training, by temperament and life, Newman was essentially a religious genius, a prophet to whom doors of vision stood wide where other men saw only impenetrable darkness; yet so sensitively sympathetic, that he knew the weight of darkness which crushed others, although he never once succumbed to it; and it is by virtue of this temperament and genius that he will always be reckoned the greatest religious writer whom England has produced—perhaps also the greatest since Augustine and Aquinas.

CHAPTER XXII

FREDERICK W. ROBERTSON

[Born in London, February 3, 1816. Ordained, July 1840. Curate at
Christ Church, Cheltenham, 1842. Incumbent of Trinity Chapel,
Brighton, 1847. Died August 15, 1853. Life by Stopford
Brooke published, 1865.]

ROBERTSON of Brighton, as he is familiarly known,
shares with John Henry Newman the distinction of
having profoundly affected the religious thought of
the latter half of the nineteenth century. The
small brown volumes containing the sermons which
he preached to a relatively insignificant congregation
in Brighton, about the time of the early fifties, are
known throughout the world. They are found in
libraries where no other sermons have a chance of
admittance, and are read by men who hold in scorn
the average productions of the religious press. They
have had a popularity exceeding that of many of
the best-known novels, and a more lasting sale than
that of the most familiar biographies. They have
influenced the theological thought of their time in
an extraordinary degree, and have given a new
impulse, character, and fashion to the preaching of
the age itself. Men of all creeds, parties, and sects
have derived inspiration from them, and while much
that seemed startling in their statements forty years
ago has now become commonplace, yet there is no

sign of diminished influence. Probably, in the entire history of literature, no sermons have ever attained a success so wide and wonderful; and it has not been that sort of fame which depends on personal reputation, but the steadier and more enduring fame which works of great literary art and genius alone can hope to secure.

Yet, it is singular to reflect, authorship formed no part of the purpose or employment of Robertson's life. Publicity he detested, and even pulpit popularity pained him. In one of his letters he regrets that he has been over-persuaded into publishing a sermon—the only sermon he ever published—and speaks of his weakness as a folly not to be repeated. It is by one of the fortunate accidents of literature that his pulpit utterances have been preserved at all. At one time he formed a habit of writing what he could recall of a discourse immediately after its delivery; from these papers, and from certain short-hand reports of his sermons, all our knowledge of his genius has been gained. For his sermons were in the strictest sense 'utterances.' He was not an extempore preacher in the loose acceptation of that phrase, since every discourse was elaborated with the most painstaking care of a singularly exact and analytic mind, but his method of delivery was extempore. Standing perfectly still, speaking in a low and beautifully modulated voice, at first he made some use of his notes; but before he had spoken many minutes he had discarded them. He spoke with intense passion, yet with perfect restraint. At the very height of oratory he never ceased to be the calm, lucid thinker, the austere worshipper of exact truth. Loose statement was as abhorrent to him as loose living. Perhaps more abhorrent still was cheap praise; the sort of adulation which follows the popular orator among those who are in love with his gift, but indifferent to his message.

It is necessary to notice these characteristics of the man if we are rightly to estimate the nature of his genius. Most readers of Mr. Stopford Brooke's admirable biography derive from it an impression of some curious and unusual element in Robertson, which they can only describe as 'morbid.' A more correct term would perhaps be 'super-sensitive,' for morbidity carries with it a suggestion of unwholesomeness and bitterness quite foreign to Robertson's temperament. The facts of the case appear to be these. Robertson came from a military stock, and was always in love with a life of action and adventure. He writes in one of his letters that he ought now to be at rest with the heroes of Moodkee, over whose bosoms the grass is growing; and goes on to explain himself by saying that he supposes that his desire for a soldier's life really means a desire to see his foe concrete and palpable before him. In such a confession we find the keynote of Robertson's character. By temperament he was a man of action and a fighter; circumstances made him the perpetual curate of an insignificant chapel-of-ease in a fashionable watering-place. He soon found himself an object of suspicion and slander, and of that intensely spiteful sort of hatred which is peculiar to the clerical mind. No doubt he also met much that made him aware of the hollowness and insincerity of conventional religion. Robertson was not the sort of man whose nature could be subdued to the element in which it worked. In such a situation a little judicious egotism, even a little rational vanity, is an invaluable defence. Robertson united with the strongest will a real distrust of himself. He could take up a position which he believed to be right, and stand by it inflexibly, but not without much secret self-torture. And with all his humility, there was also in his character a certain strain of scorn; scorn of the pettiness of the controversies into which he was forced, scorn of the untruthfulness and meanness of his opponents, scorn even of himself, that he who would have welcomed a soldier's death upon the battlefield, should have become a popular preacher in a gossiping watering-place.

Such a state of mind is no doubt uncommon, but genius also is uncommon, and its outlook upon life is peculiar. It is quite certain that in no case could a man of Robertson's temperament have taken life easily. Perhaps he expected too much of life—it is the way with idealists and enthusiasts, yet what would the world be without them? That he could enjoy intensely, that he knew occasional hours of pure light-heartedness, his letters show; but essentially he was not a happy man. The ordinary robust man knows that life is a rough business, expects a few blows and bruises, learns to laugh at them, and at last judges his fellows in the spirit of Luther's tolerant axiom that 'you must take men as they are, you cannot alter their natures.' But to the super-sensitive man no such course is possible. Folly in the wise, rancour in the good, weakness in the amiable, are to him hideous discoveries and crushing blows. The robust man works with the buzzing of the flies of slander round his head and takes no notice; with the sensitive man each sting is felt, each tiny wound inflames, and slander is a veritable *torment of flies* in the dark. One cannot well call this state of feeling morbid. The impression made upon us by Robertson's Brighton career is of some exceeding fine and delicate instrument put to uses too rough for it. He was ill-fitted for controversy, especially for the pettiness of religious controversy; ill-fitted for the glare of a public life even; a man essentially modest and reticent—guarding his feelings from the scrutiny of the crowd, yet compelled by the necessities of his position to reveal them, and suffering torture in the process. And his feelings were all intense, so that he could not help pouring himself out emotionally upon every subject that interested him, to a degree quite incredible to colder, perhaps one might say more restrained and better-balanced, natures. Thus, that which was his power as a preacher was his martyrdom as a man.

One other element also may be noticed. Probably Robertson was not wrong in his predilection for a soldier's life: in an obscure way he appears to have been conscious that he was not naturally fitted for the life of the thinker. Most men of genius who have attained fame in literature have very early in life indulged in literary expression. Even when the power of expression has come late, it has soon grown into a passion, and become the joy and occupation of life. But, as we have already seen, the pursuit of literature formed no part of Robertson's life. He is a quite singular instance of a man of genius entirely unconscious of his own gift. One might easily speculate on what might have happened if Robertson had not been a preacher; would he have died with all his music in him? Would he have found some literary ambition suited to his mind? As it was, his whole genius flowed into his preaching. Twice, perhaps thrice a week, he was forced into expression. Few people have the least conception of what such a task implies. No doubt it is often done, but it is very seldom done in Robertson's fashion. He put all the fulness of his mind into his task. No wonder he speaks sometimes of the strain of his work, no wonder that there are frequent fits of dejection and melancholy. And, one may add, no wonder that a man so sensitively organised broke down under the burden and died young. Sad as the end of Robertson was, yet one cannot but feel that it was mercy that cut his life short, and that his release was well-earned. Human lives may be measured by diffusion or intensity; between an aged Lear and Robertson there appears to yawn the widest gulf; yet of the end of each it might be said—

> O let him pass! He hates him
> That would upon the rack of this rough world
> Stretch him out longer.

Perhaps also, when we justly measure the infinite capacity of suffering which lies in super-sensitiveness, we may add the final verdict of Kent—

> The wonder is he hath endured so long.

The sermons of Robertson are at once intimate and catholic. They are catholic in the sense that they treat great questions in a great manner; they are intimate in the sense that they vividly express the characteristics of his own mind. The quality which has done more than anything else to preserve them is no doubt the power which emanates from the moral nature of the preacher. It is said that a small tradesman in Brighton kept in his shop-parlour a portrait of Robertson ; whenever he was tempted to do some dishonourable business trick, he looked upon his portrait, and, with those austere but kindly eyes gazing into his, felt he could not do it. This anecdote is very typical of the sort of influence which Robertson has exerted over many minds. He was a great gentleman, with very lofty and inflexible ideals of truth, honour, and chivalry. He hated shams, cant, hypocrisy, meanness, evasion, prevarication, and all kindred sins with a perfect hatred. He allowed no illusions to impose themselves on his own reason or conscience, and he laboured to remove all illusions from the minds and consciences of others. He himself possessed and kept the priceless gift of individuality, which is but another phrase for fearless liberty of conviction. He was not deceived, on the one hand, by popular praise, nor, on the other hand, turned aside by a hair's-breadth from his purpose by popular suspicion. He urged a course right onward, and made even his most virulent adversaries feel his absolute honesty. And this invincible honesty characterised not only his motives but his thinking. He went to the Bible with no views to support : he was a searcher after truth, and the truth he found he preached. The result is that his sermons have a freshness and force which lifts them quite out of the rut of the best pulpit literature, and gives them world-wide application. Not only are they alive with his own keenness of thought, but they are filled with his own moral energy, and are aglow with his own beautiful chivalry of spirit.

Together with this great endowment of a sincere and unvitiated nature Robertson brought to his life-work a rare combination of intellectual gifts. Chief among these must rank his lucidity. The most complicated and difficult theme resolves itself before his acute analysis. In a manner peculiarly his own, he seizes upon the most baffling problems of Christianity and pours on them a flood of light. One of his most constant hearers once said that he had never heard him without having some difficulty explained, or some stumbling-block removed. His very method of stating a difficulty, so candid, tolerant, sympathetic, and complete, often takes you half-way to its solution. It is not that there is anything startlingly original or unconventional in form or phrase; so far as sermon form goes Robertson was conventional, and he was much too fastidious in taste to permit the least eccentricity of phrase. It is rather by clearness, candour, and unaffected simplicity that Robertson wins the mind. The effect of one of his greater sermons is like the gradual growth of light. The darkness is not shattered suddenly: it slowly melts and dissolves. By what seems magic, so potent and imperceptible is the process, the distant grows into nearness, the vague into distinctness, the confused into orderliness, and the general harmony of things is felt. Perhaps no preacher has ever had so rare a faculty of irradiating a subject.

With his extreme lucidity of intellect there is joined strong sympathy—a combination very far from common. If I were asked to state what is the most acute sort of pain that human nature can know, I think I should reply, 'the pain of sympathy.' All sympathy is pain, and in the degree that sympathy is intense, pain is intense. Robertson, far more than any other preacher whose work has lived, felt the pain of the world, the tears that are in mortal things. The poor, the disinherited, the unconsidered; the timid, the doubtful, and the weak; the lonely and the uncomprehended in life and character; lives that are narrow and barren of opportunity; lives that either by their own weakness or by the wickedness of others endure shameful injuries—for all these, Robertson felt with that sacrificial fulness of sympathy which almost literally bears the sicknesses and carries the griefs of others. It is quite characteristic of him that at one time he spent long hours of the night in walking the streets of Brighton, endeavouring to redeem fallen women. Any tale of wrong done to women moved him to a paroxysm of rage, and those who witnessed these terrible outbursts never forgot them. He knew that sort of anger which is virtue enraged, pity enraged, sympathy suddenly fanned into white heat: the anger of the Lamb! His sermons bear witness to these things. Multitudes who are no scholars and have not the wit to recognise Robertson's rare quality of intellect, have read these sermons, saying, ' Here is one who understands *me*!' He who can comprehend the spiritual tragedy that underlies commonplace lives is sure of a wide audience; for who is without his inner secret of pain, who that does not yearn to be understood? Robertson's own lonely and uncomprehended life taught him intense sympathy with all who suffered, and gave him the key by which the secrets of many hearts were revealed.

In point of literary charm and grace these discourses hold their own against the best specimens of pulpit literature in any age. It is true that one cannot pick out from them gorgeous passages of eloquence as one may easily do from the sermons of Jeremy Taylor or Bossuet. Passage for passage, there is nothing perhaps that strikes so full a note of lyric beauty as some half a dozen pages of Newman. Rhetoric, as mere rhetoric, was abhorrent to Robertson. The bare suspicion that people thought he was saying something fine was sufficient to reduce him to silence. In reading Newman, one feels that he had a certain conscious delight in the exercise of his genius, that here and there he must have written with a pleasurable sense of his own powers. Robertson is never thinking of himself, never even thinking of the form in which he expresses himself. If, as a literary artist, he had any conscious aim, it was to say what he had to say in the simplest form. The result on the reader is an impression of delightful naturalness. The language is refined, fervent, cogent, but there is no effort at fineness. His illustrations are drawn from every source, yet each is manifestly chosen not for its beauty but its pertinence. Yet the beauty is there: a touch of poetry, a tenderness of phrase, something that lingers on the ear like music, all the more remarkable by contrast with the austerity of its setting. If one may be permitted a metaphor, which must not be too closely pressed, Robertson's sermons have something of the perennial freshness and simplicity of the flowers of the field about them. A rare orchid is more wonderful, but not so sweet; men may tire of the meretricious splendour of the orchid, but they do not tire of violets and primroses.

Probably the reason of the sustained popularity of these discourses lies more than we imagine in their simplicity and naturalness. We read them, re-read them, and come back to them after many years, always with a new delight, for they possess this highest characteristic of classic literature that their charm is inexhaustible.

Robertson died at the very fulness of his powers, having in his lifetime received no commensurate recognition of his genius. His intensity of living wore him out, and the overwrought and sensitive brain developed disease of an agonising nature. He hoped to live, for love of life was strong in him to the last. When he could scarcely move, he crawled to the window to look out once more upon 'the blessed day.' But the mischief had gone too deep, and the brain was too dreadfully injured to admit the hope of recovery. 'Let me rest. I must die. Let God do His work!' were his last words. He was only thirty-seven. Over his grave his friends inscribed three words that expressed the spirit of his life: *Love*, *Truth*, *Duty*. But even his friends scarcely recognised in him one of the master-spirits of the age. Years passed away, and then at length came the publication of his sermons, followed by the sympathetic biography of Mr. Stopford Brooke, and England knew that once more a man of genius had been in her midst. Brighton had not known it, Brighton does not know it now. If the stranger asks for the humble little Chapel of Ease, in Ship Street, where Robertson once preached, no one remembers where it is, or remembers the man who once made it the shrine of genius. Perhaps, after all, it is more fitting that Robertson should be remembered not by the local and accidental associations of his life, but as a spiritual force, as the soldier-saint of truth, as the clearest and most honest interpreter of Christianity which the nineteenth century has produced.

Printed by T. and A. CONSTABLE, Printers to Her Majesty
at the Edinburgh University Press

Works by the same Author

THE MAKING OF MANHOOD

Fifth Thousand. Crown 8vo. Cloth. 3s. 6d.

'There is a manly outspokenness in this book, as well as vision and sympathy, and an evident understanding of the needs and aspirations which determine the point of view in youth towards religion and literature, work and play, and the give and take of society. There are sensible and stimulating addresses in the volume, on patriotism, the gains of drudgery, the ministry of books, courage, the power of purpose, and allied themes. Everywhere Mr. Dawson succeeds in making his meaning clear and his subject attractive. We like the book because of its freshness and its force, its candour of statement, and its courage in appeal.'—**Speaker.**

TABLE TALK WITH YOUNG MEN

Crown 8vo. Cloth. 3s. 6d.

'A very good book to put into the hands of young men.'—**Times.**

'A highly helpful and stimulating book.'—**Glasgow Herald.**

'Is a manly, honest, outspoken book, and deserves a welcome. . . . It is exactly the volume likely to prove of service to young men.'—**Speaker.**

'A better book to give to a young man would be difficult to find.'—**Westminster Gazette.**

'Very enjoyable and readable essays. The chapters all contain sound sense, well expressed. The book ought to sell, and contains a good deal that young men both need and are seeking.'—**Methodist Times.**

'There is on every page the sweet reasonableness of friend conversing with friend.'—**Dundee Advertiser.**

THE THRESHOLD OF MANHOOD

A Young Man's Words to Young Men

Ninth Edition.   Crown 8vo.   Cloth.   3s. 6d.

'Among the many valuable homilies to young men now issuing from the press, these addresses take the first place. Brilliant, thoughtful, apposite, thoroughly abreast of the age, with its many perplexing problems, no better book could be put into the hands of those on the threshold of manhood.'—**Aberdeen Free Press.**

'The dramatic and pictorial power of the discourses bears witness to the fact that the writer is poet and preacher in one. Heartfelt sympathy for the peculiar difficulties of a young man's life in a great city gives the pulpit counsels a claim to attention, which all will allow. They are full of force, penetrated with Christian manliness, unsparing in their denunciations of vice, and throb with desire for the salvation of the young. These are sermons for the times, which should nerve many young soldiers for the good fight of faith.'—**London Quarterly Review.**

'A most inspiring volume. His words glow with generous sympathy, and the whole book is quite remarkable for the freshness of its style and the brilliancy of its language.'—**Young Man.**

'It is a splendid book, full of a warm, sympathetic appreciation of a young man's trials. Every page of it is worth reading. It never descends to mere commonplace platitude, and often rises to a glowing eloquence that can hardly be read without producing some practical effect on the life of the reader.'—**Church Bells.**

'The writer's evident sympathy with young men increases his success in grappling alike with their intellectual difficulties and their peculiar perils. These sermons are rare helps to building up character.'—**Methodist Recorder.**

QUEST AND VISION

Second Edition.   Crown 8vo.   Cloth.   3s. 6d.

'The marks of wide reading pervade the volume, and Mr. Dawson is in the main singularly adroit in his allusions. The "New Realism" is an essay in which Mr. Dawson gets into tolerably close quarters with the writers concerned; indeed, it is an acute and significant piece of criticism. The book as a whole is always attractive in theme, often felicitous in expression, and sometimes subtle and penetrating in judgment.'—**Speaker**.

THE MAKERS OF MODERN POETRY

A Popular Handbook to the English Poets of the Century

Seventh Edition.   Crown 8vo.   Cloth.   6s.

'We have found Mr. Dawson well balanced in his critical judgments, neither betrayed into rhapsody by his admiration, nor sacrificing an intelligent and appreciative sympathy to a just reserve.'—**Daily News**.

'The author has carried out his purpose most ably, and shown a soundness of judgment, and a subtle and clear insight into the essential characteristics of modern English poetry, which leaves little to be desired.'—**Morning Post**.

'Mr. Dawson has evidently made a careful study of his subject, and has read widely and with considerable range of sympathy. He shows a fairness in estimating the worth of poets such as Byron, Southey, or Scott, whose claims are now often denied or questioned, whilst at the same time he can do justice to the varied beauty and power displayed in the work of Shelley and Keats, of Wordsworth and Tennyson and Browning. As far as it goes, his work contains a good deal of really useful and unpretending information, likely to be of considerable service to the readers whose wellbeing he has at heart; and with this is combined a sound and appreciative judgment which ought not to be left unnoticed.'—**Guardian**.

'Mr. Dawson is a safe guide.'—**Spectator**.

'It is thorough and honest, in every sense the result of careful and loving study of the subject.'—**Glasgow Herald**.

'Mr. Dawson's book is a most impartial, discriminating, careful, and sympathetic survey; and should prove immensely useful to multitudes of capable readers whose leisure for systematic study is short.'—**Echo**.

U

THE REDEMPTION OF EDWARD STRAHAN

Cheap Edition. 1s.

SELECTIONS FROM SOME PRESS NOTICES.

'Mr. Gladstone describes this work as "a powerful book with a pure and high aim," and all must admit that Mr. Dawson . . . has produced a book very much above the average. There is something in it that is profoundly moving, and at the same time stimulating. It appeals to the divine spark which lies (in many cases dormant) in every human being. The book is written with an overmastering earnestness which carries all before it. The writer has seen and heard and felt the things that he so vividly portrays. It is written with a purpose—that of awakening a slumbering world to the mighty forces that lie about and under our feet ; of the volcanoes on which we so lightly tread ; of the misery, sin, and degradation that lie close about us as we sing and dance life away.'—**Speaker.**

'A powerful and serious story by a thoughtful writer. . . . As a psychological study of various types, the novel is both ingenious and interesting, and it deals with difficult social questions from a thoroughly rational point of view.'—**Times.**

'A book of more than ordinary merit dealing with the social question. The writer treats familiar topics with lively freshness, and his book is thoughtful and stimulating throughout.'—**Academy.**

'It has several points of undoubted excellence. In the first place, it bears the impression of thorough sincerity ; in the next, it is written in a style as clear and vigorous as it is polished and correct. No work in which these qualities are united can prove unprofitable reading.'—**Glasgow Herald.**

'Is in its way an able work. He is outspoken in laying before his readers the phase of human misery that especially occupies the philanthropist, and writes feelingly of the sufferings for which he evidently has the deepest sympathy. The pictures of low middle-class life at Middleham are faithfully realistic, but the author is at his best when portraying the mental experiences of his hero Strahan, which, after convincing him of the futility of his own efforts, lead him to believe in the power of an "Unseen Helper."'—**Morning Post.**

THE STORY OF HANNAH

Crown 8vo. Gilt top. 6s.

'One feels a growing power in Mr. Dawson's writing. He is coming into his own—which is a place not far behind any of the minister-novelists. The character-drawing, the subtle insight into the human heart, and the broad and tolerant art of goodness that pervades the story are its chief features.'—**Sheffield Independent.**

'*The Story of Hannah* is full of charm. It has such qualities as entitle it to be called literature. . . . A perusal of this tender, pensive story will be a counter-action to the unclean pessimism of some modern fictionists. . . . None can follow the fortunes of Hannah without realising what, in the estimation of the author, are the true goals of life. . . . We trust that such writers as Mr. Dawson will be generously encouraged by the Christian public, for their aim is evidently to take account of whatsoever things are pure and beautiful and of good report.'—**Methodist Times.**

'This is a story of great power. The portraiture is specially skilful, and the central character is certainly one of Mr. Dawson's finest creations. . . . Mr. Dawson is evidently writing about what he has seen, and he writes about it with an intensity which holds our interest all through.'—**Glasgow Herald.**

'A most attractive feature of the work lies in the delightful sketches of the country (north-west Devon), which Mr. Dawson has elaborated with the pen of an artist and a true lover of Nature. The novel is at once healthy, interesting, and instructive, and will well repay perusal.'—**Scotsman.**

'There is much that is graceful and striking in this new story, both in the conception of it and in the way in which it is worked out.'—**North British Daily Mail.**

'The best piece of work Mr. Dawson has given us.'—**Literary World.**

THRO' LATTICE WINDOWS

Third Edition. Crown 8vo. Cloth. 6s.

Ian Maclaren writes of it as 'THAT DELIGHTFUL BOOK,' and says, 'I wish to place on record my sober opinion, that if any man can read therein "The Tired Wife" and be not a better husband, he is hopeless, and that the congregational library, in the city as much as in the country, which has not *Lattice Windows*, ought to appoint a new librarian.'

'This is Mr. Dawson's very best book. He has already made brilliant contributions to fiction, so brilliant that they ought to have achieved an even more marked success. Yet both in England and America, there are many discerning readers who recognise in him one of the few writers who may add something to our permanent English literature.'— **British Weekly.**

'But that space forbids, we would take Sydney readers seriously to task for neglect of this last charming writer. Always quiet and unostentatious in method, the author of *London Idylls* and *The Story of Hannah* has yet a positive genius in depicting English village life. He should rank as the English J. M. Barrie. It is simply a case of over-modesty and popular caprice.'—**Sydney Daily Telegraph.**

LONDON IDYLLS

Second Thousand. Crown 8vo. Cloth. 5s.

'A collection of stories of much promise. Mr. Dawson has a pleasant style, an easy command of effective expression, and he passes lightly from pathos to humour, or rather he can blend the two with no sensible transition.'—**Times.**

'Of the idylls themselves little may be written to convey any real sense of their charm. The themes on which they turn are such as only London could have supplied.'—**Dundee Advertiser.**

'Mr. Dawson is an artist; his idylls are moments of crisis— summaries of a life.'—**Guardian.**

'In them all Mr. Dawson shows a true sympathy with the life of modern London, and no mean skill in presenting it, in certain of its aspects, to his readers. He has produced his effect in his own way, and done so with considerable force and power.'—**Scotsman.**

THE FOUR MEN

By the Rev. JAMES STALKER, D.D.

Second Edition, completing 10,000. *Crown 8vo, cloth,* 2s. 6d.

CONTENTS

Temptation.

Conscience.

The Religion for To-day.

Christ and the Wants of Humanity.

Public Spirit.

The Evidences of Religion.

Youth and Age.

'When I was in America last year, delivering the Lyman Beecher Lectures on Preaching in Yale University, the first of these discourses was given at the academic service in the university chapel on Sunday morning, April 12, 1891. Mr. D. L. Moody, the evangelist, who chanced to be present, insisted on having it printed, and he sent copies, I believe, to all the students of the university. In the same irresistible way he got the addresses on *Temptation* and *Conscience* published. As these addresses are in circulation in America, I have thought that they may be useful and acceptable in this country also.'—*From the Preface.*

'As a guide to self-knowledge, this book ought to be in the hands of every young man who has not lost faith in religion, and has some aspiration to attain to the highest type of manhood.'—**Christian.**

'There is a manly and godly tone about the teaching of the book which makes it interesting. Easy to read and likely to be useful. Young men especially would be sure to be captivated by it.'—**Record.**

'The subjects are such as attract young men, and it need scarcely be said that they are treated in a lively, lucid, and vigorous manner.'—**Expositor.**

'More thoughtful, suggestive addresses than the eight gathered in the compass of this dainty volume it would be hard to find.'—**Queen.**

9 783337 366346